KIDS ON-LINE

150 WAYS
FOR KIDS TO
SURF THE NET FOR FUN
AND INFORMATION

MARIAN SALZMAN
and ROBERT PONDISCIO

AN AVON CAMELOT BOOK

The authors and publisher have used their best efforts to research the services and products contained in this book and make no warranty of any kind, expressed or implied, with regard to these services and products.

KIDS ON-LINE: 150 WAYS FOR KIDS TO SURF THE NET FOR FUN AND IN-FORMATION is an original publication of Avon Books. This work has never before appeared in book form.

AVON BOOKS
A division of
The Hearst Corporation
1350 Avenue of the Americas
New York, New York 10019

Copyright © 1995 by Marian Salzman and Robert Pondiscio
Published by arrangement with the authors
Library of Congress Catalog Card Number: 95-15007
ISBN: 0-380-78231-6

Library of Congress Cataloging in Publication Data:

Salzman, Marian, 1959–
    Kids on-line / Marian Salzman and Robert Pondiscio.
        p.   cm.
Includes index.
1. Computers and children. 2. Videotext systems. I. Pondiscio, Robert. II. Title.
QA76.55.S35   1995   95-15007
004.69—dc20   CIP
                                                               AC

First Avon Camelot Printing: September 1995

CAMELOT TRADEMARK REG. U.S. PAT. OFF. AND IN OTHER COUNTRIES, MARCA REGISTRADA, HECHO EN U.S.A.

Printed in the U.S.A.

OPM   10   9   8   7   6   5   4   3   2   1

Acknowledgments

Special thanks to Renee Cho of McIntosh & Otis for helping to craft the book proposal and for selling it quickly; to Gwen Montgomery of Avon Books, for acting fast and bringing the book into her able care; to Ann O'Reilly, for painstakingly tending the final manuscript, ignoring the clock when her fax rang, and endlessly editing, revising, and often rewriting the "DRAFTS" that kept coming; and to Jessica Neal, for spending a month of her life holding together the pieces of the Chiat/Day Emerging Media Department since Marian was constantly virtual—virtually trying to do three jobs at once (C/D, American Dialogue™, and write two books, both due in February 1995). And, most of all, Marian never would have been able to hold any of this together without the help of her (working) partner in American Dialogue, Cindy Fazio, who managed also to do three jobs at once (American Dialogue chief operating officer, chief quantitative researcher, and also feeder of "things to do on-line" to Marian, as well as mom to not-yet-two-year-old Cassidy, who is *always* curious "But WHY?" unless, of course, someone will join her in dancing to Jerry Garcia).

Thanks also to Rachel Borer, who recruited on-line respondents on a moment's notice whenever we needed clarification; to Mary Beth Solomon and Mike Balagur, each of whom conducted and brilliantly analyzed the findings of several on-line

focus groups with kids and their parents on the subject of
" 'Netting''; and to Christy Lane, who is Marian's proverbial
sounding board (''So, seriously, what do you think of . . .'').

And there is also a Major League thank-you owed to the
other partners in American Dialogue: Bruce Schnitzer and An-
drew Penn of WAND/Yankelovich, Tom Cohen, Gary
Goldstein of AFGL International, and, especially, Jay Chiat,
who somehow manages to understand Marian even when she
talks almost as fast as she types: a hundred plus words a minute.
Chiat/Day (it's often called Chiat/Day+Night—and for good
reason) is the only place in which a book like this could have
been conceived and hatched; it's an idea factory where the
thinking never stops and where the opportunity to banter about
''Imagine this . . .'' is limitless. Thanks also to C/D Managing
Director Ira Matathia, who invited Marian inside the agency
last December knowing full well that she had these two books
to finish and also knowing full well that she was on information
overload when it came to exactly the discipline she spearheads:
emerging media. Marian's determined to turn Ira into a 'Net
head and marvels at her progress to date—''at least he no longer
laughs when I suggest solving this or that problem using on-
line.''

Trademarks and Service Marks

Trademarked names appear throughout this book. Rather than insert a registered trademark symbol with each mention of the trademarked name, the publisher states that it is using the names only for editorial purposes and to the benefit of the trademark owner with no intention of infringing upon that trademark.

America Online is a registered trademark and service mark of America Online Inc.

CompuServe is a registered trademark and service mark of CompuServe Inc.

Delphi is a registered trademark of Delphi Internet Services Corporation.

eWorld is a registered trademark of Apple Computer, Inc.

GEnie is a registered trademark of the General Electric Corporation.

Prodigy is a registered trademark and service mark of Prodigy Services Co.

Contents

Foreword from a Fourth Grade Friend

I may never know what *she* looks like and may never meet her in person, but I sure know how her dog looks. It looks just like mine—a white Jack Russell terrier mix with one black eye that we found at the pound. She found hers there too, and that's what's brought us together on-line.

I found her in the KIDS ONLY section of America Online under "Hobbies/Clubs." I found other kids who share my interest in horses, cats, drawing, saving the environment, and the overall joys and problems of being a ten-year-old girl in America.

I've found a lot of pen pals (though I'm not really good at keeping up), stored up a lot of (bad) jokes, gotten some kool recipes, and even advice on what new bike to buy.

I also found out about *Fear Street* from the "Goosebumps" bulletin board. R. L. Stine wrote both. And I don't think I'll ever look at *National Velvet* or *Black Beauty* the same way after hearing from other cyber-kids about how they treat the horses on the set.

I was never into flying planes but figured I'd see why other people were: I'm still not interested.

I found out I'm not the only one in the world who likes *The*

Lion King though my mother goes on and on about how artistically it's nowhere near as good as *Beauty and the Beast* or *The Little Mermaid*.

I've also listened to problems kids my age have. Some of them I share; others I try to think of how I'd solve them and sometimes even make a suggestion. Other times I'm just glad I can walk away from it.

I've read *Disney Adventures, National Geographic,* and *Sports Illustrated For Kids* on-line, thought about sending in some of my own poems, e-mailed my best friend, and gotten *real* excited when there's mail waiting for me. And I've looked up things in *Compton's Encyclopedia.* Today, my teacher told me my biographical report on Thomas Edison was super: Thanks for the help cyberspace!

Being on-line can get pretty expensive and my mom insists I do my homework and piano (which I *hate*) before I can go there. I think of it as sort of a cross between ice cream and carrots—good for you and fun.

A funny thing: On one of these bulletin boards deaf people wrote in. Someone said that "here you don't need to say you can't hear because no one is talking to you orally. I almost feel I can hear people." Well, I almost feel I can hear her.

Elisabeth Cuming, a fourth grader,
New York, New York

Preface

There is a great story behind the idea for *Kids On-line*. In August 1994, I was on a business trip in San Francisco. Since San Francisco is such a wonderful city, I had decided to bring along a young friend of mine named Karina Meckel. At the time, she was twelve years old.

That Saturday afternoon, we were cooped up in our hotel room. I had tons of work to do before we could go out and explore the city. Like many kids her age (and many adults my age!), Karina is a bit of a television junkie—and that afternoon she was hooked on HBO. Have you ever tried to do homework while a TV is blaring nearby? I thought I was going to lose my mind! Instead, I tried to lure Karina away from the TV by offering to let her log on to my account on America Online. It's fun, I assured her, and most important, it's *quiet*.

No such luck. Karina wasn't at all interested in spending time on-line. "What would I do on-line?" she asked me. "It gets boring." Karina has a Mac Quadra at home, and I knew that her father had gotten her an AOL account so that she could do research for school papers. It seemed that she hadn't explored enough, though, to find anything on AOL that really grabbed her attention.

"There's lots of stuff to do on-line," I told her, only to be stumped two seconds later when she said, "Like what? I mean for kids my age." The truth is, I knew what I liked to do on-line, but I had no idea what was *really* available for younger people. Surely, there had to be hangouts for kids and teens and fun magazines to read. And I knew there must be gaming forums and places with trivia quizzes and other things that might interest a sophisticated twelve-year-old, but I had no idea where they were—or how to find them.

That's when the brainstorm hit. Since I'd already written a bunch of books for kids and teens, Karina said, "Why not write a book that tells kids about all the fun things they can do online?" Surely, I told her, *someone* must have already written a book like that, but when we tromped on down to a couple of bookstores in Union Square, we couldn't find a single one. There were plenty of books teaching people how to use computers. And there was even a whole shelf of books that showed adults about all the stuff they could do on-line. But there wasn't a single book for kids. Not one. I couldn't believe it.

As soon as I got back to the East Coast, I called my literary agent and told her about Karina's idea. She loved it and suggested that I get started on it right away. Then a very lucky thing happened. I had dinner with a friend of mine named Robert Pondiscio; he works for *Time* magazine. As I was telling him about the book, I realized that Robert was the perfect person to help me write it. After all, Robert knows lots about computers and the on-line world. One of his jobs as *Time*'s public affairs director is to host the magazine's on-line conferences on AOL. That's actually how I met Robert—we were on-line friends long before we ever met face-to-face.

Luckily, Robert jumped at the idea of writing this book. He knew how useful it would be to kids and he also knew it would be a lot of fun to write. Next thing I knew, Robert and I were swapping tons of e-mails. (For those of you who don't know what e-mail is, it's notes or letters that you type on your computer and then send over the modem to someone's electronic mailbox. We'll tell you all about e-mail in Chapter 5 of this book.) Robert and I have really kept the AOL postmaster busy!

For the past few months, we've been swapping insights, interview transcripts, and news clippings—all by electronic mail.

That's one of the things that's so cool about cyberspace. Robert and I were able to write this book together even though we were almost never in the same room. We'd send each other chapters while he was in New York and I was in San Francisco or Chicago or Detroit. It was so easy! And that is just the sort of thing you can do on-line, too. If one of your friends moves to another town or state—or even another country—you can send him or her e-mails and can even create a private on-line room in which the two of you can chat directly. If you're stumped by one of your homework problems for math, you can go to AOL's Homework Helper room and ask one of the experts there for guidance. And, of course, there are all sorts of fun games to play, bulletin boards to check out, and magazines to read.

This book is jam-packed with all kinds of ideas for cool things you can do on the Internet and on AOL, CompuServe, Prodigy, or any of the other on-line services. For those of you who don't already subscribe to a service, we've included phone numbers you can call to sign up with all the major national commercial on-line services. You can find those numbers on pages 13-25. And because you've bought this book, they'll send you the software for free! What a deal!

Once you've had time to get comfortable roaming the corridors of the on-line world, we'd love it if you would keep in touch with us. You can use our e-mail addresses to give us ideas for future editions of the book. We'd love to hear from you. (Robert can be reached through America Online: RPondiscio@aol.com. You'll find my e-mail address below.)

In the meantime, read up, log on, and have a blast in cyberspace! See you on-line!

Marian Salzman [Marian_Salzman@chiat.com]
New York City/San Francisco
February 15, 1995

Getting Started

When we began working on this book we talked with kids and parents, and also with staff/guides on all the major services. Here are just a few excerpts from those conversations:

Matthew, age twelve, is from Minnesota (near the Canadian border) and Megan, age twelve, is from Franklin, Wisconsin. Carly, age eleven, is from Tulsa, Oklahoma, and eleven-year-old Brian is from Annapolis, Maryland.

How did you come to have an on-line account? What do you like to do on-line?

MATTHEW: My mom has the on-line account, and signed me on; I like going in the teens' chat rooms.

MEGAN: We got America Online and Prodigy and now we just have AOL; it's fun. A LOT of fun. And we also tried eWorld as a tester and then got rid of that. AOL only right now.

What do you do first when you log on?

MATTHEW: I look for my mail first.

CARLY: I check my mail and go to Disney. I usually meet my e-mail friends in focus groups. One of my friends from school is on-line.

MEGAN: I go to the homework help room. The only thing I don't like is it seems like the teachers take a long time just so you have a higher bill.

What's cool about on-line? Do you like the people you've met?

MATTHEW: The on-line people are nice. My mom blocks instant messages so I don't get the weirdos.

BRIAN: It's nice chatting with the rest of the country.

MATTHEW: People can send mail quicker and cheaper.

MEGAN: I think eventually we won't have paper mail or newspapers anymore.

And here are a few comments we heard while talking to parents:

Caroline, thirty-five, from Simi Valley, California: "I have three kids and they only go on-line under my sign-on; otherwise, it's too expensive. I received my AOL software when I bought a modem/fax. I use it the most in my house. My kids like to 'shop' the shareware areas for games. They have also used the teacher help area. And, my thirteen-year-old occasionally goes to teen chat. He loves it!" She went on to share a story about how her oldest child completed a term paper with the help of AOL. "The subject was Neil Armstrong, and they found outstanding resources on-line to help him prepare a first-rate report."

Robb, thirty-eight, from St. Petersburg, Florida: "My Internet use got my child, aged eleven, interested in going on-line. I have two kids, a ten-year-old boy and an eleven-year-old daughter. Right now we all share one computer; at present it's in my office. The kids use Disney, KOOL, and BKG [American Dialogue]. They actually consider on-line their major source of income since they do focus groups regularly for a company or two through BKG. I am quite [supportive of] their use of AOL for it expands the children's horizons. They get to meet children with other similar interests. My daughter, Jessica, met another girl on-line who is her age, and also Jewish, and they share similar problems. That has made a difference. Jessica attends a magnet school which encourages use. [In comparison], my son needs no motivation, outside or otherwise, to pursue anything game connected.''

''Shadowfax'' is a desktop publisher from Shipman, Virginia: ''We are in a rural area and on-line opens up whole worlds and resources, and communications! The only thing I worry about is my fourteen-year-old running up my bill. Yes, and we have had a bit of trouble with e-mail [unwelcome]. Parent control is needed at all ages. Actually, I often feel that the teen chats are too suggestive; we've had trouble [which led to the e-mails], so I don't allow much of that. [I'm not as uptight about it as I sound; it's just that I want my daughter to exercise good judgment in terms of where she heads on-line and with whom she talks.] We feel very connected and I'm thrilled by the worlds on-line has opened up for both of us.''

KIDS ON-LINE

Introduction

"We got a new computer for Christmas and it came with a CD-ROM player and a modem. My dad got us onto Prodigy and we have lots of fun talking to other kids through the message boards. Now I have a pen friend, I mean an e-mail friend, in Oregon. She's very funny and pretty. We snail mailed each other pictures of ourselves and our dogs a couple of weeks ago. Now I feel like I know her better."

—Megan, twelve, Baton Rouge, Louisiana

WELCOME TO CYBERSPACE

You can almost hear the wires humming! Without leaving home, kids are visiting the best libraries in the world, downloading cool computer software, and getting on-line help with their homework. They're talking with other kids all over the world about school, annoying brothers and sisters, and their favorite TV stars. Kids with problems they're too embarrassed to discuss with their parents and friends are getting advice from other kids with the same problems. They're keeping in touch with friends and relatives. And they're getting all the latest news on their favorite musicians and bands.

There's a lot going on in cyberspace:

1

• In the small town of Grand Marais, Minnesota, near the Canadian border, twelve-year-old Matthew hears from his grandmother in Arizona every day via computer. Electronic mail is keeping his family in touch. "My uncle is moving to Russia, and he has an e-mail address," says Matthew, "so I'll get to send him mail, too."

• The kids who go to the Boulder Valley School District in Louisville, Colorado, can apply for a free Internet account. "Most of my friends have accounts," says Mike, a freshman in Fairview High. "The Internet is a gold mine for any software known to man."

• Tia, thirteen, talks with kids all across the country about all kinds of things as a "chat host" in the Kids Only OnLine (KOOL) area of American Online. She keeps in touch with lots of friends she's made on-line.

• Patrick, a minister in West Virginia, says cyberspace has opened up a whole new world to his daughter. "My daughter, Kara, is able to study her Gaelic and French with native speakers or with university students and professors who are studying or teaching the language," he says. Kara logs on to America Online and uses the service's Internet gateway and AOL's reference section to keep up-to-date on current events, history, and geography. The Kids Only OnLine area puts her in touch with pen pals from all over, gets her the latest corny jokes, and gives her access to software to help her write and draw more creatively. She can also download books, articles, and pictures.

"In the last few months Kara has downloaded from NASA, the Vatican Library, the British Museum, the Museum of Antiquities in Jerusalem, the Library of Congress, and others," he raves. "And this is an eleven-year-old girl on top of the highest mountain in north-central West Virginia making a local phone call! There has never been a better bargain than the on-line world."

Sound incredible? It is. But kids everywhere are doing it. And you can, too!

You're about to begin an amazing adventure. With your personal computer and a modem, you can travel anywhere in the world, meet just about any type of person, learn *anything*. It's like having access to a huge brain that can answer any question and a rocket ship that can whisk you anywhere in the world.

The best news is that you don't need to know a gigabyte from a mouse to surf with ease through cyberspace. With this book you'll learn how easy it is to navigate your way through this new world. Your computer keyboard is your steering wheel; the mouse or trackball your stick shift to drive down the information superhighway you've heard so much about. This book will be your road map. Along the way we'll visit far-off places, explore a variety of fun and fascinating destinations, and learn rules of the road that will help you travel safely and get the most out of your trip.

DAWN OF A NEW AGE

One of the most exciting things about cyberspace today is that it's still under construction. Right now, only about six percent of U.S. households are hooked up to an on-line service. And those of us who are in cyberspace are witnessing an incredible revolution. Even as you're reading this book, interactive technology is changing the way we communicate, learn, work, buy and sell things, and play. We're not talking about some distant future. The future is happening *right here, right now*.

Over the next few years, more and more people are expected to join on-line services. Some people think that being on-line will eventually be as common as owning a telephone or a TV. And, just think: You can say that you were one of the first on-line explorers. You're a pioneer!

3

FUN FACTS

Communications Revolutions in History

Invention	Date	Impact
Writing	3500 B.C.	Storage of information
Movable type	Mid-1400s	Multiplied information
Telegraph	1844	Instantaneous communication
Television	1939	Single-point-to-mass communication
Information superhighway	Today	Mass-to-mass communication

. . . .

WHAT IS CYBERSPACE?

Is it a place? A thing? The word *cyberspace* was first used by William Gibson in his novel *Neuromancer*. It refers to the world you are in when you are on-line. If I'm in New York and you are in Los Angeles, and we're carrying on a conversation over the computer (or over the phone, for that matter) the place where we connect is called cyberspace.

There are plenty of other names for it: the *information super-highway*, the *infobahn*, the *electronic highway*—but they all refer to the same thing. Cyberspace is simply the place where information lives.

In cyberspace, time and distance no longer exist. When you're on-line, Japan is just as close as the house down the street. Electronic mail gets across town, across the country, or around the world in seconds, not days or weeks.

Everything you see and do in cyberspace comes down to two

simple things: communication and information. You communicate with other people, and you provide and receive information.

WHAT'S IN IT FOR ME?

Imagine having an electronic post office that's open twenty-four hours a day, seven days a week, that delivers mail anywhere in the world in the blink of an eye. Then toss in an incredibly huge library of computer software—much of which you can get for free. Add encyclopedias, dictionaries, newspapers, magazines, games, bulletin boards, clubs, stores, concerts, discussion groups, and contests with prizes, and you're beginning to get some idea of what's available to you in cyberspace.

The most important resource in cyberspace, though, is people. Millions and millions of them. It's impossible to be sure just how many people are out there, but most experts estimate that there are probably 20–30 million men and women, boys and girls in cyberspace. You'll have a chance to meet people who are almost exactly like you—and you'll also have a chance to meet people who are so different from you that you probably would never, ever run across them in the real world.

"I have a couple pen pals, but the one I always write to is my pen pal Susanna who lives in Sweden," says Courtney, who attends Safety Harbor Middle School in Florida. "I use e-mail to keep in touch. We write about all different things like our families, friends, and school. We also talk about boys!!"

HOW DO I GET THERE?

A personal computer, a modem, communications software (usually provided by the on-line service) and a telephone line are all you need to travel into cyberspace.

5

Personal Computer. The fact that you're reading this book probably means that you already own or have access to a personal computer. So, we're not going to talk about computer hardware here. If you don't yet have a computer and would like to learn more about them, we recommend the "Dummies" series (published by IDG Books), including *Windows for Dummies, Mac for Dummies,* etc. The best bet may be to visit a local bookstore and ask the salesperson to recommend his or her favorite EASY book about choosing the computer that's right for you.

There are also lots of great magazines about computers, a few of which focus on computers for families. Our favorite is *Family PC*, published by Ziff-Davis. It's sold on newsstands everywhere and is also on America Online (KEYWORD: FAMILYPC). Within each issue of *Family PC,* there's a cool insert written especially for kids. For more information or if you have questions you just can't seem to get answered, contact the magazine's editor at 244 Main Street, Northampton, Massachusetts 01060. Or, you can reach the editors by fax (413-582-9070) or e-mail (FamilyPC@aol.com).

Modem. Modem is short for *MO*dulate/*DEM*odulate. All you really need to know about modems is that they allow your computer to talk to another computer over the phone lines. You'll use your modem to dial a local phone number that connects you to one of the on-line services.

Not all modems are the same. Like people, some move faster than others. Speed is very important because it will determine how fast you can send and receive data over your computer. Modem speeds are described in bps—"bits per second," or bauds. A "bit" is the smallest possible unit of information. And eight bits make up a "byte," which is roughly equivalent to a single letter or number. Getting too technical for you? Don't worry about it. All you need to know is that the higher the bps or baud, the faster the modem can transmit data. For example, while a 2400 bps/baud modem can only transmit 3,000 words a minute, a 9600-baud modem can transmit 12,000 words in that time.

If you already own a 1200-baud or 2400-baud modem, that will connect you to any of the on-line services. The only drawback is that it will take you a long time to perform some functions. For example, downloading some types of software will take you an hour or more! That's why, if you don't yet own a modem, we recommend that you buy one that's at least 9600 bps. Some services have even begun to offer 14,400 speeds.

● ●

FUN FACTS
A Computer Timeline

Mid-1800s: Charles Babbage invents "Analytical Engine"
1930s: "Mechanical calculators" introduced
1947: Invention of transistor
1950s and 1960s: Computers still huge and highly technical
1969: Foundation for the Internet established
1977: Twenty-one-year-old Bill Gates and twenty-four-year-old Paul Allen launch Microsoft in Redmond, Washington
1984: Macintosh introduced to the world at Superbowl XVIII
1994: America Online membership crosses the one million mark
1995: More than twenty-five million people log on to the 'Net worldwide

● ●

Software. Before a modem can connect two computers, it needs communications software. America Online and Prodigy provide their own software that members use to hook up to those services. CompuServe, GEnie, and Delphi can be reached with any communications software (MicroPhone™ is an example). But each is now offering optional software to make the

7

service easier to use. CompuServe offers CompuServe Information-tion Manager (CIM) software, Delphi has D-Lite, and GEnie offers Aladdin software. (See Chapter 2 for a discussion of the major on-line services; this will give you a better idea of the software you'll require.)

Phone Lines. In order for it to work, your modem must be connected to a phone jack. The data you send and receive will actually be traveling along the same lines you use when you make a phone call. Modems are finicky creatures. If you have call waiting and another call comes through, you will lose your on-line connection. That's why it's a good idea to disconnect call waiting before you go on-line. Your phone company or on-line service can tell you how to do it.

You may also lose your phone connection if someone picks up an extension of the phone line your computer is hooked up to. And, of course, the whole time you're on-line, the phone line is tied up. That's why having a separate phone line for your computer is a good idea. It will cost a bit more, but it will save a lot of hassle. Talk with your parents about whether having a separate line makes sense for your family.

IT'S EASY!

Some people are scared of computers because they don't realize how simple they can be to use. A computer is an appliance, just like a washing machine or a stove. And nobody's scared of a stove, right? The fact is, computers are getting easier and easier to use every day—and so is going on-line. Traveling in cyberspace these days can be as simple as pointing and clicking on your mouse. Being on-line has nothing to do with being a computer whiz. It's about communicating and interacting with people and information.

No book, including this one, can tell you everything there is to do in cyberspace. For one thing, more and more things are added every day. The best we can do is give you an idea of the kinds of things that are out there, while also giving you the tools you need to explore cyberspace further on your own. We've been on-line for a while, so we think we can show you some pretty cool places in which to hang out and some pretty fun things to do. By the time you've finished this book, you'll have a better idea of what the various on-line services and the Internet offer, so you can decide which service is best for you. We'll also teach you a few rules of the road and some money-saving tips. Then it's up to you to log on and blast off into cyberspace. Have fun!!

You Should Know ... The authors of this book are "IPs"—information providers—on AOL. Robert helps run the *Time* magazine area, and Marian runs the American Dialogue™ area. We use just about all the online services, however, and we think we can be fair in judging all of them. Just because we like AOL doesn't mean we don't think there are some things the other services do better! [*Time* has recently added a site on the World Wide Web (www.pathfinder.com.time) and so has Chiat/Day, Marian's employer (www.chiatday.com). So visit us on the 'Net, too!]

2

Commercial On-line Services

"The first time I realized that I was typing to my friend, instead of talking to her, well, it made me think, this is cool. 'Chat' is a great way to find out about other people. I also write letters on-line to a couple of cousins who live in Connecticut. And I research my school papers on-line sometimes by using the encyclopedia and a few of the magazines and newspapers."

—Amanda, Canton, Ohio

WHAT'S OUT THERE?

In a word: Everything.

With your personal computer and a modem, you can look up information about your favorite celebrities, go shopping, play games, and work on school projects with kids around the country.

You can also communicate with people all over the world by posting messages on bulletin boards, sending e-mail, or talking directly with people in chat rooms. Cyberspace is an entire world waiting to be explored. No matter what it is you want to talk about or learn, you can be sure there's someone out there who shares your interest.

One thing that surprises a lot of people is how easy it is to make friends on-line. The authors of this book met on AOL and have been friends ever since. Some people who have met on-line have even gotten married. Talk show host Rush Limbaugh married a woman he met on CompuServe!

One of the coolest things about cyberspace is that every day, people think of new ways to use it. They create new services and form new areas, and they add more and more information to the systems, so that the on-line databases are always growing. Here are just a few of the creative things people have done in cyberspace:

• When Los Angeles was hit by an earthquake in January 1994, the phone lines were jammed with calls, so it was very difficult for people to reach their loved ones in other parts of the country to let them know they were OK. The solution? They posted messages on bulletin boards, asking people in other states to place the phone calls for them.

• Subscribers to Prodigy were able to send each other electronic Christmas cards this year!

• On AOL, teachers swap ideas for fun lessons. They also download software that their students can use in the classroom.

• When actor Kevin Costner turned forty, Prodigy opened up a special bulletin board where people could post "Happy Birthday" notes. Prodigy then forwarded all the notes to Kevin on his birthday.

• Rosa Parks and Gerald Ford are just two very famous people who met with kids on America Online in early 1995 as guests of the Scholastic Network.

COMMERCIAL ON-LINE SERVICES

Now that you know about some of the fun and interesting things you can do in cyberspace, it's time to get started. The first thing you need to do is decide how you want to hook up to cyber-space. The easiest way to do it is through a commercial on-line service such as America Online or Prodigy. Each of these services charges its members a fee to dial in via modem and gain access to the wealth of information and services it offers.

Not all on-line services are the same. Though most of them offer the same basic services, they look, feel, and operate differently. You may even find that different types of people join different services. For example, Prodigy is very popular with families, while CompuServe is very popular among businesspeople. The service that is right for you will depend on what you want to do in cyberspace.

We'll look at the major commercial on-line services: America Online, Prodigy, CompuServe, GEnie, Delphi, and eWorld. Then in Chapter 3, we'll discuss the Internet.

ONE SIZE DOESN'T FIT ALL

Every city has a shopping mall, a post office, a school, and a library. But that doesn't mean all of these cities are the same. Every city or town has a look, a feel, and a personality of its own. It's the same thing with commercial on-line services. They all offer similar services, but that's where the similarities end. And just like a city that is growing quickly, on-line services are constantly changing as more and more people move into town and demand a wider variety of services.

Prodigy, for example, is like the Disney World of the on-line universe. It's bright and bold with lots of splashy graphics. It was designed to be used by people in their homes, not at work. As a result, it's very family-oriented. America Online is famous for being easy to use. Even if you've never been on a computer, you can probably figure out how to use AOL. CompuServe is known for having lots more information and bigger databases than AOL or Prodigy, but because it was also built for businesspeople to use, you might find it's not as "friendly" as the others. GEnie, Delphi, and eWorld are much smaller than the others (so far, anyway), but they also have personalities of their own. We'll talk a little about each one. We'll also talk about prices, so you and your parents can figure out which one makes most sense for your budget.

Gooey Interface? Yech!

When talking about on-line services, you'll hear a lot about the "user interface." Basically, that just means what the screen looks like. Before the Macintosh was invented, computer screens all had text interfaces, which means when you looked at a screen, all you saw was a bunch of numbers and letters. The Mac changed that by adding graphics to the screen, plus a mouse, pull-down menus, and "dialogue boxes." Until just a few years ago, on-line services were all text based, too. Now they're a lot more user-friendly. That's because most on-line services feature something called a Graphical User Interface, or GUI (pronounced "gooey"). It's sometimes called a "front end." Whatever the name, it's a lot easier to use than a text interface.

If you're new to cyberspace, a good interface—one that's simple and easy to understand—can be the difference between enjoying your visit and feeling totally lost and frustrated. If you've never been on-line and aren't a computer expert, you probably shouldn't venture into cyberspace without a gooey front end!

Let's take a closer look at each of the major on-line services. . . .

AMERICA ONLINE

COOL: It's hard to imagine an on-line service that could be easier to use than AOL. The user interface is clean, simple, and self-explanatory. It's also the easiest service for meeting and communicating with other people. AOL has the simplest e-mail system. Its search mechanisms make it a breeze to find files and software to download. You get to pick your own screen-name, instead of being assigned a meaningless series of numbers and letters. It's got the best and widest variety of live chat rooms, including the ability to send and receive "Instant Messages." And it's also pretty cheap unless you spend a lot of time chatting on-line.

NOT SO COOL: It's easy to use, but there's not as much stuff to do on AOL as on CompuServe, and it's not as colorful as Prodigy. (The authors are a bit divided here: Robert likes Prodigy's colorful interface, while Marian prefers the graphics on AOL's new version and those on eWorld. If you can, check them all out to see which you like best.) And one of AOL's best features is also its worst: Live chat is so much fun on AOL that it's addictive. And it can quickly drive your bill into the stratosphere!

WHAT DO I NEED TO GET ON?: You need America Online software, which is available for free in Macintosh, Windows, and DOS versions. AOL advertises heavily in computer magazines and elsewhere, offering ten free hours to try it out. Or you can call AOL at 800-827-6364 to order your copy. Within a few days, a disk with instructions for getting on-line will arrive in the mail.

GETTING AROUND: AOL's point-and-click interface is simple, and virtually self-explanatory. When you log on, a voice comes out of your computer that says, "Welcome!" The opening screen gives "In the Spotlight" tips about events and features on AOL, so you'll know at a glance if something interesting is happening on-line. By clicking your mouse on the "Go To Main Menu," you'll call up icons for the fourteen departments AOL offers, including Education, Clubs & Interests, Computing, Reference Desk, People Connection, The Internet, and Kids Only. Click on any one of these icons, and you're automatically sent to that area!

PRICE: $9.95 per month, which includes five free hours; $2.95 for each additional hour no matter what speed your modem is. Just about everything on the service is covered in that price.

GETTING HELP: AOL's on-line help system is easy to use, and best of all, it's free. It's a great place to familiarize yourself with the service and not have to worry about your bill. By entering KEYWORD: HELP, you'll go to a free gateway where you can get technical help and tips from other users. You can also post messages and ask questions about AOL—and even get your questions answered in a live on-line forum.

WHEN ALL ELSE FAILS: If you get hopelessly stuck, can't get on-line (which occasionally happens with AOL) or are having other problems you can't seem to solve on-line, you can always call AOL's technical help desk at 800-827-6364. Recorded answers to the most common connectivity problems are available twenty-four hours a day, seven days a week. You can also speak to a technical representative who will help you with a forgotten password, a new local access number, or other problems from 9:00 A.M. to 2:00 A.M. Eastern, Monday through Friday, and from noon to 1:00 A.M. Eastern, Saturday and Sunday.

THE BOTTOM LINE: There are three basic things you should look at when choosing an on-line service: Price, content, and ease of use. AOL wins on all but content. It's the biggest and fastest-growing online service in terms of number of users because it goes out of its way to make the service easy to use and fun. If you've never been on-line before, AOL is the best place to start.

COMPUSERVE

COOL: The resources available on CompuServe are mind-boggling. Its members have access to nearly 1,500 research databases, 500 publications, and 600 discussion groups. There are plenty of hobby, entertainment, and family features, including an extensive movie database, online shopping, travel and restaurant guides, soap opera summaries, and a national phone directory—yes, the White Pages for the *entire* country. CompuServe can be a bargain: You get unlimited access to "basic services" (including news, sports, weather, and some reference libraries) for a flat monthly fee. Once you're an experienced CompuServe user (and have a full-time job!), kiss your local reference librarian good-bye. You'll never need him or her again.

NOT SO COOL: CompuServe was built primarily for business and professional use, so you won't find many games. Also, most of the best services are not part of the basic package, so you can quickly rack up hefty hourly charges for "extended services," with additional surcharges on top of that for some specialized services. If you spend a lot of time using extended services on-line, you'll understand why some people call it Compu$erve. CompuServe is not as easy to use as AOL and is not as kid-friendly as Prodigy. Finding your way around can be difficult, and the sheer volume of material can be overwhelming.

WHAT DO I NEED TO GET ON?: You don't need front-end software to use CompuServe, but it is **highly recommended**. The CompuServe Information Manager (CIM) helps you get acquainted with the service quickly and easily.

GETTING AROUND: To start exploring the service, click on "basic services" or any of the sixteen icons on the welcome or "browse" screen. Basic services is a great way to explore CompuServe without running up your bill, since there are no connect-time charges. You get unlimited access to more than a hundred different features, ranging from Grolier's Academic American Encyclopedia to The Electronic Mall to up-to-the-minute news. GO BASIC to see what's available in basic services and to read short descriptions of some of CompuServe's extended services.

PRICE: A flat monthly fee of $9.95 gets you unlimited access to "basic services" and sixty e-mail messages a month. The connect-time rate for "extended services" such as forums is $4.80/hour. In addition, CompuServe features "premium services" such as research databases that are billed *in addition* to hourly connect-time rates. Some areas can end up costing more than $20 an hour. Ouch! Luckily, the "extended" and "premium" services are clearly marked, so you know when you're entering the more expensive areas.

WARNING: CompuServe's basic service lets you send sixty free e-mail messages a month before you start running up additional charges based on message length. You also have to pay for e-mail you receive from the Internet. You may think that's no big deal, since you probably don't send sixty letters a month, even during the holiday season. But e-mail is easy to use, fun, and *addictive*. If you have lots of friends on-line and join a few on-line mailing lists, you could find yourself exceeding the sixty-letter limit in one day! So, if you think you're going to send and receive a lot of e-mail, it might pay to consider a different service.

GETTING HELP: You can send e-mail to CompuServe customer service twenty-four hours a day in the Online Feedback area. Enter GO FEEDBACK at any point on-line. The Feedback area is part of basic services, and is free of connect-time charges. Feedback messages are usually answered within 24–48 hours via CompuServe Mail. If that's not quick enough, you can look up answers to hundreds of the most frequently asked questions in the on-line Customer Service Help Database. Enter GO CSHELP to enter this area.

WHEN ALL ELSE FAILS: If you can't log on or find the answer to your problem on-line, call 800-848-8990 from 7:30 A.M. to 2:00 A.M. Eastern on Monday–Friday; or from noon until 10:00 P.M. on Saturday and Sunday.

THE BOTTOM LINE: CompuServe has it all. If you're an experienced on-line user, ready to expand your horizons, CompuServe might be for you. But it's probably not the right choice for your first on-line service. It's not as easy to use as AOL, and not as kid-friendly as Prodigy. Think CompuServe is worried about our recommending other services? Nah. They know that when you become more comfortable in cyberspace and your on-line needs become more serious, you're likely to give CompuServe a second look.

PRODIGY

COOL: Prodigy is targeted at families, so there's lots for kids to do on the service. (In fact, the third most popular area on Prodigy is the Teen area; it's always jammed with teens and kids who enjoy chat, games, swapping viewpoints, you name it.) There also are a lot of celebrities, writers, and media people who've been hired as "experts" to contribute to forums. Prodigy's colorful, appealing interface is ideal for kids, and it's reasonably simple to use. Prodigy was also the first commercial on-line service to offer access to the World Wide Web on the Internet, which is *very* cool. Unfortunately, it's only available to Windows users right now.

NOT SO COOL: Prodigy is neither as in-depth as Compu-Serve, nor as easy to use as AOL—it can sometimes be a little confusing to find your way around the system. It also accepts advertising, so while you're reading a bulletin board or sending an e-mail, you might be distracted by an ad for a car or florist service or book club. Because it's so heavy on the graphics, Prodigy is really slow at 2400 bps (that's how it got its nick-name "Plodigy"). As a result, you'll need to run it at 9600 or risk being bored to death. (As we were writing this book, Prod-igy began to offer 14,400 bps access in select cities.) Also, Prodigy's colorful interface may be a turnoff to some users—it can be a bit cartoonish.

WHAT DO I NEED TO GET ON?: You need Prodigy soft-ware to access the service. It's available in Macintosh, Win-dows, and DOS versions. You can usually order it and try it out free for a month with ten free hours of connect time—check for ads and offers in *Family PC, Home PC, Computer Life,* and other magazines, or call 800-PRODIGY.

GETTING AROUND: Click the mouse on the JUMP menu and select JUMP: LET'S EXPLORE. This is a self-guided tour through the Prodigy service that will explain the ropes to new-bies. Once you're feeling comfortable, click on the "Member Services" icon on the main screen. This will give you a list of the available services and the JUMP words (commands) you need to find your way around.

PRICE: Prodigy charges a monthly fee of $9.95, which gives you five hours of use, and an additional $2.95 for each hour after that. It also charges additional fees for some "extended" and "premium" services, such as on-line newspapers.

GETTING HELP: On-line services that have their own soft-ware usually have lots of help options built right into the basic program. That means you don't have to actually go on-line to access useful information about using the service. If you are on-line, JUMP: FOR NEW MEMBERS to get a list of information. You can find the answer to most questions in the A–Z index located there.

WHEN ALL ELSE FAILS: Call Prodigy at 800-PRODIGY. Its customer service center operates twenty-four hours a day, seven days a week.

THE BOTTOM LINE: All those brightly colored graphics can be confusing, and it's not quite as easy to use as AOL, but if you're a new infonaut, chances are pretty good you'll like Prodigy. It helped pioneer the use of on-line services for people other than librarians and gearheads. The amount of time and attention Prodigy has spent trying to appeal to families and kids makes it worth a try. As this book went to press, Prodigy was promising a cleaner, smarter on-screen appearance, to make the system a little less confusing. It's promising lots of cool graphics and sounds. If it can do it, it'll be a lot easier to recommend Prodigy wholeheartedly.

America Online, CompuServe, and Prodigy are considered the big three on-line systems. Besides these three, which have nearly six million subscribers among them, there are a few other services worth considering. Delphi, GEnie, and eWorld put together don't even have a half million subscribers among them, but we wanted to let you know about them in case they offer what you're looking for—and, of course, they could well expand rapidly in the future.

DELPHI

COOL: Three words: *full Internet access.* At the moment, Delphi is the only major commercial service with complete access to the Internet. Delphi is betting its rent money that people will want full access to the Internet, and everything it offers. In fact, it now calls itself "Delphi Internet." This is a very smart move and should help attract new members.

NOT SO COOL: Delphi is not user-friendly. In fact, it can be downright user-hostile. And we mean *mean!* There is no front-end interface. Even with full Internet access, Delphi will continue to face tough competition. The other major on-line services are making real progress in their efforts to give their members Internet access, and they're going Delphi one better: They're providing Internet access that's easy to use.

WHAT DO I NEED TO GET ON?: Delphi is the only one of the major on-line services not to offer front-end software. That means that all you need to get on is your own communications software (your modem probably came with it) to dial in to Delphi and register. To get your local access number, call Delphi at 800-695-4005 from 8:00 A.M. to 11:00 P.M. Eastern.

GETTING AROUND: "Getting around Delphi is easy to do," says the guidebook that comes with your membership. Yeah, right. Delphi uses text menus to get you where you want to go—no pointing and clicking here. The main menu lets you choose from Entertainment and Games, Groups and Clubs, Reference and Education, and about a dozen other topics. Once you get comfortable with the service (about the time your second child is born), there are shortcuts you can use to get around. But learning the shortcuts isn't exactly easy either.

PRICE: Delphi offers free trial memberships, like most of the others. After that, there are two membership plans to choose from: The 10/4 plan costs $10 a month and gives you four free hours; additional hours are $4 each. The 20/20 plan costs about $20 a month with 20 free hours; additional hours are $1.80 each. The 20/20 plan also carries a $19 one-time entry fee. Both plans charge $3 a month for Internet service.

GETTING HELP: The easiest way to find help is to type HELP. Wherever you are, you can type HELP to get a list of the options you have at that point and how to use them. There's also a section on using Delphi, which you can reach from anywhere by typing GO USING. You'll get a menu of information on rates, your bill, access numbers, etc. Also try GO USING TIPS for answers to frequently asked help questions.

WHEN ALL ELSE FAILS: Call Delphi customer service at 800-695-4005. It's staffed from 8:00 A.M. to 11:00 P.M. on weekdays, and noon to 8:00 P.M. on weekends and holidays.

THE BOTTOM LINE: By the time you read this, Delphi's long-promised front-end program might be available. If that's true, give it another look. Until then, Delphi is NOT for newbies. Beginners beware!

GEnie

COOL: The best graphical, multiplayer games are on GEnie. GEnie calls its special interest groups ''RoundTables'' or ''RTs.'' There are categories within RoundTables, so that the Education RoundTable for example (KEYWORD EDUCATION) breaks down into twenty-one categories, each of which has lots of topics, as well as bulletin boards, file libraries, and real-time chats. There is lots of stuff here, but, since there is no easy topic list (Directory of RoundTables), it's downright tough to find a cyberspot on GEnie that feels just like home. One exception is the homeschool forum, within the Education RoundTable. That seems to buzz. Unlike CompuServe, however, GEnie doesn't charge extra for RTs, so if there's an RT or other feature on GEnie you're interested in, you'll save money by being a GEnie member.

NOT SO COOL: If you're looking for other kids to hang out with on-line, GEnie is not for you. *Only two percent of GEnie members are age eighteen or under.* If you're a Mac user, you have to run GEnie on some pretty funky software, which doesn't make the adventure very worthwhile—as of spring 1995, GEnie's graphical interface (front end) is only available for Windows, and even the editors of *Netguide* (January 1995) moaned about the system's navigational limitations: ". . . Wading through old messages, dating back four years in some cases, was difficult. One poster asked, 'Is anybody out there?' We couldn't tell. We saw system operators and a few random members, but not much activity . . ." GEnie also charges extra for prime-time access and 9600 bps access. Fortunately, it runs pretty well at 2400 baud, so slow down and save.

WHAT DO I NEED TO GET ON?: Call 800-638-9636 to order a start-up kit.

GETTING AROUND: Without the graphical user interface for Windows, you're stuck trying to find your way around GEnie using difficult "page numbers" or keywords. If you're a Mac user, you have no other choice.

PRICE: $8.95 and four free hours per month, $3 an hour after that. There are extra charges for a few premium services. Where GEnie really soaks you is during prime time (8:00 A.M. to 6:00 P.M. local time), which costs $9.50 an hour; there's also a $6 an hour charge for 9600-baud access.

GETTING HELP: To get help, just use keyword HELP at any prompt. If you're new to the system, stop by the GEnie Users

RoundTable (KEYWORD: GENIUS) for advice and tips from other members.

WHEN ALL ELSE FAILS: GEnie customer service is available weekdays from 8:00 A.M. to midnight, Eastern. Weekends you can get help from noon to 8:00 P.M.

THE BOTTOM LINE: Sturdy, but unspectacular. GEnie's not the worst in any single factor—price, content, ease-of-use—but it's not the best in any category either

eWORLD

COOL: It's just as easy to use as AOL and the graphics are fun and *very* attractive.

NOT SO COOL: It's a small service, with fewer than fifty thousand members. That's not likely to change dramatically until eWorld becomes available to more than just Mac users. It's scheduled to unveil a Windows version this year—maybe by the time you read this!

WHAT DO I NEED TO GET ON?: You need a membership packet, which may come with your new computer and/or modem. If not, the software can be ordered by calling 800-775-4556. Like AOL, the installation is fairly easy: You insert the disk and follow a very logical set of instructions, providing billing information and the basic subscriber info. *Voilà!* You're on.

GETTING AROUND: eWorld has gone to school on AOL and developed a welcome screen that's clean, fun, and easy to use. If you're logging on for the first time, click on the info booth in eWorld "Town Square." A menu will pop up which features a "Getting Started" icon. Click it to find all kinds of good stuff for beginners, including "Tips and Tricks," "Internet Info," and descriptions of eWorld services.

PRICE: Charges for eWorld consist of a monthly fee of $8.95, which includes two hours of use. Each additional hour of usage is $4.95. Pricing is based on one-minute increments. In the United States (including Alaska and Hawaii) and Canada, a business hour surcharge of $2.95 per hour applies to all daytime use. Daytime hours are 6:00 A.M. to 6:00 P.M., Monday through Friday, local time. An international network surcharge of $7.95 per hour is applied to all eWorld use outside the U.S. and Canada.

GETTING HELP: The 800 number—800-775-4556—is also a help line offering a range of solutions. It is staffed Monday–Friday from 6:00 A.M. to 8:00 P.M. (To get help more quickly, as soon as the phone is answered hit 3, to be connected with technical assistance.)

THE BOTTOM LINE: It's a good service and in some ways, it out-AOLs AOL. But the bad news is that hardly anybody logs on to eWorld; Marian insists she could only find eight people on-line one afternoon when she visited eWorld. 1995 is supposed to be the year eWorld opens its doors to Windows users. If the service draws more people on-line, eWorld will be worth another look.

STUFF TO THINK ABOUT . . .

THE BILLS

Remember, on-line services cost money and your chatting and researching can and will add up. To check on how much damage you've done to your bank account—or to your parents' bank account—here's the quick way to check your charges on the big three on-line services:

America Online: KEYWORD: BILLING. Almost all AOL services are billed at a standard rate—just fax and mail service, charges from the on-line stores (for things you've bought), and the news library (KEYWORD: MERCURY) are billed at a premium rate.

CompuServe: MacCIM and WinCIM both have status bars that tell you how long you've been on-line during the current session. To find out your total charges for the current month, GO BILLING.

Prodigy: JUMP: ACCOUNT INFORMATION. Then click the Member Services icon and choose Account Status. (In this area, you can see total bills, including how much additional charges you've racked up in Plus Service time.)

Things Change

The on-line services business is *extremely* competitive. AOL, Prodigy, CompuServe, and the rest fight tooth and nail, constantly upgrading software, offering new services, cutting prices, etc. This means it's possible some of the information you just read could get out of date quickly. It's a good idea to watch for free offers from on-line services so you can go back and sample different services as they continue to evolve. Also, as this book was going to press, Microsoft, the 800-pound gorilla of the computer software business, was making plans to stand cyberspace on its ear by starting up a brand-new on-line service. Stay tuned!

CHOOSING THE SERVICE THAT'S
RIGHT FOR YOU

In deciding which service is right for you, you and your parents
need to consider a number of factors, including the following:

* Price
* What you want to do on-line
* How much time you plan to spend on-line

Pricing can be pretty complicated. Especially on Compu-
Serve. Some examples:

Absolute Newbie. Brian goes on-line twice a month. Typically, he logs on in the evening on a Sunday night at 6:00 P.M.
at 2400 baud, reads six e-mails from his keypals and responds
to them. He spends a half hour using an on-line encyclopedia
for a school project, then goes into a chat room for a half hour.
Then he goes into a sports forum, and reads and posts messages
on the bulletin board for an hour.

THE BILL

America Online:	$9.95	Delphi:	$10
Prodigy:	$9.95	GEnie:	$8.95
CompuServe:	$14.75	eWorld:	$8.95

Infonaut. Jill logs on two or three times a week in the
afternoon when she gets home from school, and spends an average of twelve hours a month on-line. She's got a 9600-baud
modem. Last month she hung out in a teen chat room for four
hours, sent and received about half a dozen e-mails every time
she logged on (fifty messages, two hours online), spent two
hours looking for magazine and newspapers articles about

27

the environment for a class project, downloaded pictures and graphics from a movies forum for an hour, and passed two hours playing interactive games with her on-line friend from Ohio.

THE BILL

America Online:	$30.60	Delphi:	$20 (under the 20/20 plan)
Prodigy:	$30.60 (plus premium surcharge for some newspapers)	GEnie:	$156.95 (prime-time hours are a killer!)
		eWorld:	$87.95
CompuServe:	$53.15		

Cyberholic. Chris *lives* on-line. He's totally into his computer; he's even got a 14.4 modem. He sometimes spends two or three hours a night on-line hanging out in forums on computer games, skiing, or television. He belongs to an Internet mailing list on alternative music that generates one hundred pieces of mail a week. He downloads lots of software from the games forum and hangs out in a gaming chat room trading tips with other kids on Doom and Myst. Last month, he spent thirty hours total on-line in forums and chat rooms and sent and/or received five hundred pieces of Internet e-mail.

THE BILL

America Online:	$83.70	Delphi:	$41
Prodigy:	$83.70	GEnie:	$266.75
CompuServe:	$210	eWorld:	$147.55

Now, as you get more and more curious about each service, figure out which of the following features matter most to you, and then determine which of the on-line services best accommodate your preferred "package."

- Interface?
- Live on-line help?
- Live help over the phone?
- Free e-mail?
- Internet e-mail?
- Kids' areas?
- News?
- Weather?
- Sports?
- Live chat?
- Message boards?
- Software downloading?
- Educational areas?
- On-line encyclopedia?
- On-line dictionary?
- Homework help?
- Newspapers
- Magazines?
- Games?
- Shopping?
- Partial Internet access?
- Full Internet access?
- Price?
- Can I try it for free?

Again, each service has its own strengths and weaknesses. It would be great if you could have several different services on your computer, but since they all charge a monthly fee whether you use them or not, it's probably too expensive to have more than one or two.

Ask your friends what services they're on. What cool things are they doing on-line? What do they like and dislike about their service? How much do they end up paying each month? If you already have a friend on an on-line service, you've got a built-in guide who can show you around and make you feel at home in cyberspace.

Fortunately, none of the services requires a membership commitment, so you can always switch from one to another if you're not satisfied or if your needs change.

The Wide World of 'Netting

"The Internet is the coolest because it's like going to an amusement park which is so big that you can never run out of stuff to do. I love to log on and look for new things. Every weekend I end up spending maybe half a day on-line, checking stuff out. The Web is awesome because the graphics are great."

—Todd, fourteen, Knoxville, Tennessee

THE INTERNET

Are you a 'Netter? Have you ever surfed the 'Net? If you have, you know that what we're talking about is amazing, is awesome, and is powerful. There's a reason that it's THE news story of this year. We're talking about the mother of all computer networks.

What exactly is the Internet? Some people think of it as a giant on-line service, like AOL or CompuServe. It's not. The Internet is the connection that joins computer networks together. It's actually capable of connecting your computer to just about every other computer in the world that's hooked up to a modem. Now that's a lot of computers!

Right now, some people estimate that the Internet links more than thirty million people around the world. They get together on the Internet (The 'Net, for short) to hold discussion groups, conduct research, and exchange information and software. The key to understanding the Internet is to know that it's a route, not a place. Think of it this way: AOL, Prodigy, CompuServe, and the other on-line services are brightly lit cities that you can actually visit. The Internet is the road that connects all of these cities—as well as thousands of smaller cities (BBSs) and millions of computers in those cities.

The 'Net was developed in 1969 and originally was intended just to link computers at the Department of Defense, universities, and private companies. It was designed to help these organizations exchange information and work together easily and efficiently. Today, twenty-five years later, the Internet still links these organizations, but it also links millions of individuals. One of the neat things about the Internet is that no one entity owns it, and nobody can control access to it. That's one of the reasons it's growing so quickly. Experts estimate that by the year 2000, more than one hundred million people will be connected to the 'Net! Of course, the bad news is that the Internet is so huge, it can be disorganized and scary if you don't know where you're going.

GETTING CONNECTED

Some people are connected to the 'Net through an independent provider such as Pipeline or through the commercial services such as America Online and Prodigy. Actually, there are hundreds of "providers," or services, and each one offers a slightly different package. The problem with a lot of them is that they require an understanding of the Unix operating system, the most common system on the 'Net. Unix was designed for rocket scientists to use. It's a complicated system that takes a while to learn. It can be extremely difficult to master.

Fortunately, computer programs that make it easier to get around on the Internet are now available. Mosaic is probably the best-known program of this kind. It was invented by a twenty-three-year-old named Marc Andreessen, and it makes it easier to access graphics and photos, sounds, and text on the 'Net. It's called a "browser" program. Lots of other browser programs are available today, too.

Are you really, completely, totally into computers? Do you know lots of stuff about how they work? If not, you'll probably want to connect to the 'Net through one of the major on-line services. That's A LOT easier than doing it any other way.

At the time this book was written, all of the major on-line services were racing to provide full Internet access for their members. That's not as easy as it sounds. For one thing, the services have to figure out ways to make the system simple enough for their members to understand. AOL, for example, is using the same type of interface for the Internet as it does for its own network—it uses icons that you click on with your mouse.

SURFING THE 'NET

People surf the 'Net for a variety of reasons. Some people use it to research reports for school or work. Some people use it to make new friends and keep in touch with people around the world. Some people use it as a form of entertainment—instead of watching TV or reading a book or whatever, they visit areas on the 'Net that interest them, or they play games or download software and graphics. The 'Net is so massive and contains so many things to do that you could spend weeks surfing it and still not explore every nook and cranny. But whatever you do, don't let the size of the Internet scare you off.

"You may think that learning all of the things you need to know to get full use out of the Internet may look like it takes a while," says Eric, fourteen, of Olmstead Falls, Ohio. "But with a good friend to guide you and some patience, you will find the Internet a useful resource and a way to meet new people that you can't stop trying to learn more about.''

Couldn't have said it better ourselves. This section will give you a basic idea of the types of things available on the 'Net. We've also included definitions of some of the terms you're likely to come across.

The Internet has lots to offer even the greenest newbie:

E-mail. If you have an Internet address, you can send e-mail to any of the thirty million other Internet users in seconds. It doesn't matter if you're on Prodigy and your best friend is on GEnie. You can send e-mail to each other over the Internet.

Newsgroups. Newsgroups on the 'Net are similar to message boards on commercial on-line services. People read and post messages on hundreds—even thousands—of subjects. The big difference is that millions of people all over the world use newsgroups over the Internet.

Usenet. This is a *huge* collection of newsgroups that cover just about every topic imaginable, from astronomy to tasteless jokes. One word of caution: The language and content in Usenet newsgroups can be R-rated, or worse. They're not monitored and censored the way bulletin boards on commercial on-line services are, so you and your parents should discuss where you may and may not go. Here are some of our favorite groups:

rec.arts.comics.marketplace: Comic book exchange
rec.arts.disney: Discussions about Disney
rec.arts.startrek.info: Info about ''Star Trek''
rec.collecting.cards: For collectors of sports and collectible cards
rec.equestrian: Horses
rec.games.misc: Games and computer games
rec.games.video.nintendo: Nintendo game systems and software
rec.games.video.sega: Sega game systems and software
rec.music.video: Music videos

rec.pets: Pets and pet care
rec.skate: Ice skating and roller skating
rec.sport.basketball.misc: Basketball
alt.collecting.autographs: Celebrity autographs
alt.games.sf2: Street Fighter 2
alt.kids-talk: Discussion group for kids
alt.tv.bh90210: "Beverly Hills, 90210"
alt.tv.simpsons: "The Simpsons"
alt.tv.tiny-toon: "Tiny Toon Adventures"
k12.chat.elementary: Discussions for students in grades K-5
k12.chat.junior: Discussions for students in grades 6-8
k12.chat.senior: Discussions for high school students

If you are 'Net surfing for the first time, be extra careful. Spend a *long* time lurking before you post, and make sure you understand the newsgroup you're visiting. Longtime Internet veterans can be a cranky bunch. They think of the Internet as their personal turf and they guard it closely.

TIP: Your first stop on the Internet should be in the newsgroup: news.announce.newusers. That's where you'll find a series of articles that will explain everything you need to know about the Internet.

Mailing Lists.
These are just like newsgroups except that the messages show up in your e-mail box rather than in a newsgroup "folder." You also have to register or "subscribe" to a mailing list (almost all of them are free).

Archie.
Looking for files? Archie is a program that helps you find all the places on the Internet that have the file you want.

Gopher.
This is a huge menu system for the Internet. It's a program that was developed at the University of Minnesota, whose mascot is the Golden Gopher. It will "go-fer" information from the Internet.

Veronica, Jughead. Archie was short for "archive," which is what that program hunts for. Somebody thought the name was cute, so they developed similar programs named after the comic book character Archie's girlfriend and best buddy. Computer humor. A riot, huh?

File Transfer Protocol. Archie finds the file, FTP reels it in. FTP stands for File Transfer Protocol. It is a way to download files of software, text, and graphics from the Internet. It lets you copy files from one place to another across the Internet.

Telnet. This lets you log on to computers all over the world, and rummage around inside. In fact, even China will be hooked into the 'Net shortly since, in late January 1995, its government caved in to pressure from its scholars and agreed to develop the computer systems necessary for them to be logged on.

WORLD WIDE WEB (WWW)

Most Internet experts say the World Wide Web is the next big thing on-line. The big problem with the Internet has always been that it's a confusing jumble—it's almost impossible to find your way around unless you know exactly what you're looking for. But "the Web" changes all that. Using software such as Mosaic and Netscape, which you can download for free, even newbies can surf the 'Net and find text and pictures.

The big difference between the Web and the text surfing that experienced 'Netters can do by using Gopher is that the Web is much more entertaining—and a whole lot easier to use! Tools are available that let you search "Gopherspace" by keywords, but the sites are so popular—and, therefore, so busy—that they often cannot be searched. It's no wonder the Web is so popular: People with multimedia computers can use it to obtain great sounds and graphics, and Web "pages" include great typography, graphics, sound, and even video clips.

What makes the Web easy to use is "Hypertext," which creates links from point to point. For example, if you were reading this on the Web instead of on a printed page, you might see the words **space shuttle** in a different color or in bold type. If you clicked on the highlighted words, you would automatically be linked to a NASA computer where you could read an article about the space program. It's the closest thing yet to point-and-click Internet access! Prodigy introduced a World Wide Web "browser" (for Windows users only) as part of its service earlier this year. CompuServe and America Online are racing hard to catch up, and may have their own Web browsers on-line by the time you read this.

Here are a few other things you need to know about the Web:

• You'll keep hearing the term *home page,* and, if you're like us, the name will puzzle you. A home page is the first place your browser opens to when the computer starts up.

• There is no "best" home page; you simply choose where you want to start up, and aim your browser to begin there. But everything is connected to everything else—that's why they call it a "Web!"

• Not all Web browsers have built-in search features, but those that do allow you to search for keywords (when the system's not overloaded). One search tool that's available is called Web-Crawler. According to *Online Access* (February 1995), "You may choose any word, or combination of words. If you love to cook, you might try typing 'recipe.' WebCrawler will search for Web pages that contain that word, and return a list of links; clicking on these links will let you explore these sites. Our search for 'recipe' brought in 257 different sites!"

What's on the Web? With the right browsing tools, you can uncover almost anything, from recreation to science (hobbyist areas), to the arts and culture (everything from the Vatican to on-line art exhibits); and the Web changes constantly since anyone can add to the Web and there is no central organizing or review committee to reject content for appropriateness. And there is no charge for processing newcomers to the Web; anyone with the right equipment and technical know-how can create a Web page.

Want to learn more about the World Wide Web? Here are some on-line sites to put you in the know.

• ftp://info.cern.ch (includes a Web demo and frequently-asked questions about the WWW)

• An on-line Web book: ftp://emx.cc.utexas.edu

Networking Between Networks. As of February 1995, you cannot send files from America Online to other commercial services. Nor can you bring back files from the 'Net, though you can access newsgroups. Prodigy allows Windows users to visit the World Wide Web, but it doesn't allow you to swap text files with a friend on CompuServe. This all may have changed by the time you read this book, though. Check it out before making a final decision on the service that'll be best for you.

BULLETIN BOARD SERVICES (BBS)

In addition to the commercial on-line services, there are networks called BBSes (short for Bulletin Board Services). These are essentially mini–on-line services. They have many, many fewer members than CompuServe, Prodigy, etc., and many of them are free. There are tens of thousands of BBSes worldwide, some of which offer Internet access (but not always complete, and not always reliable).

Anybody can run a BBS, and the systems operators (also known as SYSOPS) can be computer pros or teenage hackers with a server in their bedrooms. The more phone lines the

SYSOP has, the less likely you are to get a busy signal when you log on. A typical BBS features chat rooms (often called conferences), downloadable files, and, on occasion, Internet access. Some BBSs are part of networks other than the Internet; be sure that when a SYSOP tells you that there is 'Net access that you confirm by name that it's the Internet versus FidoNet or OneNet, or something else that you're not necessarily looking for.

THE WELL

The most famous BBS is called The Well. It features live chat, electronic forums, and lots and lots of awesome bulletin boards. Recently it began a kids program, staffed by real kids. Mike Miller, of the *Wall Street Journal,* recently wrote that The Well is "one of the liveliest outposts of the electronic underground." The Well is divided into "conferences," or discussion areas. There are currently more than 250 conferences, ranging from computer journalism to virtual reality to dreams to comics and pets.

The Well features considerable Internet access. Available 'Net features include e-mail, Telnet, ftp, Usenet newsgroups, MUSE, Gopher, Web server, and a number of 'Net-searching capabilities. For more information about The Well, call 415-332-4335. The cost is $15/month plus $2/hour billed by the minute. (Your first five hours are free.)

SFNET

Based in San Francisco, SFNet is run by Wayne Gregori, a businessman in his early thirties. One of the coolest things about SFNet is that you can log on—five minutes for a quarter—in more than twenty cafés scattered around the city and in nearby Oakland. One Saturday, Marian visited Muddy Waters (a coffee shop) and found about a half dozen young teenagers drinking lattes (an espresso coffee drink) and waiting for their turn to 'Net.

As Wayne Gregori explains, "We have thousands of subscribers who log on from home, but by placing coin-operated terminals in public places, SFNet allows those who don't own computers the opportunity to plug in and be heard ... As the data highway continues to spread over the globe, SFNet will insure access to hundreds of people who don't own computers." Won't it be cool in the future when there will be computer terminals all over the place (like public pay phones today)? As you walk down the street, you can decide to log on quickly and check your e-mail or send a quick note to a friend!

For more information on SFNet, write to Wayne Gregori, SFNet, P.O. Box 460693, San Francisco, CA 94146 or call 415-695-9824. To log on to SFNet, have your modem dial 415-824-8747.

Meet a *Very* Cool 'Netter

I (Marian) met Isaac, a fourteen-year-old skater type from Newport Beach, California, at a 'Netter party in San Francisco on New Year's Eve '95. It was at The Well's "Cyberfoo," to be exact.

Here is what Isaac had to say about Cyberfoo and lots of other cybersubjects:

• **On the Cyberfoo:** "Cyberfoo is a New Year's Party on the 'Net. People from different sites all over the country and the world can get in touch with each other at this big party. There are sites here in the United States, and also sites in Rome, in Copenhagen, in Wellington, New Zealand. Their party, in New Zealand, is probably over, since their midnight was at six in the morning today. There's also a party in London. Those are the sites that we know of. And people can be logging in from home just about anywhere."

- **On his on-line use:** "Over the summer, when I didn't have much to do, I'd log in four or five times a day and be on[line] for hours. But, nowadays, since school is on, I log on maybe once in the morning and once after school, if I'm lucky. On vacation, I log on much more."

- **On The Well:** "I'm not the only kid on The Well. There are a few other kids, too. There are a couple who are older than me, sixteen- and seventeen- and eighteen-year-olds. But I'm probably the youngest active post-er. There's a number of kids who really don't post that often. I kind of run the kids' forum on The Well right now. I host and help newbies. My mom is who got me into The Well. She has known it for a long time and she was on it a year before me. So I found out about it from her."

- **On Prodigy and AOL:** "I'd been on Prodigy before but I really didn't like it because of all the advertisements. I had been doing Prodigy for around a year, but there's some censorship on Prodigy and it used to be really slow because they had all these advertisements that took up all the bandwidth and it was hard to get anything done. And the interface was bad. I also did America Online with some friends, but I've never had my own account. Some of my friends do. AOL doesn't seem to have all that much content. It's too large, has too many people, and these people don't say enough."

- **On why he values on-line content:** "I like people that are, you know, that are having intelligent conversations, not just like, 'Here's my phone number,' cause that gets old rather quick. And I also like something that has a lot of different varieties of things and where you can really get to know someone on-line. I prefer The Well because there aren't 400,000 people and you can't really know anyone. It's smaller, and more intimate. I have made several friends on The Well, and some of them I have met on this trip up to San Francisco. And I was here for a Well party last summer, too, and went to a Well party in Los Angeles at the end of the summer."

- **On how he spends his on-line time:** To have time to be on-line, "I'm giving up TV definitely, which is a pretty good trade-off. There's more content on The Well and no commercials, which is pretty good to me. It's a good thing for all kids."

- **On his Well friends:** "There are good things about having friends on-line and there are bad things. You know that the one bad thing is that you really never get to see them as often as you'd like unless you live near them. But some of the good things are, well, you kind of have a whole different dynamic than you have with friends you see every day. Maybe you just talk to those school friends, say, about little inane things that don't really matter much. But the people on-line—well, it seems that you can have a better conversation with someone on-line, because there's nothing to get in the way. No appearance. Not the kinds of biases that get in the way usually. The only thing that matters is what kind of person they are. (That you are.)"

- **On The Well Kids Conference:** "The first conference I see, after I check my e-mail, is The Well Kids Conference, which I host with one other person. It's new. And it's something that The Well hasn't done before. All the kids get together and talk about stuff that's important to them. There are adults, too, but they leave space for kids to talk. They don't dominate the conference at all. We talk about all the kid things—sports, what we did at school, all the stuff you'd expect. A lot of the kids who are logging on are younger, and they don't have all the Internet skills they need. So we talk about stuff kids can do out on the 'Net and how to do stuff. And I've set up commands in my conference that make it easier. This way they can type an easy command and do something much more difficult."

- **On kids on the 'Net:** "A lot of my friends think of computers as sort of a geek thing. And they use them mostly for school reports. They'd rather be on the phone with their friends or watching TV or something. But I do have one friend that I got turned on to the 'Net. I think in the future, as things get easier to use, and as the World Wide Web becomes more widespread, people will log on more."

•••

FREENETS

Would you believe there's a way to access the Internet without paying for an on-line service? Some cities have BBSes called Freenets which are public access computer networks. Most often, the service is open to locals only, so you'll want to check into whether your city has one.

One drawback to freenets is that they work very much like the Internet, which means that they're much tougher to navigate than AOL, CompuServe, or Prodigy. And, since freenets are run by volunteers who sign up new members in their spare time, an application to join such a system is usually allowed to age about three weeks before the new subscriber is added.

Here are a few of the freenets that are up and running right now:

BIG SKY TELEGRAPH—Dillon,
  Montana
Western Montana College
710 S. Atlantic
Dillon, MT 59725
Modem: (406) 683-7680 (1200
  baud)
Internet: 192.231.192.1
Contact Person: Frank Odasz
voice: (406) 683-7338
e-mail: franko@bigsky.dillon.mt.us

BUFFALO FREENET—Buffalo,
  New York
Town of Tonawanda
1835 Sheridan Drive
Buffalo, NY 14223
Modem: (716) 645-3085
Internet: freenet.buffalo.edu
Contact Person: James Finamore
voice: (716) 877-8800, ext. 451
e-mail:
  finamore@ubvms.cc.buffalo.edu

CIAO! FREENET—Trail, British
  Columbia, Canada
School District #11 (Trail)
2079 Columbia Avenue
Trail, BC V1R 1K7 CANADA
Modem: (604) 368-5764
Internet: 142.231.5.1
Contact Person: Ken McClean
voice: (604) 368-2233
e-mail: kmcclean@ciao.trail.bc.ca

THE CLEVELAND FREENET—
  Cleveland, Ohio
CWRU Community Telecomputing
  Laboratory
310 Wickenden Avenue
Cleveland, OH 44106
Modem: (216) 368-3888
Internet: freenet-in-a.cwru.edu
Contact Person: Jeff Gumpf
voice: (216) 368-2982
e-mail: jag@po.cwru.edu

COLUMBIA ONLINE INFORMA-
TION NETWORK (COIN)—
Columbia, Missouri
University of Missouri/Columbia
Campus Computing/200 Hinkel
Building
Columbia, MO 61211
Modem: (314) 884-7000
Internet: bigcat.missouri.edu
Contact Person: Bill Mitchell
voice: (314) 882-2000
e-mail: bill@more.net

DAYTON FREENET—Dayton,
Ohio
040 Library Annex
Wright State University
Dayton, OH 45435
Modem: (513) 229-4373
Internet: 130.108.128.174
Contact Person: Patricia Vendt
voice: (513) 873-4035
e-mail: pvendt@desire.wright.edu

DENVER FREENET—Denver,
Colorado
4200 E. Ninth Avenue, Campus
Box C-288
Denver, CO 80210
Modem: (303) 270-4865
Internet: freenet.hsc.colorado.edu
(140.226.1.8)
Contact Person: Drew Mirque
voice: (303) 270-4300
e-mail:
drew@freenet.hsc.colorado.edu

GREAT LAKES FREENET—Battle
Creek, Michigan
P.O. Box 1615
Battle Creek, MI 49016
Modem: (616) 969-GLFN (4536)

Internet: not available
Contact Person: Merritt W. Tumanis
voice: (616) 961-4166
e-mail: merritt_tumanis@fc1.glfn.org

LORAIN COUNTY FREENET—
Elyria, Ohio
32320 Stony Brook Drive
Avon Lake, OH 44012
Modem: (216) 366-9721
Internet: freenet.lorain.oberlin.edu
(132.162.32.99)
Contact Person: Thom Gould
voice: (800) 227-7113, ext. 2451 or
(216) 277-2451
e-mail:
aa003@freenet.lorain.oberlin.edu

MEDINA COUNTY FREENET—
Medina, Ohio
Medina General Hospital
1000 E. Washington Street, P.O.
Box 427
Medina, OH 44258-0427
Modem: (216) 723-6732
Internet: (not yet available)
Contact Person: Gary Linden, Me-
dina General Hospital (Project
Director)
voice: (216) 725-1000, ext. 2550
e-mail: aa001@medina.freenet.edu

NATIONAL CAPITAL
FREENET—Ottawa, Ontario,
Canada
Computing Services
Carleton University
Ottawa, ON K1S 5B6 CANADA
Modem: (613) 564-3600
Internet: freenet.carleton.ca
(134.117.1.25)
Contact Person: David Sutherland

44

voice: (613) 788-2600, ext. 3701
e-mail: aa001@freenet.carleton.ca

OCEAN STATE FREENET—
    Providence, Rhode Island
Rhode Island Department of State
    Library Services
300 Richmond Street
Providence, RI 02903
Modem: (401) 831-4640
Internet: 192.207.24.10
Contact Person: Howard
    Boksenbaum
voice: (401) 277-2726
e-mail: howardbm@dsl.rhilinet.gov

OZARK REGIONAL INFORMA-
    TION ON-LINE NETWORK—
    Springfield, Missouri
Springfield-Greene County Library
MPO Box 760
Springfield, MO 65801
Modem: (417) 869-6100
Internet: ozarks.sgcl.lib.mo.us
Contact Person: Annie Linnemeyer
voice: (417) 887-3030
e-mail: annie@ozarks.sgcl.lib.mo.us

PRAIRIENET—Champaign-
    Urbana, Illinois
Graduate School of Library and In-
    formation Science
University of Illinois at Urbana-
    Champaign
426 David Kinley Hall
1407 W. Gregory Drive
Urbana, IL 61801
Modem: (217) 255-9000
Internet: prairienet.org (192.17.3.3)
Contact Person: Ann P. Bishop
voice: (217) 244-3299
e-mail: abishop@alexia.lis.uiuc.edu

RIO GRANDE FREENET—El
    Paso, Texas
P.O. Box 20500
El Paso, TX 79998
Modem: (915) 775-5600
Internet: rgfn.epcc.edu
Contact Person: Don Furth
voice: (915) 775-6077
e-mail: donf@laguna.epcc.edu

SEATTLE COMMUNITY
    NETWORK—Seattle,
    Washington
c/o CPSR/Seattle, P.O. Box 85481
Seattle, WA 98145-1481
Modem: (not yet available)
Internet: (not yet available)
Contact Person: Randy Groves
21240 N.E. 12th
Redmond, WA 98053
voice: (206) 865-3424
e-mail: randy@cpsr.org

TALLAHASSEE FREENET—
    Tallahassee, Florida
Department of Computer Science
Florida State University
Tallahassee, FL 32306
Modem: (904) 576-6330 or
    (904) 488-5056
Internet: freenet.fsu.edu
    (144.174.128.43)
Contact Person: Hilbert Levitz
voice: (904) 644-1796
e-mail: levitz@cs.fsu.edu

TRI-CITIES ON-LINE—Tri-Cities,
    Washington
RECA Foundation
605 S. Olympia #74
Kennewick, WA 99336
Modem: (509) 375-3548

Internet: (not yet available)
Contact Person: Bruce McComb
voice: (509) 586-6481
e-mail: nelva@delphi.com

TRISTATE ONLINE—Cincinnati,
  Ohio
Cincinnati Bell Directory, Inc.
Room 102-2000
201 E. 4th Street
Cincinnati, OH 45201-2301
Modem: (513) 579-1990
Internet: tso.uc.edu
Contact Person: Michael King, TSO
  System Administrator
voice: (513) 397-1396
fax: (513) 721-5147
e-mail: sysadmin@cbos.uc.edu

VICTORIA FREENET—Victoria,
  British Columbia, Canada
Victoria Free-Net Association
C/O Vancouver Island Advanced
  Technology Centre (VIATC)
Suite 203-1110 Government Street
Victoria, British Columbia V8W
  1Y2 CANADA
Modem: (604) 595-2300
Internet: freenet.victoria.bc.ca
  (134.87.16.100)
Contact Person: Gareth Shearman
voice: (604) 385-4302
e-mail: shearman@cue.bc.ca

THE YOUNGSTOWN
  FREENET—Youngstown, Ohio
YSU Computer Center
410 Wick Avenue
Youngstown, OH 44555
Modem: (216) 742-3072
Internet: yfn2.ysu.edu
  (192.55.234.27)

Contact Person: Lou Anschuetz
voice: (216) 742-3075
e-mail: lou@yfn.ysu.edu

*NATIONAL PUBLIC TELECOM-
PUTING NETWORK*
• EDUCATIONAL AFFILIATES
  (Access limited to K-12 schools
  in their states)
• AMERITECH EXTENDED
  CLASSROOM—Chicago, Illinois
• LEARNING VILLAGE CLEVE-
  LAND—Cleveland, Ohio
• AMERITECH EXTENDED
  CLASSROOM—Detroit,
  Michigan
• AMERITECH EXTENDED
  CLASSROOM—Indianapolis,
  Indiana
• AMERITECH EXTENDED
  CLASSROOM—Milwaukee,
  Wisconsin

CORE
California Online Resources for
  Education
Machine located in Los Alamitos,
  CA
Contact Person: Keith Vogt
P.O. Box 3842, 4665 Lampson
  Avenue
Seal Beach, CA 90740
voice: (800) 272-8743
e-mail: kvogt@eis.calstate.edu

EDUCATION CENTRAL
Education Central
Machine located in Mount Pleasant,
  MI
Contact Person: Hal Crawley
204 Ronan Hall
Central Michigan University

Mount Pleasant, MI 48859
voice: 517-774-3975
e-mail:
  374cylb@cmuvm.csu.cmich.edu

PEN
Public Education Network
Machine located in Richmond, VA
Contact Person: Dr. Harold Cothern
P.O. Box 6Q
Richmond, VA 23216
voice: (804) 225-2921
e-mail:
  hcothern@vdoe386.vak12ed.edu

SENDIT
North Dakota's K-12 Educational
  Telecommunication Network
Machine located in Fargo, ND
Contact Person: Gleason Sackman
Box 5146
North Dakota State University Com-
  puter Center
Fargo, ND 58105
voice: (701) 237-8109
e-mail: sackman@sendit.nodak.edu

. . . .

FUN FACTS

Internet servers—the 1.5 million computers which make up this network which reaches all the way around the world—can be broken down into the following types:

- Research servers—44%
- Commercial servers—31%
- Defense servers—10%
- Education servers—8%
- Government servers—7%

It's important to note that the Internet Society keeps count of servers on the net, and then approximates users by using a 10:1 ratio. Unfortunately, there is no evidence to substantiate this ratio. For example, consider on-line services such as AOL and Compuserve, with direct Internet connections, providing potentially millions of users from one server. It's also clear that educational servers would have many more than a 10:1 ratio.
                    —The Internet Society, September 1994

. . . .

47

SEORF
South Eastern Ohio Regional Free-
   Net
Machine located in Athens, OH
Contact Person: Damien O. Bawn
P.O. Box 5621
Athens, OH 45701
voice: (614) 662-3211
e-mail: bawn@oucsace.cs.ohiou.edu

UMASSK12
Machine located in Amherst, MA
Contact Person: Morton M.
   Sternheim
Physics Department, Lederle
University of Massachusetts
Amherst, MA 01003
voice: (413) 545-1908
e-mail: mms@k12.ucs.umass.edu

4

Playing It Safe On-line

"My mom always urges me to be careful when I log on to a chat service. She's right. On the news last summer, there was a story about a man who tricked kids into giving him their phone numbers. He even visited a few of them—and it sure sounded like he wasn't a nice normal man. That scared me plenty. Now I always think twice before telling anyone anything very personal about myself until I feel like, well, I know them pretty much. And I never ever talk to adults on-line other than my uncles. They're both away at college and we send lots of e-mails to them."

—David, twelve, Farmington Hills, Michigan

RULES OF THE ROAD

Cyberspace is part of the "information superhighway." And it has rules and regulations just as a regular highway does. Don't worry, no one's going to pull you over for speeding or for running a red light! And the cyberpolice don't hand out tickets. In fact, in some parts there are no cyberpolice at all. That's why there are some rules you need to follow so you don't get in trouble or put yourself in danger.

Rule Number 1: No Personal Info

You know how your parents are always telling you not to talk to strangers? Well, there are good reasons for that. Most people you meet are probably very nice, but some people aren't. They may want to scare you or steal from you or even hurt you. The thing to remember is that these people are in cyberspace, too.

Of course, in cyberspace it's very difficult to know who you're talking to. People can pretend to be anyone they want. A boy can pretend to be a girl, a girl can pretend to be a boy, and a grown-up can pretend to be a child. Some people do this just for fun, but you need to be aware that not everyone is who he or she says he/she is.

Does this mean you shouldn't talk to anyone in cyberspace? No, no, no! Meeting new people on-line is one of the things that's most fun about cyberspace. Of course, you should talk to people! You just need to take a simple precaution: **NEVER GIVE OUT PERSONAL INFORMATION.** What's personal information? It's things like your real name (it's OK to tell your first name, just don't tell your last), your address and phone number, where you go to school—things like that. The reason for this is that people may use that information in a bad way.

Can't happen to you? Check out this true story from the Kids Only OnLine message board on America Online. This kid learned the hard way to take on-line safety seriously:

I was in a public chat room talking to a man who seemed pretty nice. After a while, he started going on and on about how he knew a man who has the same last name as I do. He then asked me my dad's name, saying he thought it might be him. Once I told him, he starting saying how it was my dad he knew and that he had my phone number and was going to call me. At first I didn't believe him, but then he told me what my phone number was. So, I believed him. But then the phone rang. I just sat there for a minute; for

50

some reason I was afraid to answer it. Finally, I picked up the phone. It only took the first three words out of the guy's mouth before I knew that he definitely did not know my father. I couldn't really hear what he was saying, my heart was beating like mad, but I do remember some of what he said, and it wasn't very nice. Finally, I hung up the phone and went outside for a long walk—I didn't want to be around if the phone rang again.

Nothing terrible happened, but it really shook me up. I had listed my name and my city and state in my on-line profile; once he had that information, all the man needed was my father's first name, so he could call information and get our phone number. He could have easily gotten my address and showed up on my doorstep! I don't want that to happen to anyone. It scares me to think that it has happened to people before, and that it could happen again. I told my parents what happened, and we deleted my name and city and state from the profile. Now no one will know where I live unless I tell them. And you better believe I'm never going to do that!

If you belong to a service that lets you fill out a member profile, be sure that you don't include any information people can use to find out who you are and where you live. It's OK to list stuff like your favorite hobby or what type of computer you use. That way, people who like the same things as you do can get in touch with you. But there's no need to broadcast who you are.

You may also want to choose a screenname that doesn't tell anything about you. Let's say someone's screenname is "KatieL13." Chances are pretty good that the person who has that account is a thirteen-year-old girl whose first name is Katie and whose last name begins with the letter L. That's quite a bit of information! But if this same girl used the screenname "Fandango" or "Explorer," you wouldn't know much about her at all, would you? You wouldn't even know if this person was male or female.

Pen Pals-Keypals

So, what happens if you meet someone on-line and want to become pen pals? The best thing to do is send e-mails to one another rather than regular letters. Just think of all the paper and postage you'll save! If there's someone that you'd really like to talk with on the phone or if someone wants to send you something in the mail, ask your parents first. They can help you figure out if the person you're talking to is for real or a creep.

Rule Number 2: Be Careful Out There

We've already talked about not giving out your phone number and other personal information. That's very important. But it's also important to keep yourself safe in other ways. Anyone can send you an e-mail or instant message on-line. And it's possible that they may be saying things that make you scared or uncomfortable. If that happens, tell your parents right away. No one should have to put up with that stuff.

One of the best things to do is learn how to save a "log" of on-line chats, e-mails, and instant messages. That way, if someone says something that makes you scared or uncomfortable or nervous, you can record that person's words and then make a report to the on-line service. AOL, CompuServe, Prodigy, and the other services don't want creepolas hanging around, so they want us to tell them if anyone is causing trouble or doing bad things. When you turn these people in, you'll be doing a favor for everyone!

"The built-in anonymity makes things easy for child molesters," Ruben Rodriguez, an analyst with the National Center for Exploited and Missing Children, told the *Miami Herald*. "They monitor the junior chat lines. They get to know the age group, what the kids like to do. Then, they start speaking to them as a peer."

You may go on-line for years and never run into a person

who's a creep. But it's good that you know this stuff just in case you ever do run into a problem. On-line services such as AOL, Prodigy, and CompuServe do their best to keep creeps out, but privacy laws make it very difficult. The Internet, which has no real rules, is even harder to police. Your best protection is to play it safe by following all the guidelines we've listed in this chapter.

RULE NUMBER 3: NO FOUL LANGUAGE

One of the easiest ways to get into trouble on-line is to write curse words. Your on-line service probably has rules about what you can and can't do and say on-line. If you break these rules, and someone complains, you might get a warning—they may even boot you off the system!

And it's not just in chat rooms that you have to be careful. Prodigy, CompuServe, America Online, and the other services have monitors who read messages posted on bulletin boards. They don't take kindly to foul language. The punishment can range from having your posting censored to having your account canceled. Try explaining that to your parents when your whole family's account gets canceled because of your on-line antics.

One Westchester County, New York, dad told us about how his eighth grader and her friend managed to have his accounts on AOL, CompuServe, and Prodigy canceled in one night by romping through rooms using swear words. Needless to say, he was more than a bit angry with his daughter, especially when AOL refused to sign him back up immediately, despite his written apology. And, Rosie O'Donnell, a celebrity chatter, says that she was kicked off AOL more than once for using, that is typing, "bad words." So, don't dismiss this tip unless you want to miss on-line for a few weeks or more—most of the services cancel subscriptions for a minimum of a month if their service terms are violated.

The best advice we can give you is never to do or say anything on-line that you wouldn't want your parents to find out about. That's a pretty simple rule!

RULE NUMBER 4: WATCH THE CLOCK

Most of the on-line services charge a fee that lets you go on-line for a certain number of hours each month. Once you go over that amount of time, they bill you by the minute. Some online providers also charge extra for certain services.

WARNING: *These charges can really add up! Have you ever heard the expression "Time is money"? Well, that's certainly true in cyberspace.*

Going on-line is a lot of fun, and it's really easy to lose track of the time. If this becomes a problem for you, you might want to develop a system to remind you when you should log off. If you have a watch with a timer on it, you could set it to start beeping after a certain number of minutes. Or you could set a kitchen timer. You should also write down how many minutes you spend on-line each month, so you'll know when you've gone over the "free" period.

Your on-line service probably has a built-in system to tell you how long you've been logged on for. On America Online, KEYWORD: CLOCK shows you how long the meter has been running. On CompuServe, the toolbar at the top of your screen (when you log on with CIM) shows you your total on-line time and alerts you when you've left basic services.

RULE NUMBER 5: NEVER TELL ANYONE YOUR PASSWORD

Your password is a secret. You should be the only person who knows what it is. The reason for this is that anyone who knows your password can log on to your account, read your e-mail, and run up charges that you and your parents will have to pay for. They can even do nasty things on-line that you'll end up getting in trouble for. Believe us: It's not worth it!

Here are some simple tips to help you make sure your password doesn't fall into the wrong hands:

• If possible, don't write down your password. Make it something easy to remember. (If you do have to write it, put it in a secret place and don't label it as a password. For example, don't write "CompuServe password: Banana." Instead, just write "Banana." You'll know what it means, but no one else will.)

• Don't choose a password that will be easy for other people to guess. For example, you shouldn't use your first name, the name of your dog, or anything like that.

• Beware of tricksters. If someone calls you claiming to work for your on-line service and asks for your password, don't give it out. This person may even say he or she needs it to correct a "problem" with your account. Baloney! That's one of the oldest scams in cyberspace. Your on-line service will never, ever call you to ask what your password is; they already know it.

RULE NUMBER 6: KNOW YOUR 'NETIQUETTE

Cyberspace can be a little strange at first. It's full of quirky little rules that newcomers (called "newbies") may not know anything about. These rules are known as Internet etiquette, or "'Netiquette" for short. Some of them may not seem very important, but people who don't follow them can catch a lot of flak. This is especially true on the Internet, where people sometimes aren't very nice to newbies. Don't worry: You won't be a newbie for long!

Here are some basic rules of 'Netiquette that you should follow:

• NEVER TYPE IN ALL CAPS. If you do, people will think you are SHOUTING AT THEM!!! If you accidentally hit the

CAPS LOCK key on your keyboard while chatting, don't be surprised if people start responding, "Stop yelling at us!"

• Lurk before you leap. When you come across an ongoing discussion in a bulletin board or chat room, read the postings for a while before you put in your two cents worth. That way, you'll understand more about what the discussion is about and whether people will be angry if you go off on a tangent.

• Don't forget your smileys. A little humor goes a long way on-line. Some terrible misunderstandings happen because people aren't always sure when someone is joking. That's because they can't see the expression on your face or hear you laughing. What's the solution? Smile when you say that! By using "emoticons" or "smileys," you can indicate:

:-) A smile
;-) A wink
:-(Sadness
:-D Laughter

Tilt your head sideways to look at those symbols and you'll see how they work. You can also use a <g> to indicate a grin or <vbg> for "very big grin." A smiley at the end of a sentence can turn an insult—"Hey Buttface!"—into good-natured ribbing—"Hey Buttface! :-)." These symbols will stop people's feelings from getting hurt when you're saying something they might otherwise consider offensive. (See Chapter 6 for a more complete list of smileys.)

• Don't create a new message board folder unless you're absolutely sure one doesn't already exist on that topic. Many forums have limited bulletin board space, and the SYSOPS (short for system operators—the people who run the forum) won't appreciate it if you start a new topic when the same subject is already being discussed elsewhere. If someone closes the folder you started and tells you to post in the area where your topic is already being discussed, don't give them a hard time about it. They're just trying to make sure that no bulletin board space goes to waste.

- Don't try to sell stuff on a bulletin board. Message boards are places to trade ideas, not make a fast buck. Unless the area is specifically set up for on-line classified ads—where people buy, sell, and trade things—you're not allowed to use message boards for commercial purposes.

- Don't upload commercial software or other copyrighted material. It's illegal. Your on-line service has libraries with tons of shareware, freeware, and "public domain" material. That's OK because those things aren't copyrighted. Copyrighted materials are an entirely different story—you can get into a whole lot of trouble if you distribute them illegally. And we're not just talking about software. Posting your own words on a message board is A-OK, but posting other people's words or materials (for example, a magazine article) is illegal unless you have their permission.

- Don't scroll! This may be the most annoying and immature thing you can do in a chat room. Scrolling is when someone repeatedly hits the return key. It makes chat room messages move too quickly for people to read. It's totally obnoxious, and people will let you know it!

- Be polite. Being rude or harassing someone—either in a chat room, on a message board, or via e-mail—is considered disruptive, and could get you in trouble. Just as in the "real world," disagreements will happen in cyberspace, but there's no reason to let them get out of hand. Don't turn a difference of opinion into a personal feud. That takes all the fun out of a good debate. And if someone is harassing you, don't fight fire with fire. Some services let you ignore or block messages from the offending jerk. It's a good idea to learn how!

- Learn—and follow—the rules set forth by your on-line service. These are usually pretty basic and easy to follow. If you can't remember what they are, reread them.

- And, finally, the most important rule of 'Netiquette we can share with you comes from author Virginia Shea, who has been dubbed the "Miss Manners of Cyberspace." Her number one rule is: "Remember the human. Never forget that the person reading your mail or posting is, indeed, a person, with feelings that can be hurt." It sounds like a simple rule, but you'd be amazed how quickly people forget it once they go on-line. Don't let that happen to you!

Rule Number 7: Keep a Fire Extinguisher Handy!

It's going to happen to you sooner or later. You go on-line, open your e-mail box, and see a letter from an unfamiliar person. You open it up, and your eyes nearly pop out of your head. . . .

"Dear Clueless Idiot: You have the intelligence of a handball. Your head is so far up your butt that you obviously can't see . . ."

Aaaaarrrrggggggghhhhh! *You've been flamed!* Don't panic. And, most important, don't take it personally. There is something about cyberspace that makes some people downright nasty. They think it's fun to pick on other people and write mean things. *Ignore them.* In the real world, these people are probably quiet and shy and maybe even polite. But some strange process takes place when they're hiding safely behind a screen-name. No one knows who they are or what they look like, so they transform themselves into the Terminator. At home they're probably Pee-wee Herman. In cyberspace, they're Ah-nold!

No matter how friendly you are on-line, eventually someone is going to disagree with you about something and take a few verbal swings at you. We call this getting "flamed." Flames can range from a minor dissing to an on-line drive-by shooting. Flames can be funny or mean. Or both.

People flame each other for lots of reasons: Sometimes they really disagree with something you said. Sometimes they're just bored and want to stir up trouble. And if you venture onto the Internet, some veteran cybernauts will attack you just because you have an AOL or Prodigy e-mail address! Just remember: Even though it may feel like it, they're not attacking you personally. They don't know anything about you, so how could they really hate you? That would be ridiculous.

How should you handle a flame? "Take a deep breath and decide whether it's really worth responding to," advises Adam Gaffin, author of *The Big Dummy's Guide to the Internet*. He notes that "nothing puts flames out quicker than ignoring them."

So you'll know what to expect, here are some of the most common flames:

- **The Newbie Flame.** These are directed at newcomers to an on-line forum, bulletin board, or Usenet newsgroup. If you post a question that already has been answered by the veterans dozens of times, they might send you a flame that says, "RTFM," which stands for "Read the @#$%! Manual!" In this case, it probably is a good idea to take their advice (no matter how rude it is) and read the Frequently Asked Questions (FAQs) for that area.

- **The Ad Hominem Flame.** Ad hominem is a Latin phrase. It refers to someone attacking someone else's character rather than using logic to win an argument. For example, let's say you were arguing with someone about a movie you saw together. If you said, "I liked the movie because the special effects were really cool," that person might argue by saying, "Yeah, but the dialogue was so fake." That's a normal discussion. If, on the other hand, that person said, "The only reason you liked that movie is because you're a complete and total idiot," that would be an ad hominem attack. He's not attacking the movie, he's attacking YOU. Don't worry if someone sends you an ad hominem flame. All it means is that the flamer can't come up with a logical way to counter your argument. If you get an ad hominem flame, consider it a victory!

- **The Nit-picking Flame.** This is when someone takes apart your post or e-mail, sentence by sentence, word by word, leaving no letter unturned. The flamer might pick on your grammar or spelling or logic—or all of those things. Again, your best response is to ignore it. Obviously, that person has WAY too much time on his or her hands.

- *The "Stealth" Flame.* Some of the best and funniest flames are disguised. You might get a letter that starts out friendly and helpful, then suddenly turns into a flame.

Virginia Shea, author of the on-line manners guide *'Netiquette,* thinks flames are only bad when they become personal attacks. "If you're going to flame, make it fun, make it funny, don't be serious, and don't be abusive," Shea says. "Always be aware of the fact that some people are more sensitive than others. Be ready to pull back when it's time to pull back."

One thing to remember before starting or joining a flame war: Unlike a nasty argument with a friend that is forgotten as soon as it's over, a flame hangs around for a long, long time. When you post an insulting or nasty flame in an on-line forum, it stays on the bulletin board for people to read. That makes it hard to forgive, and impossible to forget!

A lot of people get upset when they are flamed. Other people, though, think it's a lot of fun. It's like a game to them. If you're the type of person who likes to give and get flames, check out one of the on-line areas dedicated to flaming (and don't pick on the rest of us!). There are entire newsgroups on the Internet devoted to nothing more than attacking annoying people and things. There's even a "Hall of Flame" on Usenet—alt.flame.hall-of-flame—dedicated to collecting some of the cleverest, hottest flames on the 'Net.

RULES FOR ON-LINE SAFETY

The National Center for Missing and Exploited Children last year published an excellent brochure titled "Child Safety on the Information Highway." It's written by Lawrence J. Magid, a columnist for the *Los Angeles Times,* who is author of *Cruising Online: Larry Magid's Guide to the New Digital Highway* (Random House, 1994). He suggests kids make the following on-line pledge:

1. I will not give out personal information such as my address, telephone number, parents' work address/telephone number, or the name and location of my school without my parents' permission.

2. I will tell my parents right away if I come across any information that makes me feel uncomfortable.

3. I will never agree to get together with someone I "meet" on-line without first checking with my parents. If my parents agree to the meeting, I will be sure that it is in a public place and bring my mother or father along.

4. I will never send a person my picture or anything else without first checking with my parents.

5. I will not respond to any messages that are mean or in any way make me feel uncomfortable. It is not my fault if I get a message like that. If I do, I will tell my parents right away so that they can contact the on-line service.

6. I will talk with my parents so that we can set up rules for going on-line. We will decide upon the time of day that I can be on-line, the length of time I can be on-line, and appropriate areas for me to visit. I will not access other areas or break these rules without their permission.

Free copies of "Child Safety on the Information Highway" can be obtained from the National Center for Missing and Exploited Children at 1-800-THE-LOST (1-800-843-5678). Larry suggests keeping this pledge by your computer. If you follow no other piece of advice in this book, make it that one!

Note to Parents

Just as in the real world, there are lots of places on-line you probably don't want your children to visit. There are bulletin boards, forums, and chat rooms that aren't appropriate for kids. In addition to talking with your kids about where they may and may not go, you might want to actually block their access to certain areas. America Online and Prodigy allow parents to make chat rooms, instant messages, and other functions inaccessible on their kids' accounts. Stay on the lookout for new "Parental Controls" on the other on-line services, too.

5

E-mail

"I have a lot of friends that I write to. We use e-mail to keep in touch. We write about anything that comes to mind. It's just like writing a note to someone at school. We write back to each other almost as soon as we get the letter."

—Sandra, fifteen, Seneca, Missouri

KEEP IN TOUCH!

Your computer offers lots of ways to "reach out and touch" people. The simplest way is through electronic mail, or "e-mail."

"I like the fact that you can talk to people all around the U.S.," says Nikki, thirteen, who logs on to Prodigy from Dousman, Wisconsin. "I have a lot of friends on-line, so we write almost every day."

"The coolest thing about being on-line is the access I have to people and places, not just locally, but around the world," says Eric, who goes to Olmstead Falls Middle School in Ohio. Eric has been on-line for over two years. He keeps in touch with friends via e-mail on Cleveland's FreeNet.

"I'm subscribed to Kidlink, which links kids between the ages of ten and fifteen all over the world," says Heidi, fourteen, from

Bryn-Athyn, Pennsylvania. "I've made tons of new friends through it. I even received a Christmas card from Denmark!"

TIP: You can order Connect Soft—Kidmail™ [which uses whatever online service you have (from among CompuServe, Prodigy, and MCI Mail)] by calling 1-800-889-3499. The package includes special offers from CompuServe, Prodigy, and MCI Mail and is also for sale at Egghead Software, Electronics Boutique, Micro Center, and other software retailers. The best thing about Kidmail is the way cool "letterhead," created just for kids!

E-mail is even easier than sending a regular letter. You don't need paper, and there's nothing to sign, no envelope to stuff, and no stamp to lick. All you have to do is hit a few keys on your keyboard, and your letters are on their way, zipping through cyberspace at the speed of light!

Not so long ago, letter writing was considered a dying art. Why write when you can pick up the phone and talk? But the PC and modem have brought letter writing back in a big way. E-mail is just as fast as a phone call, and usually cheaper.

Another great thing about e-mail is that you can read and respond to it whenever you want. And, unlike the phone, you don't have to worry about waking someone up or interrupting them in the middle of dinner. YOU decide when you want to check your e-mail box, and YOU decide whether to reply to the letter or delete it.

INSTANT COMMUNICATION

Do you have friends or family who live far away? Most of us do. And sometimes it can be difficult to stay in touch. But with e-mail, people who live far away from you are just a few computer keys away. You can send notes to your older brother or sister in college, send a birthday greeting to your grandfather in another state, and keep in touch with an old friend who moved to another town. As long as they have a computer and modem, you can keep in touch with anybody, anywhere!

"I have two pen pals that I keep in touch with over e-mail. One is from Puerto Rico and the other is from Israel," writes Lisa from California. "We just started to contact each other so we are telling each other about ourselves. I write to them as soon as I receive mail."

Another cool thing about cyberspace is that the post office never closes. You can send and receive e-mail twenty-four hours a day, every day—even on Sundays and holidays! And you don't have to worry about writing a long letter that tells the person everything you've been doing over the past year. E-mail is so easy that most people just write a few lines and send it off. Later on, if you think of something you forgot to say in your letter, you can just send another one.

Once you become an e-mail junkie, you'll find yourself rushing to your computer when you get up in the morning, when you get home from school, and before you go to bed. You know how much fun it can be to get your own mail at home? Well, it's just as much fun to get your own e-mail. And don't think e-mail is just for formal letters. You can use it to arrange dates, plan a party, gather information, send holiday greetings, and meet new people. In fact, just about all the quotes we've used in this book were sent to us via e-mail. Maybe we should get out more . . .

WARNING: E-mail is so fast and so easy that sometimes people send e-mail messages before they really think them through. It's way too easy to send a nasty note and hurt someone's feelings. So if you're mad at someone, try sleeping on that angry e-mail before you click and send it!

INTERNET E-MAIL

If you've got an account on AOL, Prodigy, CompuServe, or any other major on-line service, you're all set to send and receive Internet e-mail. You can write and receive letters, and subscribe to on-line mailing lists on thousands of different topics.

What you may not realize is that you can also write to people who belong to a *different on-line service.* Most commercial on-line services now let you send and receive e-mail to and from—and through—the Internet. This means that if you are on AOL and your best friend is on Prodigy, you can still e-mail each other simply and easily. You can also e-mail anyone who has an account on the Internet. The main difference is that when you mail to someone outside your service, it may not be delivered instantly. Sometimes it can take a few hours. But Marian now receives notes from Tokyo over the 'Net in minutes, maybe even seconds!

"Through the Internet, I was able to communicate with students from Europe and Israel," says Terry, a tenth grader at Bethel High School in Hampton, Virginia. Terry's English class had access to use the Internet. "I was also able to talk to other students from high schools in the U.S. The Internet is a different and new way of communicating with other people all around the world."

To send e-mail along the Internet, all you need is the "Internet address" of the person you are trying to reach. Every on-line address follows a simple format: **username@domain**

First is the username—this is your screenname on AOL, or your user ID (sometimes spelled "userid") on Prodigy or CompuServe. The "@" sign simply tells you that this is a valid Internet address. The next few letters are called the "domain." The domain is the on-line system where you have your account. When you think about it, it's not all that different from a regular mail address. The username is the name of the person you're writing the letter to. The domain is the name of the service where he or she "lives."

If you write a letter to a friend on another system, all you need to know is his or her screenname or user ID, and the domain name of the on-line service he or she uses. Here are the major ones:

America Online—@aol.com
CompuServe—@compuserve.com
Delphi—@delphi.com
GEnie—@genie.geis.com
Prodigy—@prodigy.com
eWorld—@eworld.com

So, Robert's on Prodigy and his userid is YGBCO7A.* If he wanted to send a letter to Marian on America Online, he'd send it to MarianS104@aol.com.* If she wanted to write back, she would send her letter to YGBCO7A@prodigy.com.

Hold it. What's with this "dot-com" business? The only time you need to worry about that is when you're sending mail to a different system from the one you're on. The three letters after the dot indicate to what kind of on-line service you're sending your mail. "Com" means it's a **com**mercial service, like AOL or Prodigy. Here are some other common codes:

edu: an **edu**cational computer system, like the ones found at most colleges
org: a nonprofit **org**anization
int: an overseas group ("int" stands for **int**ernational)
mil: a **mil**itary site
gov: a **gov**ernment address (President Clinton's e-mail address, for example, is president@whitehouse.gov. Yep, it's true—you can write him any time you want!)

IMPORTANT TIP! User IDs on CompuServe contain a comma, which confuses Internet addressing. If you are sending e-mail to a CompuServe member from another service, replace

---

* Authors' user names are subject to change.

67

the comma in the address with a period. Robert's CompuServe ID is 75672,1540. So if you were writing to him from another service, you'd send it to 75672.1540@compuserve.com.

When you think about it, it's pretty amazing. Once you sign up with an on-line service, you can send and receive e-mail with *every* other person in the world who has an Internet address. That's more than thirty million people, with thousands more coming on-line every day!

Chances are pretty good that you already know someone you can send an e-mail to. If not, you can always find a ''keypal'' (you're not using a pen, so why call them pen pals?) in another town, another state, or a country halfway around the world! It's easy to do and it's fun. And, of course, you can always write to us!

E-MAIL STYLE

As we mentioned, e-mail is usually less formal than regular letter writing. Lots of people use ''computer shorthand'' and ''smileys'' for on-line writing. (See Chapter 6). Also, you don't need to write things like ''Dear Amber,'' and ''Sincerely, Joe'' (unless the person you're writing to won't recognize your e-mail name).

Many e-mail messages are just a sentence or two long. For example, you could e-mail a message to a friend that said, ''Go see *Terminator 3*—it's AWESOME!'' or ''Who are you rooting for in the Super Bowl?'' You can also send funny jokes you've heard and stuff like that.

Here are just a few suggestions about e-mails:

• Be yourself. Don't worry as much about spelling or punctuation as about putting your whole person into your correspondence. You can take advantage of all the emoticons to convey laughing, teasing, thinking, etc.

• Put yourself in the place of the person you're writing to. Make sure he or she will understand what you're saying and the manner in which you're saying it.

• Take time addressing the letter because it's pretty darn easy to send a letter you intend for AmandaP11 to AmandaO1—and it's hard and sometimes impossible to retrieve a misaddressed e-mail. In the best case, it goes into the "Dead E-mail Office," somewhere in cyberland. In the worst case, the wrong Amanda knows that you're dying because your father is dating the wicked witch of Tennessee and you overheard your grandmother telling someone she thinks he'll marry her.

EXTRA FEATURES

Basic e-mail is simple. On most on-line services, it's as easy as write, click, send. But once you've mastered the basics, there are extra bells and whistles that will help you get even more out of e-mail.

FAXING

Need to send a fax? Most on-line services allow you to send e-mail directly to fax machines. It's usually as simple as adding the fax number with the area code to the e-mail address of the person you're trying to reach. Be warned, though: There's usually an extra fee of a few dollars for fax service.

ATTACH FILES

Every day, businesspeople spend millions of dollars to send documents all over the world. With e-mail, you can send documents in seconds for the cost of a local phone call. Most e-mail systems allow you to "attach files," which means that you can send a document, electronic picture, or piece of software along with your letter. If you're really proud of a story you've written, for example, you can send it via e-mail to your grandmother or one of your old teachers. You can also send artwork that you've created on Kid Pix™, MacDraw™, or another graphics program.

Return Receipt

A return receipt is something you can use to track your e-mail. If you use this option, you'll receive an electronic message as soon as the person at the other end reads your letter. That way, you'll know that your friend got it and has read it. Some services also let you check the "status" of mail you've sent to see whether it's been read yet.

Multiple Recipients, CCs, and BCCs

This feature lets you send a piece of e-mail to more than one person at a time. You can either list everyone as the "addressee" or send CCs or BCCs. CC is a "carbon copy." Before photocopy machines were invented, people used to use carbon paper to make copies of things they wrote on a typewriter. That name is still used, even though we can make copies now without having to use carbon paper. If you're writing a letter to someone and want another person to receive it, too, send a CC. "Blind" carbon copies—or BCCs—are just like CCs, except that the person you're sending the e-mail to won't know that you've sent a copy to someone else.

America Online lets you send the same message to several people at once by stringing their names together separated by commas. By putting a user name in parentheses in the CC box, you can send a blind carbon copy or BCC. People listed in the TO box won't know the BCC recipient got a copy of the e-mail.

Writing Off-line

If you belong to a service that charges you for time you spend on-line, you should write any long e-mails you want to send *before* you log on to the service. That way you can take all the time that you want to write the e-mail, without worrying that it's going to cost you an arm and a leg. You can also read e-mail off-line; when you receive an e-mail, simply save it to your disk. That way, long-winded friends won't cost you lots of money. Services with their own software like AOL and Prodigy let you write your e-mail without logging on. Just open the software, write your message, then log on and send.

Outbox

Suppose you write to a friend and ask a question. Three days later, the answer comes back—but you've forgotten what you asked! Not to worry if your on-line service gives you an "outbox" which stores mail you sent for up to a week.

Flashmail, Etc.

Flashmail on AOL lets you send and receive e-mail on a schedule you set. You program your computer to log itself on at whatever time of day you want it to; it will download all your mail very quickly and then, at your convenience, you can read this mail, create your responses off-line, and log back on to "mail" your responses. If you're big on e-mail correspondence, this will save you some bucks after a few days/weeks.

E-MAIL ON EACH OF THE SERVICES

All of the major on-line services let you send e-mail, but there are some minor differences in their rules and procedures. Here's a quick look at each of their e-mail systems:

71

ON-LINE SERVICE FEES AND FEATURES

	America Online	CompuServe	Prodigy
SERVICE FEES			
Start-up fee	$0	$39.95	$4.95
Monthly rate	$9.95	$8.95	$9.95
Hourly prime-time fees	$2.95	$4.80–$9.60	$2.95
Hourly non–prime-time fees	$2.95	$4.80–$9.60	$2.95
MESSAGE FEES			
Included with monthly fee	Unlimited	$60	Unlimited
Additional electronic messages	$0.00	$0.15	N/A
Attached 10K file	$0.00	$0.20	$0.10
SPECIAL SOFTWARE			
Required	Yes	No	Yes
Available	Yes	Yes	Yes
COMMUNICATIONS FEATURES			
E-mail	Yes	Yes	Yes
File attachments	Yes	Yes	Yes
Fax	Yes	Yes	Yes

AMERICA ONLINE

"You've got mail!" says a voice from within your computer. That's how you know there's e-mail waiting for you when you log on to America Online. (Marian points out that this is exactly the sound that sends her bloodhound, Sam, over the edge. When he hears the ping, he tries to cover his floppy long ears.) Click on the mailbox icon, and a list of e-mail waiting to be read appears on your screen. Click again to read each letter. To reply, simply click on the reply button, and AOL automatically addresses a form for your return e-mail.

Sending mail is just as simple:

1. Click on the Mail menu at the top of the screen, then choose Compose Mail. (Or hit command-M.)

2. Type the AOL or Internet address that you wish to send your e-mail to in the TO field; an address book stores names and electronic addresses of on-line friends, so you don't have to worry about remembering them all. Then, tab to the Subject field and add a subject name (AOL won't let you send the letter if it's blank), and tab to the message field and type in your message.

3. Now click the ''Send'' button to send the message on its way.

IMPORTANT TIP! You can do steps 1 and 2 before you log on. Since you're paying by the minute on AOL (after the first five hours each month), it saves you money to write your letter off-line, then log on to send it. On AOL, sending and receiving e-mail is free, and there's no limit to how many you can send and receive each month.

COMPUSERVE

If you use CIM, you will see a Mail icon on the screen to alert you to incoming mail. Click on the icon or select Get New Mail from the Mail pull-down window. You can save, forward, or delete your messages. To reply, simply click on the reply button, and CIM automatically addresses a form for your return e-mail.

You can compose mail off-line with the CIM editor by selecting "Create Mail" from the Mail pull-down window. Then you can store your outgoing messages in the CIM Outbasket.

CompuServe Mail has an upload feature that allows you to compose e-mail off-line and send files from a personal computer. An address book stores names and electronic addresses of on-line friends, which is useful, because CompuServe e-mail addresses are a long series of numbers that are difficult to remember.

PRODIGY

Prodigy's e-mail is easy to use. A small box on the welcome screen lets you know you have mail. When you click on the window, you go straight to a list of incoming mail. Click on each piece of mail to read messages. A series of icons on the bottom of the screen allows you to reply, forward, save, or delete the message. Just click on the one you want. You can also attach files from your computer to send to other Prodigy members, and send Internet e-mail.

To write messages click on the "Write" icon underneath your list of incoming mail. A new message screen will pop up. Just type in the address, write your message and send. Simple!

Prodigy's e-mail does have one or two annoying extra steps. When you send e-mail, the message stays on the screen. You have to click on "clear" to write a new message. Likewise, when you delete a message from your list of incoming mail, it stays on the screen until you leave the mail area.

eWORLD

eWorld's e-mail is worth mentioning because it's so simple. A little red mail truck pulls up in front of the eMail Center in eWorld's "town square" welcome screen to indicate there are messages waiting for you. Point at the truck and click to see your list of unopened mail. Click on "Open" to read messages.

E-mail on eWorld is a breeze to send:

1. Click "eMail" on the menu at the top of the screen, and choose "New Message."
2. Type the eWorld or Internet address of the person you're writing to in the TO field, tab to the Subject field, and add a subject (you can't send it without a subject), then tab to the message field and type in your message.
3. Click the "Send Now" button to send your mail to its destination.

Like AOL, eWorld lets you write your letters off-line, then log on to send them. Since you're paying for connect time, not per e-mail, always write mail off-line, then log on to send.

DELPHI

When it comes to Delphi, Alfred Glosbrenner, author of *The Little Online Book*, said it all: "The best advice I can give you regarding using Delphi e-mail is don't—if you can at all avoid it. It is a truly terrible system." We'll explain it to you as soon as someone explains it to us! Seriously—we think we're smart and we sure don't get it!

E-MAIL PRICES

E-mail prices can get complicated. Some services charge you for the time you spend on-line, regardless of whether you're writing e-mail, chatting, or playing games. Others charge on a per-message basis. Some allow unlimited free e-mail. Some have extra charges for letters sent and received over the Internet. And that's just the easy stuff.

If you're going to send and receive a lot of e-mail (more than two or three messages a day), you should probably consider signing up with America Online, Prodigy, or eWorld. Each charges a flat monthly fee that includes unlimited e-mail. CompuServe, by comparison, is downright stingy. You can send up to sixty messages for free to other CompuServe members every month. That may sound like a lot, but some people can send more Internet e-mail than that before their first bowl of cornflakes in the morning! Plus, CompuServe charges ten cents for every piece of e-mail you send or receive through the Internet—even if it's junk mail you didn't ask for! If you sign up for even one Internet mailing list (cool ones are scattered throughout the book—but check the Address Book for your specific areas of interest), you'll save money by subscribing to a service with unlimited free e-mail.

6

Live Chat—Reach Out and Stay in Touch

"Some people who think they have better things to do than spend their time on-line think that people who use it frequently have no life. I say, I've met TONS of interesting people who have become really good friends and all you people who 'have a life' probably never met half the number of people I have. I think all kinds of people hang out on-line."

—Eric, fourteen, Olmstead Falls, Ohio

The other day, I (Marian) talked with Sean, a ninth grader who had worked with me on an earlier book. Sean and I gabbed about a lot of things, including his job as White House correspondent for "Kid Company" (a radio show in Boston—see more about some of its contents in Chapter 8) and the fact that he is in a new movie starring Diane Keaton. Pretty cool for a fourteen-year-old!

But I think the coolest thing about my conversation with Sean is that it took place in cyberspace. I was doing some work on America Online, and Sean logged on and sent me an Instant Message, or IM. He asked me if I had time to talk, and I said yes, so we decided to create a "room" on-line in which we could have a private conversation. (Later on in this chapter, we'll tell you how you and your friends can create private chat rooms, too.)

LIVE CHAT

We've already given you lots of information about ways you can communicate with other people on-line—particularly through e-mail and bulletin boards. With e-mail, you send messages to specific people. With bulletin boards, you post messages that anyone on the system can read. Live chat is kind of a combination of the two: If you want to talk privately you can, but you can also talk in public "rooms" that are open to anyone who wants to drop by.

We're using a lot of words—like "room" and "drop by" and "conversation"—that you may not usually think of when talking about computers. To understand what we're saying, it might help you to think of cyberspace as a huge building with thousands and thousands of rooms. In each of these rooms, people are talking about different things. So, for example, there might be a room where people are talking about the Super Bowl, a room where people are talking about "Beavis & Butt-Head," and a room where people are talking about cooking or Ultimate Frisbee™ or karate.

Some of these rooms are bulletin board rooms. People go in there and read messages that other people have posted about the room's subject. No one's actually in the room when you get there; it's just filled with messages and maybe some software to download. But there are also rooms that are filled with people who are actually talking with one another. These are called "chat rooms." If you go into one of these rooms, you can read what everyone is saying and type in responses of your own. The other people in the room are sitting in front of their computers just as you are—it's like talking on the phone with a whole bunch of people at once, but instead of using your mouth to say words, you're typing words into your keyboard.

Trevor, a seventh grader from Houston, enjoys on-line chat because it lets people speak freely and honestly. Jeff, a sixth grader from Long Island, New York, agrees: "You can say anything. Everybody's equal here because you can't tell who they are." And, Annie, an eighth grader from San Francisco, says that she chats with some older friends on SFNet. "I like being able to tell them really personal stuff without having to look them right in the eye. They give me great advice, and I never end up feeling embarrassed."

Eleven-year-old Aaron from northern Michigan agrees that on-line chat is often more comfortable than face-to-face conversations. It doesn't matter what you look like or what you're wearing; people judge you simply based on what you say. And, because nobody knows who you are, you can talk about things that you might be too shy to discuss otherwise.

How do you get involved in on-line chat? It's simple. Here are some of the main ways:

PUBLIC ROOMS

Entering a "public room" on-line is like walking into a noisy, crowded room where (sometimes) everyone is talking at once. It's fun and easy, once you get the hang of it. Too much fun, sometimes. Live computer chat can eat up time and money in what seems like an instant.

Public rooms are usually organized by topic. On America Online, for example, you can go into a "lobby," a place for general chitchat, or enter rooms set up to talk about a particular TV show or hobby or other topic. These rooms have names like "Game Parlor" and "Teen Chat," so you'll know what the topic is. CompuServe's chat rooms are part of what they call their "CB Simulator." Channels 7 and 17 are for kids. eWorld's chat works just like AOL's. Prodigy, a latecomer to the on-line chat game, offers lots of chat rooms, but you have to dig through several levels of screens to get to them. Delphi has chat rooms called "conferences"—they're harder to communicate in because you need to learn a bunch of commands first. The discussions in all of these rooms are "unmoderated," which means that no one is in charge of the room. You can enter and "lurk" (just listen), or you can join in the conversation.

When you enter one of these public rooms, your user ID or screenname shows up on the screen to let people know you're there. Don't be surprised, then, if some people say "hi" to you right away. The screen will also tell you how many people are in the room. Some rooms seems like they're packed with people no matter what time of day you show up; other rooms may be pretty empty from time to time.

When you first check out the chat rooms, it's probably a good idea to cruise from room to room for a while, so you can decide which ones grab your interest. Of course, this may change every day—or even every minute—because a chat room is only as interesting as the people who are in it at that particular time.

Private Rooms

Several of the online services allow you to set up private rooms to carry on one-on-one conversations without being interrupted by all the other people in a public room. Let's say, for example, that you're in a room where everyone is talking about music. You and one other person in the room LOVE Boyz II Men, but most of the people in the room are talking about rappers like Snoop Doggy Dogg and Dr. Dre. If you're tired of hearing about rap, you might decide to ask the other person in the room who likes Boyz II Men to join you in a private room. That way you can talk about your favorite group to your heart's content.

How do you go about it? First you have to invite someone to go into a room with you. You can post a message in the public room, saying, "Hey, [whatever the person's screenname is], do you want to create a private room so we can talk about

Boyz?'' Then that person can send a message saying yes or no. If you want to be more private about your invitation, you can send that person an instant message (this service is available on AOL, Prodigy, and eWorld). A note will appear on that person's screen that only he or she can see. That person can then send you an IM back to tell you whether or not he or she wants to "go private."

IMPORTANT: If someone asks you to "go private," remember all the safety rules we discussed in Chapter 4 before you agree.

Conferences

You know how we told you there are millions of people on-line? Well, we're talking about all kinds of people—even celebrities. Some celebrities who are on-line like to remain anonymous. You could be talking to your favorite actor or athlete in a chat room and you wouldn't even know it was he or she!

So, which celebrities hang out on-line? There's really no way of knowing unless the celebrity makes an announcement that he or she is on-line. (And remember: People who say they are celebrities aren't necessarily telling the truth. So, if someone says he's Macaulay Culkin or she's Janet Jackson, you shouldn't necessarily believe it!) Celebrities who are known to hang out in cyberspace for fun and relaxation include Madonna, author Tom Clancy, Rosie O'Donnell, and talk show host Rush Limbaugh. Singer Courtney Love told an interviewer from *Rolling Stone* that the only human contact she had in the weeks after her husband, Kurt Cobain, committed suicide was chatting on-line. (And would you believe that Marian and her friend, Cat Doran, who also works at Chiat/Day, actually cohosted a special event on America Online the night Cobain's body was found?) "We thought of it as an on-line celebration of life—a wake, if you will, to channel grief more positively," says Marian.

In addition to hanging out on-line, a lot of celebrities come on-line for scheduled conferences. One of the on-line services will arrange for the celebrity to enter an on-line auditorium at a particular time to answer questions posed by people in the audience. For example, America Online has several live conferences every night, many of which feature celebrity guests. Center Stage is AOL's theater district; it has four on-line auditoriums—Coliseum, Odeon, Globe, and Rotunda—each of which can hold up to two thousand people at a time. Guests have included musicians (Garth Brooks, Melissa Etheridge, Arrested Development), actors (Pauly Shore, Terry Hatcher of "Lois & Clark," Ben Savage of "Boy Meets World," Zachery Ty Bryan of "Home Improvement"), athletes (Dan Jansen, Bonnie Blair), and others. Everyone who attends can send questions for the moderator to ask the guest. What happens if you miss the conference? No problem. You can download the transcript (and possibly a photo) to read later on.

What do celebrities talk about on-line? Lots of stuff. Some celebrities come on-line to talk about their new movie or TV show. Others just want a chance to meet their fans. And sometimes celebrities take part in conferences on a particular topic such as music censorship or a particular organization they're working with.

Here are a few samples of on-line conferences:

MICK JAGGER OF THE ROLLING STONES

Question: Hey Mick, are you ever going to retire or are you going to be like the Energizer Bunny?

MICKJAGGER: I'm still running on the battery pack I was born with and I have no plans to retire before next year when we go to Europe. After that, who knows?

HAKEEM OLAJUWON OF THE HOUSTON ROCKETS

Question: First I would like to say you are a great player. I know you don't talk trash while you are playing. How do you stay calm while every other player talks trash?

HAKEEMNBA: Well, you understand, you have to have a professional and sportsmanlike conduct, where the sportsman is supposed to watch his moral conduct and be a good example for the audience. It is something that is very important to me. It is also part of my faith.

CLAIRE DANES (MTV's "MY SO-CALLED LIFE")

Question: Being fifteen myself, I was wondering how you can juggle school and your career?

CLAIREDNES: It's difficult. My hours on the set are strictly regulated 'cause I'm a minor—five hrs. in front of camera, three hrs. in school (a room with a tutor), one hour rest and recreation and a half hour of lunch. And they're not in blocks of time—they are split up into different like twenty-minute increments. I go from a crying scene to studying geometry and vice versa all day. It's hard to focus.

Question: Hi Claire, how do you like this computer on-line crap?

CLAIREDNES: This is fun man—typing is a blast—and I love hearing what audiences have to say. Feedback is great!

STEVEN TYLER OF AEROSMITH

Question: What advice can you give struggling cats like myself who feel they have what it takes to get signed but the industry gives us the short end of the stick?

STEVENLIVE: The road of a thousand miles starts with the first step. Do the clubs, and whatever it takes. Set up in a mall. Fake it till you make it, if you have to.

ACTRESS/COMEDIENNE ROSIE O'DONNELL

Question: Rosie, what led you on-line?

ROSIE OH O: I was doing *Another Stakeout* and the entire cast and crew were members. They turned me on to it. And now I am hooked.

Question: How often do you use the service? Where do you go?

ROSIE OH O: At first I was on five hours a day, then I cut down as it was affecting my life. Now I am on about five hours a week. I go into the chat rooms, use e-mail, and read reviews. I had an account last year, and got two TOS violations for arguing with a bigot. (*que sera*). I have behaved myself since.

America Online and CompuServe offer the most live conferences. Prodigy, which was late getting into the live chat game, lets fans post message board questions to stars in their "Guest Spotlight." Among their dozens of special guests have been quarterback Terry Bradshaw, former President Jimmy Carter, the cast of NBC's "Cheers," and Jerry Seinfeld. Just recently Phil Donahue was working the boards.

CYBERCOMMUNICATION

So, do you think you're ready to start chatting it up on the 'Net? Well, you *almost* are. There's still one more thing to learn: how to cyberchat. Oh, sure, you could just use words like you normally do. But there's also an entire language on the 'Net that's been developed to help people communicate more easily. Only in cyberspace do people ;-) at each other, LOL at a good joke, answer a smart-aleck remark with a :-P or express themselves brilliantly, IMHO. This part of the book is going to teach you about some of the symbols and acronyms used most commonly in cyberspace.

Join American Dialogue™ on AOL

Did you know that some companies actually pay people to talk with them about their products? That's right, it's called "market research," and it's something you can sign up for on AOL. All you have to do is enter the American Dialogue™ area (KEYWORD: DIALOGUE) and fill out a short questionnaire. Then BKG—a company founded by Marian and the creator of American Dialogue™—will send you an e-mail or call you on the phone when it has a project that might interest you.

Let's say that BKG wanted to talk with you about sneakers. Someone at the company would ask you if you would like to be in an on-line focus group. If you decided to do it, you would be asked to log on to AOL and go into a particular "room" at a certain time. There might be anywhere from five to twelve other people in the "room" with you, and you would all be typing answers to questions asked by BKG. You might be asked, for example, to tell BKG what your favorite sneakers look like, how much they cost, what the coolest sneaker brands are, etc.

And the best part? You actually get paid for it! Depending on things like how long the session lasts, you could earn anywhere from $10-$75. Great deal, huh?

"My mom and little brother and I were all in separate focus groups about orange juice. They asked us stuff like how much OJ we drink every day, what we drink with dinner, and what foods taste really gross with OJ (I said, 'Pizza'—YUCK!). Afterwards, I got a check for $20. I had a really fun time doing it, and I LOVED earning money!"

—Ashley, eleven, Dayton, Ohio

SMILEYS (OR EMOTICONS)

You might not realize it, but when you talk with a person face-to-face, you use a lot of visual cues to let that person know what you mean. For example, you might frown and shake your finger to let someone know you're angry, or you might grin to let someone know that you're just kidding. In cyberspace, people can't see each other's body language, so it's easy to misunderstand a person's attitude. That's where smileys come in.

Smileys, also known as emoticons, take the place of facial expressions and vocal inflections on-line. They help people understand each other's meanings better. Here's an example: Let's say you were talking in one of the chat rooms with your cousin who lives in another state. If you usually goof around together, you might greet her by saying, "Hey, Dogbreath." If you were talking to your cousin in person, you could let her know you were just joking by smiling when you said it. Well, you can do that in cyberspace, too, simply by adding a smiley. You'd say, "Hey, Dogbreath:-)."

To view a smiley, tilt your head to the left. You should be seeing something that looks like a human face. A smile is just one of hundreds of smileys used in cyberspace. And more seem to be invented every day.

The following list contains some of the most common smileys—the ones you're most likely to use. It also contains some smileys that aren't used very often. We wanted to show them to you since some of them are pretty clever!

:-)	Your basic smiley (used to show humor or happiness)
;-)	A wink (shows you're being a flirt or sarcastic)
:-(	A frown (means you're sad, depressed, or have hurt feelings)
:'-(	Crying
:-D	Laughter, or a really big grin
:-*	A kiss
:-P	Sticking out your tongue
%-)	Confused

86

:-/	Perplexed
:-|	Bored
:-x	Your lips are sealed
:-$	Put your money where your mouth is
:-0	Astonished
=:O	Frightened/hair standing on end
=8o	Bug-eyed/hair standing on end
:-!	Put your foot in your mouth
:-}	Embarrassed smile
O:)	You're an angel
>:->	You're a devil
;-^)	Tongue in cheek

Putting someone's name in brackets like this: {Lindsay} means you're giving her a hug. Lots of brackets {{{{{Lindsay}}}}} is a really big hug.

Some people have turned smileys into an art form!

—<—@	A rose
\(((((())))))/	Bowl of chips
\~~~~~~~/	Bowl of dip or salsa
[:-l]	A robot
:-)8	Man with a bow tie
8:-)	Little girl with a bow in her hair
(:V	A duck
(-:l:-)	Siamese twins
d:-)	Baseball player
9:-)	Baseball catcher
-{}	Man with a mustache
:-[	Vampire
:-#	wearing braces
Cl:-=	Charlie Chaplin
=l:-)=	Abe Lincoln
C=:-)	Chef
*<:-)	Santa Claus
*:o)	Bozo

[:-)	Wearing a Walkman		
+-(:-)´	The Pope		
=l:-)=	Uncle Sam		
(:)-)	Scuba diver		

SHORTHAND

Another thing people use a lot on-line is shorthand. Sometimes it can be a pain in the neck to type out all the words, so people use shorthand for commonly used phrases. On-line shorthand is a little more common than smileys and can be very useful—plus, you don't get a sore neck looking at your computer!

Using just the first letter of each word in a common phrase is an online habit. The reason for this is speed: Why type out "by the way" if BTW means something to your cyberpals? Just don't assume that your English teacher will be happy to see this terminology creep into your next book report!

Here are some common shorthand phrases:

ADN	Any Day Now	DIKU	Do I Know You?
AFK	Away From Keyboard	F2F	Face-to-Face
ASAP	As Soon As Possible	FAQ	Frequently Asked Question
B4N	Bye For Now		
BAK	Back At Keyboard	FISH	First In, Still Here
BBL	Be Back Later	FWIW	For What It's Worth
BBS	Bulletin Board System	FYI	For Your Information
BIOYIOP	Blow It Out Your I/O Port	<g>	Grin
		G, BG, VGB	Grin, Big Grin, Very Big Grin
BL	Belly Laughing!		
BRB	Be Right Back	GAL	Get A Life
BTA	But Then Again	GD&R	Grinning, Ducking, And Running
BTW	By The Way		
CU	See You	GIWIST	Gee, I Wish I'd Said That
CUL or CUL8ER	See You Later	GMTA	Great Minds Think Alike

88

GTRM	Going To Read Mail	PU	That Stinks!
IAC	In Any Case	ROFL	Rolling On Floor Laughing
IC	I See		
ILY	I Love You	ROTFL	Rolling On The Floor Laughing
IMO	In My Opinion		
IMHO	In My Humble Opinion	ROFLWTIME	Rolling On Floor With Tears In My Eyes
IMNSHO	In My Not-So-Humble Opinion		
		RPG	Role Playing Games
IOW	In Other Words	RSN	Real Soon Now
J/K	Just Kidding	RTFM	Read The #$%@! Manual
L8R	Later		
LD	Later, Dude	S/AC	Sex/Age Check
LDR	Long-Distance Relationship	SIG	Special Interest Group
		SO	Significant Other
LLTA	Lots and Lots Of Thunderous Applause	TAFN	That's All For Now
		TANJ	There Ain't No Justice
LOL	Laughing Out Loud		
LTIP	Laughed Till I Puked	TGIF	Thank God It's Friday
MOSS	Member Of Same Sex	TLK2UL8R	Talk To You Later
MOTOS	Member Of The Opposite Sex	TTFN	Ta-Ta For Now!
		TTUL	Talk To You Later
OIC	Oh I See	Txs	Thanks
OTF	On The Floor	WFM	Works for Me
OTOH	On The Other Hand	WU?	What's Up?
OLL	On-Line Love	WUF	Where Are You From?
PDA	Public Display Of Affection		
::POOF::	Good-bye (leaving room)	WYSIWYG	What You See Is What You Get
PMJI	Pardon My Jumping In		

LIVE CHAT DOS—AND DON'TS

Now that you're set to enter the wonderful and wacky world of on-line chat, we wanted to remind you of a few basic rules. Following these will help make sure that your cyberchats are fun and positive. [If they sound familiar, think of this as a review session:-)]

- **Remember the "rules of the road" (see Chapter 4).** You'll really need them here. Don't give out personal information such as your phone number, real-world address, or last name unless you are very, very sure that you know who you're giving it to. And never give it to anyone without permission from your parents. If you're going to run into any nasty people on-line, it's most likely you'll find them in a chat room. If someone starts to pick on you or if someone frightens you in any way, tell him or her nicely that you don't want to talk. If that person doesn't go away after a second warning, log off and call customer service. Be sure to write down the person's exact screenname or user ID so the on-line service can contact the troublemaker.

- **Don't forget your 'Netiquette.** Don't use foul language. It can get you kicked off your on-line service pronto. If someone in the chat room is offended by a word you use or a really mean thing you say, that person could report you to the service. We've heard stories about parents who've come home and discovered that their kids have gotten the entire family kicked off an on-line service!

- **No scrolling.** No programming in sounds, and repeating them, again, and again, and again.

- **Be helpful.** If a newbie doesn't understand a smiley or acronym you use, explain it.

- **Watch the clock.** Lots of people think that live chat is the most fun thing to do on-line. It's easy to get hooked—and that means it's easy to run up your bills. Don't let that happen to you. Watch your time carefully. It's also a good idea to talk with your parents about how much time it's OK for you to spend on-line each month.

7

On-line Connecting—SIGs, Forums, and RoundTables

"I love the area called 'KOOL,' for Kids Only Online. I post in the Teen Scene, too. My favorite areas are the message boards. I've met a lot of people through them. I usually hang out in the chat rooms KOOL Treehouse or the KOOL Gameroom. The people there are friendly, especially the staff."

—Johanna, thirteen

CONNECT!

People are people. We love to chat, gossip, meet new people, make friends, discuss what's important to us, get advice, and hear other opinions. We need to laugh, cry, and feel as though other people care about us. In short, people need to *connect*. Making connections is the real magic of cyberspace.

"My favorite place to be is the Treehouse, which is a kids chat room under the topic Kids Only on AOL," says Sarah, ten, of Bethesda, Maryland. "I like it because I have met a lot of friends. I even met someone who lives near me!"

Josh, fourteen, of Herndon, Virginia, hangs out in a PC Games forum. "It is a lot of fun, I enjoy it, and there are many frequent users so they must enjoy it to keep coming back," he says. "When I log on I check mail, see if any friends are on-line, then go to the downloading areas. You can get mail, games, gifs, and new friends all in the first sign-on."

"I usually hang out on NBC On-Line or Critic's Choice," says fifteen-year-old Jaclyn of Brunswick, Maine. "I hang out here because these are my favorite areas. I like the message boards and I get to voice my opinions about TV shows or whatever the subject matter is."

These on-line meeting places have lots of different names. CompuServe calls them SIGs (special interest groups) or forums. America Online calls them message boards. Prodigy calls them clubs or bulletin boards (BBs). They're also known as newsgroups, RoundTables, and discussion groups. No matter what they're called, they're all the same—places to go on-line to meet people who are interested in the same thing—anything from backpacking and bicycling to science fiction and sports.

But it's usually not the subject, it's the people that make on-line forums special. You can get information about "Star Trek" anywhere. But if you know people who are as into "Voyager" as you are, and are fun to hang out with, it's a lot more interesting. Plan on spending some time "cruising the boards" and checking out lots of different forums. And be open-minded. There are a lot of forums on cool subjects that are totally boring because the people in the forum aren't active and involved. On the other hand, you can find forums full of interesting and fun people in places you never dreamed.

For millions of cybernauts, a forum is their on-line home. It's the place you hang out, make and meet friends, and learn more about things you're interested in. The best forums are like clubs where you know everyone and everyone knows you. "I like to hang out in Teen Chat," says AOL member Anna Frances, thirteen, "because I can actually talk to people my age who may have my same likes and dislikes.'' Finding a forum to call your own is how the real magic of cyberspace comes alive.

JOINING AN ON-LINE FORUM

Again, remember your 'Netiquette from Chapter 4. When you're new to a forum, it's often a good idea to "lurk" for a while. That is, explore and read what others have had to say before adding your own questions or comments. It's not a good idea just to show up in a new forum and start polluting the bulletin boards with your messages. That's the on-line equivalent of showing up at a party and being a loud, obnoxious show-off—a surefire way to get flamed!

Come in and have a look around. Introduce yourself on the message boards. Most people you'll meet on-line are friendly and helpful. But some forums can be like a foreign country, full of their own rules and customs. By lurking for a while before getting involved in the conversation, you can get an idea of how to act. The last thing you want to do is make yourself unwelcome in a forum because you made a lousy entrance.

Once you've lurked around a bit to get a feel for the place, you can start to jump in!

Here's how it works: Check out a bulletin board, read what other people have to say about the topic being discussed, then respond with your own comments. Contributions to a bulletin board are called "posts." Check back in a little while to see if anyone answers your post. It can sometimes be a few hours or days, so be patient. When someone responds to what you wrote, you can answer back. Bulletin board conversations can go on for days, weeks, or months, and sometimes longer.

You also can respond to messages that have been left by someone else. It doesn't matter if they're not addressed to you—on-line bulletin boards are free-flowing discussions that anyone can join.

When you are reading through the message boards in a

forum, you may come across a post that asks a question. If you know the answer, don't be shy—post it! That's the whole point of an on-line forum. It's a place to share ideas and information, and everyone's encouraged to join in.

FORUM FAST FACTS

Forums aren't just about hanging out and chatting. They're also some of the best places to get practical information and help.

You might find a forum or two on-line where you spend most of your time, getting to know the regulars and making on-line friends. But forums can also be a great place to "hit and run"—get the answer to a specific question in a hurry.

There are many different ways to get information from an on-line club or forum. The simplest way is to just spend a little time browsing through what other members have already posted. You'd be surprised how many times someone has asked the same question and received an answer from another member. A lot of forums have something called an "FAQ" list. FAQ stands for "Frequently Asked Questions." It should always be your first stop if you're new to a forum.

The best forums offer lots more than message boards. A lot of them feature live chat rooms and libraries of files, pictures, and software for downloading. They're great places to meet experts and get up-to-the-minute information on a subject.

FINDING A FORUM

OK. You're ready to find a forum. What do you want to talk about? Let's say you saw "The Simpsons" last night. Nobody at school agrees that Homer is deep down an OK person. You want to see if you're the only person in the world who thinks he's a regular father of the year—just a carbon copy of your dear old dad. Let's find a conversation about it.

On America Online, the first thing to do is check out the Departments. Click on Main Menu and check it out. There's a department called "Entertainment" and another one called "Kids." Nothing specifically about television. Go to the top of the screen and pull down the "Go To" menu. Choose "Directory of Services." This lets you enter in words that describe what you're looking for and AOL will do all the work for you. Type in the word "television" and thirty different forums pop up! There's "Television News." It contains the top television news, soap opera summaries, a list of the top ten television shows, and a message board where members can discuss their favorite shows. That's a possibility. There's also an area run by "Extra," the entertainment TV show. Click on the message boards and there it is! A folder dedicated to messages about "The Simpsons." ABC, NBC, and MTV all have very cool areas on-line.

Here's the best thing: On the way to the Extra area, we saw a list of thirty areas when we typed in "television." The list included things like National Geographic On-line, "Geraldo," "The Ricki Lake Show," CNN Newsroom, and "Comedy Central"—areas you might never have known about if you didn't go looking for a place to dish about "The Simpsons." You might even decide some of these areas were more interesting than what you were looking for! Happens all the time in cyberspace. For example, could you resist the opportunity to put your two cents in about the antics of Beavis & Butt-Head, or maybe to swap reactions to the latest on Court TV?

FORUMS FOR KIDS ON COMMERCIAL ON-LINE SERVICES

There are tons of forums for on-line kids—and many more that welcome kids' participation. You'll find lots more in Chapter

10, "Special Interests, A to Z—And Even More Great On-line Places."

PRODIGY

Just Kids (JUMP:KIDS) Prodigy is the champ for the sheer volume of stuff for kids to do, and you can get to most of it through the Just Kids screen. It's the gateway to Games, the "Kids Talk" message boards, Stories, Activities, Kids News, Humor, and Contests & Quizzes.

NOVA (JUMP: NOVA) Who says science isn't fun? Each month, the NOVA Feature takes you on an entertaining adventure that explains a little about the universe we live in.

Baby-sitters Club (JUMP: BSC) What can you do when a two-year-old has a tantrum? How do you entertain five-year-olds when it's raining? You'll find these answers and more in BSC Tips & Tactics. Browse almost two hundred articles offering advice, how-tos, suggestions, games, activities, and more. A really cool feature is "Make a Date." Enter the dates of baby-sitting jobs, parties, or school assignments, and BSC Date Reminder will send you an e-mail message one week in advance to remind you where you need to be and when!

SI For Kids (JUMP: SI KIDS) brings the world of sports to kids. Post questions about sports, and get answers in "Letters to the Editor." Write about what you'd like to know about your favorite athletes through "Ask the Athlete." The "Pro & Con Debate" lets you vote on important sports questions, and lets you see how other kids voted. If there's a sports event you don't want to miss, check out "This Month in Sports." And go "Behind the Scenes" with the writers and editors of *SI For Kids*.

Ask Beth (JUMP: ASK BETH) is a great place to talk about problems you don't want to discuss with your friends and family. "Ask Beth" is Elizabeth Winship, the advice columnist for teenagers and parents. Having launched "Ask Beth" for the *Boston Globe,* where she was children's books editor, Winship brings more than twenty years of experience in writing about adolescent concerns to Prodigy. You can read daily advice plus new questions and answers on Tuesdays and Fridays.

AMERICA ONLINE

Kids Only Online (KEYWORD: KIDS) is ground zero for kids on AOL, and arguably the best on-line service for kids anywhere. It's where most of the kids on AOL hang out, and it offers point-and-click access to dozens of other areas of interest to kids—from the Cartoon Network and *Disney Adventures* to Compton's Encyclopedia and Homework Help. There are on-line clubs on astronomy, the environment, and Star Trek. Plus the "Treehouse," "Playground," and "Jellybean Park"—three "Kids Only" chat rooms for live conversation, games, special guests, special topics.

KIDSNET (KEYWORD: KIDSNET) features a very active "Kids Talk about TV" message board for discussions of your favorite shows. This forum is a place to get information on children's audio, video, radio, and television programming.

National Geographic Online (KEYWORD: NGS) gives you on-line selections from *National Geographic* magazine and *National Geographic Traveler* and *World* magazines. It also has great resources for school projects—NGS Kids Network, Geographic Interactive, Geographic TV, or the Geography Education Program. *National Geographic* is also available on-line on Prodigy.

Tomorrow's Morning (KEYWORD: TOMORROW) is America's only weekly home-delivery newspaper written and designed just for kids. You can read the paper on-line, and discuss it with others on the message board.

COMPUSERVE

There are no forums specifically for kids on CompuServe, but there are more than six hundred forums on such diverse topics as humor, rock music, auto racing, handicapped PC users, and science fiction. All of these are "extended services," meaning they will cost you extra to hang out there.

Students' Forum (GO STUFO) is worth visiting so you get to type STUFO. Seriously, this is a forum for students to share their ideas and interests with other students around the world.

Education Forum (GO EDFORUM) is where teachers, students, parents, and other interested people meet. Mostly for adults, but older kids might find it interesting and useful. One of the hottest topics is how computers and high technology is changing the way kids learn.

Dinosaur Forum (GO DINO) Not a kids forum, but an area set up by the Dinosaur Club with message boards on everything from "Dinosaur Science" to "Dinosaur Humor." What makes this forum really cool is the forum libraries, which include computer graphics of dinosaurs.

IBM Special Needs Forum (GO IBMSPECIAL) Do you know someone with special learning needs? The IBM Special Needs forum addresses all aspects of special education—from education of the handicapped to bilingual education and more, from kindergarten through twelfth grade and adult literacy programs. The forum includes information on IBM educational programs such as Write to Read, Listen to Learn, and PALS.

FORUMS FOR KIDS ON OTHER SERVICES

eWorld's Youth Central (SHORTCUT: YOUTH) is the place where kids hang on eWorld. There are two main message boards: Central Beat, where music is the subject, and the Coastin' Collage, which covers every topic from high school wrestling to "Melrose Place" to a place to post on-line smileys. There are daily conferences in the Central Conversation chat room and weekly polls for forum members (Sample: Has "Saturday Night Live" lost its spark? Yes! 63%; No! 27.6%). There's also an easy-to-use feedback section that lets you make suggestions on how to improve the forum.

Blackberry Creek (SHORTCUT: BLACKBERRY) The Kids' Creativity Community—Blackberry Creek on eWorld—is for kids who use computers for fun and creativity. The emphasis is on computer projects like *The Blackberry Creek Gazette,* a forum newspaper; the Kids' Hangout, where kids can share ideas and information, write stories, and tell jokes; and the Hungry Ear, a "live performance space," featuring "chats" to create group stories, a Comedy Club, and more. One of the most original offerings is the Party and Gift Shop, where you can get ideas for gifts you can make with your computer, such as coupons, calendars, and more.

FORUM DOS—AND DONT'S

• *DO have respect for the opinions of others.* Some of the best forums are filled with smart, funny, opinionated people who are not shy about expressing themselves. Disagreements are not against the rules. In fact, they're usually encouraged!

But you can disagree with someone without attacking him personally. It's extremely rude. If you make a habit of personal attacks, your posts will probably end up being ignored.

- *DO remember your 'Netiquette.* Foul language is not acceptable. On most services, the forum host will remove your post if it is rude, crude, or offensive. **DON'T forget you're in public.** A forum or bulletin board is in full view of anyone who happens by. You should not post anything about yourself that you would not want everyone to know. Don't forget that unlike live chat, which scrolls off the bottom of the screen in a few minutes, your on-line posts in a forum or SIG will stay there in full public view for months or years—maybe even forever!

- *DON'T stray from the subject.* If you want to talk about your favorite TV shows, go to bulletin/message boards about TV, either within the specific areas programmed by the television networks or in locations where kids and teens have staked out space to chat it up about stuff which matters to them. Do not go to the pets forums if you're looking to discuss "60 Minutes," "The Simpsons," or "House of Style," or anything else. Also, if everyone in a discussion thread is talking about Nick at Nite programs, don't try to steer the conversation to what's new on your favorite soap. Samantha Stevens is a bewitching subject but Erica just won't keep the thread running! Then again, if no one is talking about a subject you are interested in, start a new topic.

ONCE YOU KNOW YOUR WAY AROUND

Once you have learned your way around, you'll find on-line forums are the coolest places in cyberspace. It's where the magic of a "virtual community" really happens. If you spend a little time exploring, you're sure to find an on-line hangout that's right for you, where the people are friendly, and the conversation interesting.

But whatever you do, try to surprise yourself. From time to time, visit different forums and expand your horizons. The wealth of information on-line and the number of on-line communities is nearly endless. You'll enjoy life in cyberspace a lot more if you get out of your own on-line neighborhood and see more of what's out there!

Talk About Friends and Foes On-line

Is someone at your school really bugging you? Has your best friend turned into a total creep? Don't worry—you're not alone! Check out the "Friends and Foes" board on AOL to see what we mean! (KEYWORD: KOOL)

"I have this friend named Travis that lives down the street from me; we got into a water fight and I don't know how, but we got into a fistfight. Luckily I bailed out before his dad came"
—Re: Friends and Foes, by Velvet

"Anyone that lives in the Kansas City or Topeka area watch out for R__ Q__. I think I got his name right. He is so WHINEY! He was about four feet tall about a year ago. The other is H__ J__. He uses people like C__ S__ used BigFoot. But it is different. He feeds off of friendship and rules everyone by pouting if he doesn't get his way. He had me captured and I got away. He now has my friend."
—Re: Foe, by FunnyGirl

"I have a friend (EX-friend to be exact!) that won't stop bragging about the last incidents that I accidentally did!!! I hate to have a friend (Justin's my ex-friend!!!) that brags about some things that involve mischief!!! I just haaaatttteeee that Justin!!! He insulted me, he hurted my feelings soooo bad, I just wish somebody would come along and make him feel the same exact feelings that I have!!!! What's worse, he makes me feel stupid enough to make me feel like I'm nobody but a geek-faced, nincompoop, stupid obnoxious jerk who don't know nothing! But I'm not any of those. I'm a somebody. I can do things that he can't. It's just not fair!!! What should I do? Should I put him behind me?"

—Re: Justin that dweebhead, by Sasquatch

"There is this girl who keeps annoying me because I'm not in the 'cool' group. My friends are also in the 'cool' group so . . . they won't get bugged when she is around. I ignore her, but it doesn't help. I tell teachers, but they don't do a darn thing about it! My parents are no good either. Please help me get this little moron out of my hair!!!"

—Re: The "in" crowd, by HiStar

• •

8

Just for Fun—
Games, Multimedia,
Sports, and Shopping

Had a tough day at school? Tired of the tube? Want some *real* entertainment? Well, you came to the right place! Cyberspace is a movie theater, amusement park, video arcade, and sports arena all rolled into one. No matter what you like to do for fun, no matter what your special interests, you're almost guaranteed to find something along those lines in cyberspace.

Each of the major on-line services has areas devoted to hobbies of all kinds. On CompuServe, they're called SIGs (special-interest groups) and there are more than six hundred of them! For a complete list, GO INDEX. On AOL, special-interest areas are called clubs and forums, and they include—among many, many other topics—Comedy, Cooking, Debate, Emergency Response, Environment, Free-Form Gaming, Gadget Guru Electronics Forum, Ham Radio, Pet Care, Photography, Role-Playing Games, Science Fiction, Scuba, Star Trek, Travel, Trivia, and Writers. Phew! Try to read that out loud without taking a breath!

Delphi's SIGs include Amiga, Apple II, Atari Advantage, Environment, Golf, Hobby Shop, Internet, Language and Cultures, Music City, Radio, Science Fiction, Software Reviews, Sports Connection Online, TV and Movies, U.S.A. Gymnastics, and World of Video Games. Delphi also has unique custom forums ranging from All-Star Sports, Comedy Club Online, Comics, Scotland Online, Soap Operas, Star Trek, Teens and Youth to Wargaming and Military Strategy.

GEnie has what it calls "RoundTables" on such things as Computer Game Design, Disney, Fantasy Sports Leagues, Genealogy, History, Japan, MPGames, Modeling, Motorcycling, Outdoors, Pet Net, Scuba, Space and Science, Sports, Stamp Collecting, Video Games, and White House.

And the Prodigy Bulletin Boards cover such topics as Books and Arts, Cars and Motorcycles, Collecting, Crafts, Games, Movies, Pets, Radios, Science Fiction and Fantasy, Sports, Sports Play, Teens, Trading Cards, and TV. (See Chapter 7 for complete info on how you can locate and use these areas.)

As you can see, there's never any excuse to be bored in cyberspace—provided you're curious and willing to hack and crack your way through all of the areas appropriate for kids of your age who have similar interests! Since we couldn't possibly list all the fun areas available on-line, this chapter will touch on just a few of the areas that we think will be of greatest interest to you, particularly on-line gaming, media, sports, and shopping. If your particular hobby or interest isn't mentioned, don't assume you're out of luck. As we've said again and again in this book, just about every topic under the sun is covered to one degree or another in cyberspace. If you can't find it on one of the commercial services, you're almost sure to find it on the 'Net. And if you don't find it on the 'Net, you can always start your own newsgroup!

ON-LINE GAMING

First there were board games. Then came role-playing adventure games and video games and computer games. But did you know you can play all of these types of games on-line? That's right— there are hundreds and hundreds of games you can play in cyberspace, either alone, with a partner, or with a large group. Here are the major types:

Role-playing (Fantasy) Games.
These are games in which you pretend to be a particular character faced with various situations. Dungeons & Dragons is one example.

SAMPLE SITES			
America Online	KEYWORD: RPG	Live on-line fantasy games
	KEYWORD: RD	Visit in character, or stop by to gather information or discuss games, interactive play, and creative development
	KEYWORD: ADD	On-line version of "Neverwinter Nights" (Dungeons & Dragons)
GEnie	KEYWORD: TSR	Info from the company that created "Dungeons & Dragons"
	KEYWORD: GS3	Enter the world of Kulthea and interact in real time with other people as you seek treasure and glory
CompuServe	GO RPGAMES	Discuss and play board, paper, and role-playing games

Card and Board Games.
These are on-line versions of games you're probably already familiar with—games like chess and poker and crossword puzzles. Some of these you can play by yourself or against the computer; others you can play against other kids or adults on-line.

SAMPLE SITES

Delphi	GO ENT BOA	Computer simulations; board and strategy games
America Online	KEYWORD: GAME DESIGN	Learn more about game design: computer and non-computer games
	KEYWORD: GAMEBASE	Database with gaming info
Prodigy	JUMP: CHESS	Chess tutorials and new updates
CompuServe	GO CHESSFORUM	Play e-mail chess and get updated chess news
	GO RPGAMES	Discuss and play board, paper, and role-playing games
GEnie	KEYWORD: CHESS	Play chess on-line and participate in tournaments

Play-by-Mail Games. These are games played by groups of people all over the country using e-mail and bulletin boards. The actual amount of time people spend playing on-line is relatively short (good news for those of us on a strict budget). You do all your planning and strategizing off-line and then post your next move. It's a great way to play games, because you can post your moves whenever you want—you don't need to wait for the other players to show up.

All of the major on-line services offer on-line gaming, but you'll probably find that the best gaming for kids right now is on Prodigy and CompuServe. The other services also offer lots of gaming, but they don't have as many games that are specifically designed for kids—at least not yet.

PRODIGY

Since Prodigy is widely considered the "family" on-line service, it's no surprise that it's probably the best gaming source for kids. To find out about all the games available (JUMP:JUST KIDS) or (JUMP:GAME CENTER) or, for discussion, (JUMP:GAMES BB). If you're interested in sports simulations, click the "fantasy games" button on the Sports-ESPNET page (JUMP:ESPNET).

Here's a list of some of what's out there. Remember that playing some of these games may result in premium charges.

Games for younger kids
JUMP:WordType of GameAge

"Reading Magic"	reading game—action ending	School-age
"Twisted"	reading game—random words	School-age
"MadMaze"	fantasy	School-age
"Krazy"	weekly caption-writing contest	School-age
"Guts"	weekly quiz game	School-age

Games/activities for 'tweenagers

"Nova"	entertaining science facts	Junior high
"Carmen"	geography tests and intrigue	Junior high

Here are more detailed descriptions of a few of the games you might want to try out first:

MadMaze (Jump:Madmaze)

This is an adventure game in which you'll find yourself on a heroic quest to save the world. There are more than 16,000 locations you can explore in an attempt to find your way out. Your goal is to save the world by delivering a very important message to the wizard; in order to find him, you have to move through three areas of the maze, and each one is more complicated than the last. You should expect to spend 40–100 hours before you complete MadMaze. Don't worry: You can save the game and come back to it later!

"Fill in the Blanks" (Jump:Fitb)

Prodigy's version of "Hangman" lets you play with as many as four other people, all sitting around your computer. The goal is to guess a word, name, or phrase within a specific category. Five words or phrases make up a category; and each category is a clue. When you pick the right letter, it goes into the appropriate spot; and then your turn continues. But, if you guess wrong, you lose your turn. Play is at three levels: easy, hard, and goofy. FITB can last anywhere from two to thirty minutes.

Quick Games (Jump:Game Center)

Quick Game options on Prodigy are located within the Game Center menu. What makes these games "quick" is that they typically take one to five minutes, never more. In fact, when we tried them, we only wondered how many parents would think that some of the brain teasers were worth the $.50 premium Prodigy attaches to them after just one play per week. "Police Artist" is one example; it helps you develop your memory and recognition skills by having you reconstruct the face of a villain, using standard police artist tricks. As the promotional copy says, "With the (facial) parts available, you can make 100,000 different faces. But can you make this face?"

Other Prodigy quick games include: "AJ Dakota," "Frantic Guts," "Guys," "Match It," "Square Off," and "Thinker."

Game Point: Going Head-to-Head

If you want to actually play against other on-liners on Prodigy, you'll need to have a separate subscription and different access numbers (the phone numbers your modem dials). Players in Game Point can play against other people across the country and can even create their own on-line faces. You can look like a warlord, a heavy metal rocker—whatever you want. JUMP: GAME CENTER for information on this service. (Think of this service as ImagiNation Network—which we cite elsewhere in the book; ImagiNation is a premium gaming service—sort of AOL for the game junkies: easy, fun, and perhaps addictive.)

COMPUSERVE

There are lots and lots of games on CompuServe, including the Grolier Whiz Quiz, the ShowBizQuiz™, Classic Adventure, Enhanced Adventure, CastleQuest, Black Dragon, and Hangman. Here are a few in-depth look-sees at these games. CompuServe offers special pricing for those who plan to do lots of gaming on-line. For more information GO ECENTER (Entertainment) and read up on special extended entertainment (a.k.a. games) services and prices.

Take the Grolier Whiz Quiz

Sponsored by Grolier Electronic Publishing, this quiz on CompuServe (GO GROLIER) allows you to compete with up to four people. There are thirty questions to answer on such subjects as sports, music, movies, and history. Why not challenge your friends or family to a match? And, if yours is one of the top ten scores for any session, you'll automatically be entered into the Whiz Quiz Hall of Fame!

"I usually take the quiz once a week or so and compete against my sisters. My older sister is really good at the history questions, but I usually win on the music ones. Sometimes we play against our parents, too. It's pretty cool when we know something that they don't."

—Chris, thirteen, Newport Beach, California

Play BlackDragon

CompuServe's BlackDragon (GO BLACKDRAGON) is a fantasy role-playing game set in a multilevel maze. You can use magic as you encounter all kinds of "strange and wondrous creatures (most of them are deadly)." The object of the game is to accumulate treasure and gain strength. To win, you must be strong enough to conquer Arch Demon on the final level of the maze. Good luck!

AMERICA ONLINE

Though America Online offers lots of games, its selection for kids is limited to Broderbund's Masterword, a multiplayer version of Hangman. Eight people can play at a time; and fourteen others can watch the action. Its exciting graphics and sound effects make this a lot more fun than traditional Hangman. KEYWORD: MASTERWORD, then enter the word library.

THE INTERNET

The Internet contains all kinds of games. Here is just a sample:

Hey, Gamers!

Do you love to play games but have trouble finding people to play with you? Don't despair. On AOL, you can go to the Gamers' Registry (KEYWORD: OGF, which stands for "on-line gaming forum"), which provides contact information on people who want to recruit fellow players in their part of the country. Here is a random entry:

Name: Mike Dee
County: Manhattan, New York
City, State: New York, NY
Time Zone: Eastern
Screen Name(s): Beatnik903
Clubs: EMC Roleplaying Society
Genres: Fantasy, Cyberpunk, Space Travel, Present Day Horror
Games: Advanced Dungeons & Dragons (AD&D), Dark Sun, Vampire, Werewolf, Shadowrun, Cyberpunk
Additional comments: We play in NY, Queens, and Long Island and are always looking for new players. Our games are sometimes hack and slash, sometimes real dramatic. If you want to join us, e-mail me.

alt.games.tiddlywinks
rec.games.board
rec.games.chess
rec.games.misc
rec.games.pinball
rec.games.video
rec.games.video.arcade
rec.games.video.nintendo
rec.games.video.sega

111

And, don't forget ImagiNation Network—if you use an IBM compatible computer. For more information, see page 195. ImagiNation's phone number (voice) is 800-695-4002. A second gaming network is MPGNet. Its number (voice) is 800-GET GAME. And *Net Games* (a Michael Wolff Book for Random House Electronic Publishing, 1994) is a must-have for on-line gamers. According to *Net Games'* authors, here are some of the hottest on-line games:

BEST SHOOT-'EM UP

Air Warrior	GEnie	KEYWORD: AIR
CyberStrike	GEnie	KEYWORD: CYBERSTRIKE
Stellar Conquest	Delphi	GO GRO GRAM

TOUGHEST WORD GAME

sKramBle	America Online	KEYWORD: CENTER STAGE

BEST CHILDREN'S GAMES

Thinker	Prodigy	JUMP: THINKER
Where in the World Is Carmen Sandiego?	Prodigy	JUMP: CARMEN

AND, JUST A FEW MORE *GREAT* GAMING DESTINATIONS

Star Wars	Internet (telenet)	techno.stanford.edu4402, connect guest
Star Wars (in the Ten Forward Lounge)	America Online	KEYWORD: PC; member rooms—Ten Forward Lounge
WWW Hangman	Internet (WWW)	http://www.cm.cf.uk/htbin/RobH/hangman?go
Tic Tac Toe	Internet (WWW)	http://www.bu.edu/Games/tictactoe

More Game Info

For more information ... *PC Gamer:* twelve issues with HD Demo Disc in CD-ROM or floppy format, $57.95—call 415-696-1661 or write to *PC Gamer,* P.O. Box 5014, Pittsfield, MA 01203-9418. Or you may contact *PC Gamer's* editors by writing to PC Gamer Strategic Central, 300-A South Westgate Drive, Greensboro, NC 27410 or e-mailing them at peeceegee@aol.com or 74431,3433@compuserve.com.

The Net: Call 800-706-9500 for a free trial issue

Next Generation: Call 800-706-9500 for a free trial copy

The best gaming 'zines can be found on AOL (KEYWORD: PC GAMES, enter Softward Library, then search by KEYWORD: GAMEBYTE) and on CompuServe (GO GAMERS, enter Libraries, and then click on Game Magazines).

MULTIMEDIA

Do you like to read magazines and newspapers? Listen to music? Talk about movies and TV shows? Talk about computer stuff with other folks who share your passion for a supermachine named after a piece of fruit? Lucky for you, so do tons of other people in cyberspace! You can get together with fellow fans to praise or trash a new CD or movie. You can go online to check out the latest issue of lots of top magazines and papers. And you can post messages for artists, editors, and writers to read. You can even hang with fellow Mac lovers (or Windows lovers) in special chat rooms organized for intense geek speak.

It seems as though every week more and more fun multimedia stuff is added on-line. Every year there will probably be loads more things to do on-line that we can't do right now. And new techniques are sure to be developed that make things faster, better, and easier. For example, in summer 1994 it was possible to download clips of such movies as *Wyatt Earp, The Lion King,* and *The Shadow* from CompuServe (in the Entertainment Drive and Macintosh Multimedia forums). But at 2400 bps, each clip would have cost an arm and a leg to download. A clip of *Wyatt Earp,* for example, would have taken nearly two hours to download—at a cost of approximately $9.60. That's more than it would cost to see the entire movie in a theater! *The Lion King* clip would have taken nearly three hours, for a cost of approximately $14.40.

Does that mean that multimedia clips will always be so expensive? Not at all. In addition to faster and faster access rates, it seems likely that the on-line services will eventually let people view movie clips on-line instead of having to download them. The same sort of advances are taking place with on-line publications right now. Whereas they used to just be plain text, many on-line magazines and newspapers now include cover photos and other graphics. It's just a matter of time before on-line publications are as slick—or slicker—than their off-line counterparts.

All of these developments and advances are one of the reasons it's so cool to be in cyberspace right now. New things are being added at breakneck speeds, and the systems are getting faster and easier to use. It's so much fun to log on each day and find out what's new and improved. For now, though, take a look at some of the multimedia offerings already available in cyberspace. This is just a short sample to give you an idea of the kinds of things you can access:

Publications

Newspapers and magazines are a great research source in cyberspace. At least seventy daily U.S. newspapers currently have or are about to add on-line systems, and magazines running the gamut from *Sports Illustrated* to *Smithsonian* are also on-line. You can use these publications to catch up on current events or topics of interest or to do research for school projects. Here's a sample of what's out there:

Atlanta Journal Constitution (Prodigy)
Los Angeles Times (Prodigy)
People Weekly (CompuServe)
Seventeen (AOL)
Disney Adventures Magazine (AOL)
Smithsonian (AOL)
National Geographic Online (AOL and Prodigy)
Omni Magazine Online (AOL)
Sports Illustrated (CompuServe)
@times—*The New York Times* (AOL)
Time Online (AOL)
PC Novice/PC Today (AOL)
HomePC (AOL)
Stereo Review Online (AOL)
MacHome Journal (AOL)
Windows (AOL)
Wired (AOL—and find ''Hotwired'' on the Web)
Macworld (AOL)
Backpacker (AOL)
Bicycling (AOL)
Boating (AOL)
DC Comics (AOL)
Vibe (on the Web)

Radio

We wanted to be sure to tell you about the ''Kid Company'' quiz on AOL. ''Kid Company'' is a radio show that's broadcast out of WBZ Radio in Boston. The show is produced by kids for kids, and can be heard in thirty-eight states from 7:00–9:00 P.M. on Saturdays. (Remember Marian mentioned her young friend Sean, who also happens to be a friend of President Clinton? Well, Sean is "Kid Company's" White House Correspondent.) The show, which is interactive, has features, interviews, news, games, prizes, and lots of fun! If you want to send comments or questions to "Kid Company," send an e-mail to KidCompany@aol.com. "Kid Company" conducts a regular quiz on AOL, in which you can participate via e-mail or snail mail. Pages 117–19 show a few of their postings, so you can get an idea of what the quizzes are like. It looks like a lot of fun!

Get the Latest Sports Scoops On-line

When the World Cup was being played in the U.S. in summer 1994, each of the major on-line services had forums on soccer and its top players.

Disney Adventures Online (AOL) got into the act by interviewing Zachery Ty Bryan (Brad on "Home Improvement"). Zach, thirteen, is a huge soccer fan—so huge he got the job of Youth Ambassador for the World Cup '94. Zach met famous players, went to soccer clinics, and made special appearances to get other kids hyped about the Cup. Zach's been getting his kicks from soccer for eight years. He now plays for the California Flyers traveling team.

Subj: Dinosaur quiz WINNER   95-01-22 22:56:05 EST
From: KidCompany
Posted on: System

Of all the correct entries sent to "kidcompany" via e-mail, we drew
one winner: RobbyD7662.
This was the question:
Which of these would make a nice dinner for a Brachiosaurus?
A. Ferns and grass low to the ground.
B. Leaves high in the trees.
C. Smaller, slower dinosaurs.

Here's RobbyD7662's winning reply:
Date: Thu, Jan 19, 1995 6:13 PM EST
From: RobbyD7662
Subj: Answer
To: KidCompany

B. Leaves in high trees

Special congratulations go out to STARTREK BARREL and
"64416.22@compuserve.com" who also sent in correct replies.
Robby will receive a copy of *Dougal Dixon's Dinosaurs,* a full-color
illustrated guide to dinosaurs published by Boyds Mills Press. Look
here in the folder for the next quiz, where you could win a copy of
the Parker Brothers game, Bottle Topps.

Subj: MAILBOX QUIZ 1/21/95   95-01-22 22:56:53 EST
From: KidCompany
Posted on: System

The prize is a copy of the popular game from Parker Brothers Bottle
Topps. Put your balancing skill to the ultimate test as you stack
'em high and wide. This week we have a question straight out of
the newspaper.

For the last month, Russian soldiers have been attempting to gain
control of the breakaway province of Chechnya. What is the name
of Chechnya's capital city?

E-mail your answer to "KidCompany" here on AOL. Deadline for entries is end of the day (midnight) Thursday, January 26th. We'll select ONE WINNER from among all of the correct e-mail entries.

On the weekend of January 28th, the winner will be announced here in KIDS ONLY. If you live in the Northeast states, you can HEAR the winner announced live on the radio on KID COMPANY (To hear it, set your radio to receive AM transmission and tune to WBZ AM/Newsradio 1030 Saturdays from 7-9PM)

Subj: PRIZE QUIZ 1/28/95 TriBond   95-01-27 23:58:28 EST
From: KidCompany
Posted on: America Online
Here's part of the script from our radio show broadcast in Boston Saturday night, January 28th. Read along, and see how you can WIN A PRIZE THIS WEEK!

(Josh)
Time to put down the phone and pick up your pencil. It's the Mailbox Quiz, where players win not by calling, but by writing. Last week we asked about a place that's been in the news:

(David)
This was the clue: For the last month, Russian soldiers have been attempting to gain control of the breakaway province of Chechnya. What is the name of Chechnya's capital city?

(Josh)
The answer is Grozny.

(David)
We had no e-mail winner this week, but from our postal service entries, we drew the postcard sent by Rachel Weisel of Brookline, Massachusetts. Rachel will receive a copy of the popular game from Parker Brothers, Bottle Topps. "Put your balancing skill to the ultimate test as you stack 'em high and wide." Now let's hear about this week's Mailbox Quiz.

(Josh)
This week, the prize is a copy of Tribond Kids, the game that asks you to guess what three things have in common. And to qualify to win a copy of the game, we'll ask you a Tribond type question. For example, if I said gold, silver, and tuna, you'd say—

118

(David)
Fish. They're all fish! Gold-fish, silver-fish, tuna-fish.
That's how it works. We name three things, and you have to guess
what they have in common with each other.
Here's this week's question—write these three things down and figure
out what they have in common: Navy, Boston, and Jelly. That's Navy,
Boston, and Jelly.

(Josh)
One last time our three things are Navy, Boston, and Jelly. Tell us what
these three things have in common.

(David)
Write your answer on a postcard, or e-mail your answer to Kid Company by the end of the day Thursday, February 2nd. We'll select one
winner each from among all of the correct postcard AND e-mail entries.

(Josh)
To enter, send your answer to Kid Company, care of WBZ Radio, 1170
Soldiers Field Road, Boston Massachusetts, zip code 02134. And re-
member, if you're on the Internet, our e-mail address is
kidcompany@aol.com.
   It's that simple folks. Just e-mail us at kidcompany. Do it by Thurs-
day midnight, and look back here next Saturday to see if you have won.
   You may win a great prize!
[Readers: You didn't think we'd leave you hangin', did ya? The answer
is "beans."]

MOVIES AND TV

Movies cost as much as $8 in some cities. Eight bucks for
Richie Rich? Can you imagine? Since checking out a flick is
practically a major investment, go on-line before you shell out
your money. You can get movie reviews from the experts, as
well as from regular folk who've seen it ahead of you. Roger
Ebert (he's the chubby one; Siskel is the skinny one) provides
movie reviews of even the most recent box office hits and flops
in Roger Ebert's Movie Reviews on CompuServe (GO EBERT).
This moviegoer's forum also offers celebrity interviews, a movie

lover's Source List, a list of the Top Ten movies of all time, and a bulletin board to let you communicate directly with Roger.

In addition, all of the major on-line services have forums in which movie lovers can talk about their all-time favorites, best and worst actors, cult flicks, movie news, and rumors. On Prodigy, JUMP: MOVIE BB. The Well also has a great movie conference, which die-hard movie buffs swear by. The busiest place in cyberspace for movie chat is rec.arts.movies on the Internet.

On AOL, check out Hollywood Online (KEYWORD: HOLLYWOOD). You can download multimedia sneak previews of the hottest new motion pictures; collect sound bites, video clips, and pictures of your favorite stars from the "Pictures and Sounds" library; read about the cast and production notes in "Movie Notes"; and talk about the movies on the "Movie Talk" message board. Hollywood Online also offers contests to win promotional items from the movie studios, such as movie posters, complimentary movie passes, and other items. Also on AOL is Critic's Choice (KEYWORD: CRITICS), which contains an equally extensive collection of movie-related bulletin boards and info, as well as info on TV, video games, laser discs and videos, and books.

All of the major TV networks are on-line, as well. CBS is on CompuServe (JUMP:CBS), and NBC and ABC are on AOL (KEYWORDS: NBC and ABC, respectively). Each of the networks offers scheduling info so, for example, you can find out which celebrities are going to be on upcoming talk shows. They also offer message boards, photos to download, and live conferences with special guests.

SPORTS

If you're a sports fan, you'll be in hog heaven on-line. You can find all sorts of stats and reference articles on-line, and you can attend on-line conferences with some of your favorite sports stars. Each of the major services has a sports area covering the

The Late-Night War
Heats Up on the 'Net

In February 1995, both NBC and CBS opened sites on World Wide Web. Thus far, CBS's site (http://www.cbs.com/) has been dominated by items pertaining to David Letterman's "Late Show," including Top Ten lists, guest lists, press releases, and an e-mail box.

Not to be outdone, NBC opened an Internet WEB page for the "Tonight Show with Jay Leno" (http://www.nbctonightshow.com). The site features excerpts from Leno's monologues, guest listings, and behind-the-scenes clips.

• •

basics; these normally include such sports as auto racing, baseball, basketball, boxing, football, golf, and hockey. You can also find various SIGs on the commercial services and the 'Net on everything ranging from Ultimate Frisbee to lacrosse to mountain biking.

Here are some of the basics:

SPORTS NEWS

CompuServe	GO AP SPORTS	The latest in sports news
	GO UKSports	The latest on cricket, rugby, snooker, etc.
	GO NCAA	Division I, II, and III college sports news
America Online	KEYWORD: TENNIS	News on bowling, golf, and tennis
	KEYWORD: KOOL	Data Times sports reports

GEnie	KEYWORD: SPORTSNEWS	Coverage of major sporting events
Delphi	GO NEW SPO	Sports news and stats
Prodigy	JUMP:SCHAAP	Dick Schaap on sports
	JUMP:OLYMPICS	Everything you'd want to know on the subject

SPORTS TALK

America Online	KEYWORD: GRANDSTAND	Sports forums on everything from baseball, football, and hockey, to auto racing and cycling
Prodigy	JUMP:SPORTS	An elaborate array of sports and entertainment

More Prodigy Sports: Once you're within the area, there is the Sports Play BB for participation in sports discussions and the Sports BB for spectator sports discussions. Within Sports Highlights, there are top news stories; Sports Schedules are organized by sports and generically. And, for stats junkies, there are Soccer Stats, Bowling Stats, and Skiing Stats.

GEnie	KEYWORD: SPORTS	News and statistics—and libraries of info and software
CompuServe	GO FANS	Covers major league, college teams, and fantasy baseball and football leagues

MOTOR SPORTS

America Online	KEYWORD: GRANDSTAND	Racing talk every Sunday night in chat area called "The Pits," schedules galore; race team gossip on message boards
CompuServe	GO RACING	Car-racing stats, schedules, and info

GOLF

| Prodigy | JUMP:NETWORK GOLF* | Play on-line golf |
| | JUMP:AUSTADS GOLF | Info on golf equipment and supplies |

BASEBALL

America Online	KEYWORD: GRANDSTAND, click into DUGOUT	
Prodigy	JUMP:BASEBALL COVERAGE	
	JUMP:BASEBALL ODDS	
	JUMP:BASEBALL TALK	

FOOTBALL

America Online	KEYWORD: GRANDSTAND	Fantasy 50-Yard Line football, Pro Picks contest, and schedules
Prodigy	JUMP:FOOTBALL	NFL info, Canadian and college football stats, and fantasy football
	JUMP:FANTASY FOOTBALL	On-line football stats to use for off-line fantasy games (fantasy software is sold on-line)
GEnie	KEYWORD: FOOTBALL	Choose a team and earn points according to real play
	KEYWORD:QB1	Chat live about football; predict the next move of your favorite quarterback
CompuServe	GO FANS	Play fantasy football

* Charges a premium

HOCKEY

| America Online | KEYWORD: GRANDSTAND | Play fantasy hockey |
| Prodigy | JUMP:HOCKEY COVERAGE | Team news and stats |

BICYCLING

| America Online | KEYWORD: BIKE | Netbiking and racing info |
| | KEYWORD: GRANDSTAND | Racing information and views from racers and recreational cyclists |

OUTDOOR FORUM

| CompuServe | GO OUTDOORFORUM | Camping, climbing, hiking, hunting, fishing, cycling, sailing, and winter sports |
| | GO OUTNEWS | Text stories on outdoor activities |

SAILING

| CompuServe | GO SAILING | Sailing discussions, including celebrities, etc. |

SCUBA

America Online	KEYWORD: SCUBA	Info on general diving and dive destinations
CompuServe	GO DIVING	Equipment reviews, fave dive sites, and more
GEnie	KEYWORD: SCUBA	More than fifty categories of bulletin boards about diving; all scuba-related discussions

SKIING

| Prodigy | JUMP:SKI CENTER | Includes ski conditions |

And now for something completely different: Let's go cybermalling.

SHOPPING

Tired of having to wrangle a ride to the mall? Unwilling to be seen traipsing from store to store with Mom and Dad? Then why not bring the mall to you? With a few clicks of your keyboard, you can shop to your heart's content. Here are some good places for the whole family:

• Former MTV veejay Adam Curry has created a totally cool cybermall that features all kinds of shopping options. To take advantage of good deals on clothing, sporting goods, gifts, books, etc., go to http://www.onramp.net/shopping_in/on the Web. Or if you're looking to be penny-wise, try http://www.on-ramp.net/goodstuf/.

• Another good family site is "Marketplace" on America On-line; it features a full range of shopping options, from Lands' End to museum stores. Delphi offers some shopping, too, but, according to *The Hitchhiker's Guide to the Electronic Highway,* it is "like the main street of a small Midwestern town."

• And, if you're in the market for name-brand merchandise, check out NPTA (Nordstrom Personal Touch America), an e-mail shopping opportunity that makes available all of the collections sold at this department store. Nordstrom even throws in a personal shopper who will help you on each return cybershopping spree. Contact Nordstrom_PT_America@MCI-MAIL.COM.

• There are a couple of virtual malls on the Web that you might also want to check out, including The Global Electronic Music Marketplace, where you can buy and sell everything related to music, and the Speak to Me Catalog, which features weird and funky gifts. There's also World Square, a general mall; Sofcom, a shopping service from Australia; and Home Shopping Network on-line—also known as Internet Shopping Network.

9

Tapping the Resources— Getting Informed and Getting Help

"What I especially like about on-line services is the vast amount of information such as encyclopedias, and people willing to help you almost everywhere—this is a place where you can find almost anything. Also the increasing availability of services has made it so that I can do research for school for myself and friends on-line."
—Kevin, sixteen, Cupertino, California

The amount of information available at your fingertips through an on-line service is simply unbelievable. Even the people who run the services never get to see it all. No matter what information you want, from aardvarks to the signs of the Zodiac, you're almost guaranteed to find more than you need on-line. Once you know how to look, if you can't find it, you're not really trying!

ON-LINE ENCYCLOPEDIAS, MAGAZINES, DATABASES, ETC.

A few years ago, nobody—except for computer whizzes, that is—would have dreamed of an electronic dictionary or encyclopedia. But now, commercial on-line services offer a mind-boggling range of encyclopedias, newspapers and magazines, databases, and other sources of information. It's like having one of the best libraries in the world at your fingertips. It can give you a big advantage in school!

"I use CompuServe for research projects or reports," says Charlotte, thirteen, of Middle Haddam, Connecticut. "For example, I am doing some research on five French cities: Versailles, Chantilly, Mont-Saint-Michel, Fontainebleau, and Carcassonne. I looked them all up on the Academic American Encyclopedia on-line."

Going on-line can make projects fun and interesting, and help improve your work. "Having a computer and on-line encyclopedias definitely gives me an advantage in school," Charlotte says. "When I do projects, I can always get a lot of information without having the bother of going to the library. All that I have to do is type in a research term, and the computer comes up with all the articles it has concerning that topic. There's no annoying leafing through books!"

Here's a look at a few of the most helpful offerings of the major on-line services:

COMPUSERVE

CompuServe made its reputation on being *the* on-line service for information junkies. And its reference library is head and shoulders above the crowd.

Here are a few (and just a few!) highlights:

• **Academic American Encyclopedia (GO ENCYCLOPE-DIA)** is an on-line edition of Grolier's 21-volume set, featuring 33,000 articles and over 10,000,000 words. The encyclopedia is updated 4 times a year on-line, where it takes up a lot less shelf space!

• **American Heritage Dictionary (GO DICTIONARY)** contains over 200,000 word definitions, geographical descriptions, and biographical sketches of famous people. You can search the dictionary by entering the word, or just the first five letters if you're unsure of how to spell it.

• **Information USA (GO: INFOUSA)** is one of the coolest reference sources available anywhere. Want to know how to get a birthday greeting from the president? Looking for maps or info about national parks? Information USA explains how to squeeze information out of government bureaucrats and how to get free or cheap government publications. It's also full of useful tips for traveling, including information on hiking, diving, camping, and visiting historical sites. NOTE: This is an extended service, not included in CompuServe's basic rate.

• **Who's Who (GO: BIOGRAPHY)** Need info on a famous living person? Type in the name and Who's Who tells you where she was born, where she went to school, what jobs she has held, and lots more.

• **Phone*File (GO PHONEFILE)** Want to track down long-lost relatives? Phone file is the world's biggest phone book. It has the names, addresses, and phone numbers of 75 million American households. If you've got an unusual last name, you can find out in a few seconds who else across the country has your name!

• **IQUEST (GO IQUEST)** is the true information addict's dream come true. It searches magazines, newspapers, directories, books, government documents, encyclopedias, reference guides—you name it, and IQUEST will turn up everything there is to know about it in over 850 different on-line databases! Just enter in the topic, and it will find the appropriate information source and take you there. It's a great resource, but an expensive one—part of CompuServe's premium service, so you should only use it for very special information needs.

AMERICA ONLINE

AOL's menu of on-line reference tools is getting better, but it still has some big gaps. For example, there's no on-line dictionary or almanac. Some useful offerings:

• **Barron's Online (KEYWORD: BOOKNOTES)** features searchable versions of Barron's Book Notes, the company's popular guides to great works of literature. Plot summaries, author biographies, and character sketches are available for *Animal Farm, Canterbury Tales, Great Gatsby, Huckleberry Finn* and over 100 other books your teacher is going to assign to you sooner or later.

• **AskERIC Online (KEYWORD: ERIC)** is an information service provided and maintained by ERIC (Educational Resources Information Center) for AOL members. If you have a question related to education, send e-mail to AskERIC—the staff will respond to your question within 48 hours!

• **Compton's Encyclopedia (KEYWORD: ENCYCLOPEDIA)** has more than 9,000,000 words—5,274 long articles and 29,322 short ones—all of it fully and easily searchable on-line! If you search the encyclopedia for ''dinosaurs'' for example, you get a list of 54 articles. Key in ''outer space'' and 86 entries pop up. It's a great resource!

• **The Library of Congress (KEYWORD: LIBRARY)** has more than 27 million books and pamphlets, including publications and other materials in nearly 500 different languages. You can't find all of that on-line, but the Library's area on AOL features a rotating special exhibit of original documents (the

Dead Sea Scrolls, the Secret Soviet Archives, Treasures of the Vatican, etc.), an extensive interactive area in support of the exhibit, message boards, e-mail directories of scholars and experts, a direct line to the library, real-time conferences, and more.

PRODIGY

• **Academic American Encyclopedia (JUMP: ENCYC)** is the same encyclopedia CompuServe offers. Just type in the first part of the subject you're looking for information about, then hit "Return." If there is no exact match, you will see a list of articles that most closely match what you typed. There's also a feature (JUMP: BACKGROUND) that links current events to the encyclopedia.

• **Political Profile (JUMP: POLITICAL PROFILE)** is the place to find biographical information about members of the 103d U.S. Congress. Finding out how your Senator/Representative voted on key issues and what special interest groups contributed to campaigns is great stuff for reports and current events discussions. If you want to know whether your congressman is a liberal or conservative, you can see how he or she is rated by different political organizations. There's also an area that lets you write directly to Washington.

• **Total TV Online (JUMP: TOTAL TV)** is not a classic reference source, but it's an amazing resource! It's the first national on-line guide to a week's worth of television listings. You can look up what's on TV by time, category, or network and you can also view the week ahead in movies and sports. The information is updated daily for the week ahead, so it never gets old. There are also feature articles and the "Wired" column from the current week's issue of *Total TV* magazine.

eWORLD

- **TimeMachine (SHORTCUT: TIME MACHINE)** is a unique service on eWorld, which otherwise has pretty slim pickings on the reference shelf. It's a surprisingly deep library of files and documents, including ''QuoteLine,'' a fully searchable on-line dictionary of quotations. It features 450 quotes by or about Shakespeare alone! ''DocuLine'' has time-related documents and literature from around the world; and ''StatLine'' offers a source of global and US statistics, both current and historical, and more. There's a cool ''This Day in History'' feature, which will tell you important things that happened on any day of the year.

ACADEMIC ASSISTANCE

This is interactivity at its very best. If you're stumped by a math problem, don't know where to turn to find out the name of an eleven-sided figure (it's an undecagon), or want the advice of a teacher or expert on the outline for your book report, help is a few keystrokes away.

On-line forums, bulletin boards, and chat rooms give you a place to get in touch with helpful teachers, parents, and other kids across the country or around the world. Most of the on-line forums are available after school and in the evenings, so if your parents are still at work, you can log on and get help. Some of them are available twenty-four hours a day. The best ones even offer live help from real teachers on every imaginable topic.

''They allow the students to connect to the professionals and resources on any conceivable educational topic,'' says Mark A. Hulme, who helps run Interactive Education Services on America Online (KEYWORD: IES) ''They allow kids to leave their own towns and cities in search of information and to connect to scholars who have devoted their lives to researching the information the students are seeking.''

On-line homework services are staffed by real teachers who volunteer to help kids with their homework in exchange for free on-line time. The teachers' qualifications are checked out before they're allowed to become electronic tutors.

OK, about now, you're probably thinking that you've stumbled upon the Holy Grail of homework. A magic tool that will give you all the answers you need quickly and easily. Well, not exactly. If you're expecting to be spoon-fed homework answers, you're going to be disappointed. On-line teachers are no different than classroom teachers (most of them are teachers during the day). They will help you develop research skills and give advice on where to find answers to questions, using on- and off-line resources. They won't just give you the answer.

''Homework help is incredible. There is no 'do the work for you' there,'' says Genevieve Kazdin, who runs the Kids Only OnLine area on AOL (KEYWORD: KIDS). ''There is guidance, support, instruction, pointing toward reference material and an attitude of friendliness and 'hey, learning is FUN.' I can and do recommend that service often—it is available from the Kids Online screen and many of the kids avail themselves of the help there. And each one comes back to say, 'WOW Gen— they really HELP!!' ''

Kids aren't the only ones who love interactive homework help. Believe us, lots of parents who flunked algebra are glad to know there's a place where their kids can talk to someone who was paying attention in class all those years ago!

One thing to remember: You can't always get instant help. Homework help on the message boards is a cooperative service. If you post your question, it can sometimes take a day or two until someone who knows the answer sees it. If you're in a screaming rush, it pays to check out the live homework help rooms on AOL, GEnie, and Prodigy. But even there you have to be patient and wait your turn, which can take up to a couple of hours (but it's reputed to be getting better). A few kids we interviewed quipped that they know the teachers keep them waiting to get paid extra! Here's where to find homework help on-line:

AMERICA ONLINE

One of the most amazing interactive services for kids anywhere is the Academic Assistance Center and the on-line tutoring program on AOL (KEYWORD: HOMEWORK). You can get answers on a thousand topics in forty Departments from Arts to Zoology, Law, Medicine, Family Services, College and Career Guidance, and Sports. It's part of the Interactive Education Service on AOL.

The most popular area is the live Academic Assistance Rooms. Students can wander into these chat rooms and get homework help or ask questions of teachers and experts in dozens of fields. At least eight teachers are available at all times between 5:00 P.M. and 1:00 A.M. Eastern, seven days a week. Sometimes many more are available.

"I use Academic Assistance to help me with my geometry," says Malinda, 14, of Alexandria, Virginia. "It's hard being a freshman taking a tenth grade course. The teaching staff on-line help out a lot. It helps having the same material taught in a different way."

Pretty cool, huh? Wait. It gets better. Interactive Educational Services offers a "Teacher Paging" service (KEYWORD: TEACHER PAGER). Type in a question or a topic that's got you stumped, key in your grade level. Then click Send. Your message goes to a 24-hour a day clearing center where it will be forwarded to at least 3 of the experts who staff the Academic Assistance Center. Over 700 experts are available to answer your questions. Most questions get answered in just a few hours, and e-mail answers are guaranteed within 48 hours or AAC gives you an hour of free on-line time as compensation. But don't get your hopes up—these guys are good! In the last year they've only failed to get an answer 3 times!

"Just last winter we were averaging 30 to 50 questions a day through the Teacher Pager and worked quite well with a staff of 450," says Hal Rosengarten, Coordinator of the Academic Assistance Center. "Now we have exceeded 500 Pages in one day and the staff, which is approaching 800, is hard-pressed to keep up with events in the Rooms. We receive over a dozen compliments a day from users. When you consider that AOL does no advertising for the AAC, and our clients come mostly from word of mouth, someone must be happy with the services we provide."

"With tools like the Teacher Pager and the Help Rooms the students can carry on one-on-one conversations with these scholars, teachers, and professionals, which might have been impossible using any other format," adds Mark Hulme.

Occasionally, the volunteer teachers who staff the homework help areas get a surprise. "Someone came in asking about the reasoning for the math rule that states you cannot divide by zero," recalls Barbara Jorgensen, a Pittsburgh teacher who answers math questions in the Homework Help area. "Assuming that it was a middle school–age student, I went into great detail and explained the entire theory and gave long, drawn-out examples. Upon completing my lesson (which I was very proud of, I might add) the 'student' announced, 'I am a math teacher myself and just thought I would try this thing out and see if it was for real. Thanks, your answer was great!' And with that he left, never to be heard from again!"

CHECK THIS OUT! Even if you are not an AOL member, you can now take advantage of AAC's Homework Help. Homework24@aol.com is the world's access to the Teacher Pager. No matter what on-line service you're on—or through the Internet—you can get help!

MORE ON-LINE HOMEWORK HELP

The important thing to remember is that finding homework help on-line is often a simple matter of learning your way around—your entire on-line service is a potential source of information for projects and reports. Here are some good places to begin your search:

On CompuServe, check out the Student's Forum (GO STUFO). There's no formal homework help area, but you can usually find a teacher or two in the Education Forum (GO EDF-ORUM), which hosts bulletin boards for teachers and school administrators. One big plus for CompuServe: It's an international service. So if you are looking for help on the French Revolution or ninth-grade Spanish, you might be able to get in touch with kids and teachers in French or Spanish-speaking countries.

For older students, America Online's Academic Research Service (KEYWORD: RESEARCH) provides research support for students in high school, college, or graduate levels who are writing papers. The service offers assistance, leads, basic information, sources of information, search strategies, etc. to assist you in your research.

GEnie offers a strong homework help area in the Computer Assisted Learning Center (KEYWORD: M175). You can post your homework questions by subject. While not as extensive as AOL's help area, you can chat with a teacher in real time Mondays and Wednesdays 9:00 P.M. to 10:00 P.M. (Eastern), and Tuesdays and Thursdays 10:00 P.M. to 11:00 P.M.

On Prodigy, kids can get homework help on the Education bulletin board (JUMP: EDUCATION). Tammy, trying to break a case of writer's block one evening, posted a plea for help: "I am a ninth-grade student working on a research report. I'm not very good at writing introductions or conclusions. Could someone please help? Write back ASAP." A few hours later, help was on its way. "You may want to use a quotable quote book.

There are books that have topics that the quotes fall under," wrote Lori Liebl, a twelfth grade English teacher from North Dakota. "If you are writing on heroes, you look up that subject, and the book will have several quotes that support that topic. After using that quote, use a transition and then add your thesis statement."

When you think about it, that's pretty amazing. A schoolkid goes on-line looking for help, and gets it from a teacher hundreds of miles away! That's life in cyberspace.

P.S. The best is yet to come for Prodigy members. As this book went to print, Prodigy had just announced the launch of "Homework Helper," a new application which will put a virtual library of encyclopedias, books, 400 magazines, 100 newspapers, plus thousands of photos and maps on-line. The computer database, which contains about 2 billion words, is updated daily. Prodigy will offer two hours of use for $9.95 a month. Additional time will be billed at $2.95 an hour.

OTHER RESOURCES

You can find help with homework in hundreds of places on-line, not just in the areas designated for homework help. All it takes is a little creativity and imagination. You can get up-to-the-minute information on hundreds of subjects in forums and special-interest groups (see Chapter 7), where you can meet experts who might know even more than your teacher about some subjects!

You can also find the answers to homework questions in any of the dozens of newspapers and magazines that are available on-line. Publications like *Time, Newsweek, U.S. News, National Geographic,* the *New York Times,* and hundreds of others are available on-line. Many of them have searchable back issues— so you can search for stories on whatever subject you need in just seconds. And some newspapers and magazines even put

Get Published!

Scholastic's *Storybook* in-school magazine is seeking short book reviews by students in grades three through five. What a great opportunity to be published in a magazine read by kids all around the country! Plus, if your book review is published, you'll win a prize.

To get started, you should first enter the Scholastic folder on AOL (KEYWORD: SCHOLASTIC) and check out reviews that have been written by other kids. That will give you a good idea of what the magazine is looking for. Then, write your own book review and send it to screenname "Storyworks." Be sure to follow the instructions included in the folder.

their writers and editors on-line to answer questions on message boards and in chat rooms.

Join the American Folktale Project

The American Folktale Project on AOL (KEYWORD: SCHOLASTIC) is a place in which students can write their own stories and post them for discussion. You can write four types of folktales: a historical anecdote, a nonsense tale, an occupational tale, or a scary story. They even provide four Folktale Starters in case you need help beginning your story. Teachers are also allowed to come on-line and comment on the stories.

Ten Things to Do with Channel One On-line

1. Report a great local news story about your school or community.

2. Send fan e-mail to your favorite newscaster.

3. Suggest a question for the daily pop quiz. Or let them know which questions you absolutely loved. (Marian's all-time-favorite pop quiz questions are total brain teasers: What was the year of the first commercial airline flight? Who was the first African-American to win a Nobel Prize?)

4. Tip them off to a great map or an interesting piece of shareware that will help other kids really "get" the news. Your tip may find its way into the network's *Teacher's Guide,* which is mailed to 600,000 teachers in more than 11,000 schools in every state.

5. Persuade your teacher to let you conduct a "swap" or exchange program with another school. Contact Channel One and find out about cool schools in your state or in a nearby state.

6. Conduct a poll of kids in your school around the same time as your state's election primary or caucus takes place. Find out who they'd support for prez in '96 and e-mail Channel One the results.

7. Write a letter to David Neuman, president of programming at Channel One, to tell him what's right and wrong with the program. Be sure to include your snail mail address and your school's name and location. You never know which schools he'll be visiting this year.

8. Initiate a debate about an issue that matters to you mucho. How about school uniforms, for example? Or teachers' pay? Maybe you're worried about global warming or race relations or urban violence. Send an e-mail to the network—make your voice heard: LOUD AND CLEAR.

9. Submit an application to participate in Student Produced Week or another one of the Channel One in-school promotions. And it's never too soon to lobby for your school to be the supplier of a "Pop Quiz" team. Win, lose, or draw, you'll get fifteen minutes of fame—and almost half of all the students in grades five to twelve throughout the country will see your national TV debut.

10. Tell Channel One who your favorite anchor is, and why! Better still, e-mail this lucky person with an invite to your next school dance!

Send e-mail to CHANOne@aol.com. This is the network's general e-mail box. The two people you want to contact are Mike Soules, director of programming, and Jeff Rose, director of network affairs. They're the Channel One Webmasters.

Shakespeare On-line

To download or not to download? That is the question. It seems as though everyone is setting up shop in cyberspace. Even Shakespeare has a World Wide Web site on the 'Net, which can be accessed through MIT's computer server. Shakespeare lovers can click on any of the thirty-seven listed works by the Bard. Shakespeare's Internet address is http://the-tech.mit.edu/Shakespeare/works.html.

Learn About Different Careers

Do you know what you want to be when you grow up? Neither did a lot of kids in computer teacher Jean Stringer's eighth grade class at St. Julie Billiart School in Hamilton, Ohio. That's why they decided to study a variety of careers and write letters to adults over the Internet, asking them about their careers, the education they needed to get their jobs, and about the importance of computers in their work.

The kids have heard from people in dozens of different careers: computer software developer, nurse, radio commercial producer, lawyer, fire fighter, airline pilot, nuclear medicine researcher, computer programmer, religious sister, chemist, writer, truck driver, college professor, heating and electrical mechanic, and a woman who is vice president in charge of finances for a company. Whenever a student gets a reply, he or she shares it with the rest of the class.

Most of the kids in Ms. Stringer's class didn't decide what they want to be when they grow up, but they did learn a lot of other interesting things: "I know now that I need to think about what I enjoy and not just making lots of money," says Jenny. "Money isn't everything!" "I thought that the people who worked with computers were very boring and dull. The letters they wrote made me realize that they were very happy and that computers can bring you a lot in life," says Erin. "There are adults out there who care about the next generation and how we are going to survive and what we can do to succeed," says Jenni. "All the people we wrote to were very interested in us, and were ready to give us advice and information we could use." Finally, Angie writes, "I learned that all of the schooling does pay off and people really can be successful if they try hard." She concludes, "All of the people that we wrote to said that it is important to get a good education and to keep trying."—Contact: Jean Stringer, computer instructor, St. Julie Billiart School, Hamilton, Ohio; e-mail stjulie@tlcnet.muohio.edu

GET PREPPED FOR COLLEGE ON-LINE

America's college prep tests are on America Online. To check them out, stop by the College Board on-line (KEYWORD: COLLEGE BOARD), as well as the areas created by Kaplan (KEYWORD: KAPLAN) and Princeton Review (KEYWORD: PRINCETON). Also expected on AOL by the time this book is published is *U: The College Newspaper,* a national weekly that publishes the best articles from campus newspapers nationwide. If you're interested in campus newspapers that are on-line, go to http://ednews2.asa.utk.edu/papers.html. And, finally, Peterson's College Database on CompuServe is a great place to find info about 3,000 colleges (GO PETERSON). (Also try GO PBX for Peterson's Connexion—careers and educational information.)

VISIT THE LIBRARY OF CONGRESS

Pretty soon five million of the forty million treasures in the Library of Congress collection will be digitized and available to be visited and studied. You can find the first installments at KEYWORD: LIBRARY on AOL or by heading to the Web— to enter the library's stacks, type: http://lcweb.loc.gov/. For the Library of Congress Archives, a monster FTP site: ftp SEQ1.LOC.GOV,ANONYMOUS/<your e-mail address>.

MEET A SCIENTIST

Access Excellence on America Online (KEYWORD: EXCELLENCE) is a three-year, $10 million national educational program for high school biology classes. It uses AOL and the Internet to link teachers and scientists via computer. Although designed for teachers, the service is also open to students. Resources available include "What's News," a regular update of developments in biology, medicine, and the environment; "About Biotech," a listing of information resources; and the "Virtual Library," offering even more resources.

"I have been able to relay students' questions to real scientists," says one teacher. "A student asked a question about proteins, and two days later I had five responses from five different scientists in four different protein-related fields!" Access Excellence is funded solely by Genentech, Inc., a San Francisco-based biotechnology pioneer. It was developed with the assistance of many leading national scientific and educational organizations.

CREATE AN ALTERNATIVE NEWSPAPER

In 1994, when key employees at both of the daily newspapers in San Francisco went on strike, in the middle of a heavily contested Senate race, many of the writers and editors felt obliged to continue providing Bay area residents with the most important news. What did they do? They took to the 'Net with their own electronic newspaper. And you can do the same thing! You could create a paper designed to get news out to others or create a specialty newspaper. It can be focused on politics, humor—whatever you want.

Here's an example: Recently a bunch of kids in grades four through eight worked with us to create a newspaper about the future. Here's just one article from that specialty 'zine, which we called *The Millennium Reporter*.

143

COLUMN: A Day In Your Life, 2010

The alarm clock on your computer rings, as a robot arm shakes you out of your waterbed. It's Friday morning in the year 2010, time to get up and go to school.

The lights turn on when you clap. You're feeling lazy, so you summon your motorized chair and command it to roll you to the bathroom. As you step into the shower, the water comes on and you are automatically washed. You step out, and the automatic hairstyler reaches out its hands: if you're a girl, it twists your hair into a braid that looks like a zipper; boys get a buzz cut.

Back in your bedroom, your chair rolls you over to the closet, where your clothes were cleaned overnight. It's cold outside, so the first thing you put on is your temperature suit—but be careful not to turn it up too high, or you'll cook! Hmm, what else should you wear? The "in" style for girls and boys is vintage-faded jeans and a plaid flannel shirt. (But the jeans have a calculator sewn into them, and the shirt lights up in the dark.) Or you might want to go with the "modern" look: one-piece rubber outfits or clothes made from metallic materials.

Time for breakfast. You might want to start the day with the old standbys—cereal, bagels, coffee—but some of you will be more adventurous. Anyone for eggs with horseradish? No, thanks. You'd rather have some Hershey's candy cereal, and wash it down with a blueberry shake. If you're running late, you may have to settle for a food pill: Drop it into a glass of water, and it expands into a whole meal. It's expensive, but good. You grab a genetically engineered orange-apple-banana fruit as you head for the door.

If it's snowing outside, you put on your color-change boots; if not, you put on your convertible sneaker-skates with in-line wheels that come out of the bottom. You don't need a bookbag—everything you need has been electronically transferred to school. Finally you're ready to go. You can float to school in your inflatable jacket and jet-powered sneakers, but the wind is blowing, so you decide to walk. You step onto the moving sidewalk outside your house, and your traction soles grip the surface. You're on your way.

Every day you have the option of going to the school building or taking your lessons on your computer at home. Today you have decided to go to school so you can see your friends. You arrive at an oval-shaped building and head for your classroom. Your desk is a flat computer screen, hooked up to a video telephone and a virtual reality headset. You selected your own class schedule: industrial drawing, nuclear rocket propulsion, history, puzzle solving and mechanics, clothing design, physical education, world civilization, computer language, UFOs, and sciath—science and math taught together.

Most of your teachers are human, and are in the room with you. Some of your teachers run their classes from remote locations, using a big computer screen at the front of the room. Don't goof off—even though the teacher's not in the room, she can still see you! Some of your classes are taught by interactive computer programs. Some are even taught by students. You use your virtual reality headset to explore different countries for your world civilization class and to go on virtual field trips with your teachers.

Lunchtime! You head for the computerized cafeteria, where you can have the daily special served by robots, create a custom lunch with the food-making machine, or order fast food from restaurants such as Pizza Hut. You decide to go with the daily special: international cuisine with selections from Mexico, Italy, and China. You have a piña colada soda with static electricity instead of bubbles, and flavored cream for dessert. You pay for your lunch with credits.

Recess is next. You play some computer games for a while, then join a pickup game of rocket booster basketball. After recess you decide to go home and finish your schoolday from the comfort of your own room. All of your books, homework, and grades are immediately available in your computer desk at home. You have a history test, and find the answers with your computer. There's no way to cheat—you're tested on your infoseeking skills, not your ability to memorize facts. You answer questions about the collapse of the United Nations, the epidemic of birth defects caused by Gulf War Syndrome, and the evacuation of California because of earthquakes and pollution. Life in America is still rough, but these and other problems are being solved.

School is finally over, and it's time for your neighborhood sports league. Kids can get together every day for some friendly competition, and parents take turns as referee. This month, you're playing soccer—with jet sneakers, on a mile-long floating field with walls! Last month you played basketer, a combination of basketball and soccer, and next month you're playing antigravity ball. If you don't feel like playing a team sport today, you might decide to do some mountain climbing in your backyard, skate around on your hoverboard, or go to a body music class—synthesizers are hooked up to your body with wires, and you create music as you dance.

You go home and do your chores—your dad left a list of things to do on your computer. Then you finish up your homework, using your interactive-TV encyclopedia and your homework machine. At last, after a long day, you relax for a while playing virtual reality games, reading video game magazines, or watching three-dimensional television. There are no broadcast news shows anymore—they became unpopular because they never had any good news to tell. But you can still get news reports by selecting a specific topic such as "the President" with your foot-long remote control.

Dinner is meatloaf with orange sauce, and mashed potatoes with vegetables mixed in. All of the food is organically grown—it costs more, but it has more vitamins. It's Friday night, so you head to the mega mall with your friends, driving your own minicar. You chew some virtual reality gum—it tastes like whatever flavor you're thinking about—as you zoom around the mall in your antigravity suit. Time flies, and so do you—and soon it's time to head back home and go to sleep. You turn on your stereo and fall asleep listening to some oldies from the 1990s, and dream about another busy day in 2010.

ADVERTISEMENT: House For Sale

Features: Voice-activated entry with thumbprint identification lock. Automatic sliding doors. Computer terminal and video telephone in every room. Solar power. Clap-activated switches for lights and appliances. Automatic robot cleaners. Computerized climate control and food preparation.

Exterior options and additions: Swimming pool. Gazebo. Tree house. Personal mini-house with bedroom, bath, kitchen, and living room for kids.

Specialty rooms: Movie room with form-fitting reclining massage chairs and snack delivery. Feel Good Room (FGR) with waterfall, foliage, and relaxing outdoor sounds and scents. Virtual reality room. Playroom with flying toys. Video arcade with prizes.

Kid's bedroom: Waterbed with automatic bedmaker, slides into wall when not in use. Built-in multimedia unit with computer, 84-inch television, video games, stereo. Computer alarm clock with wake-up robot arm. Closet with automatic clothes cleaners. Voice-command motorized rolling desk chair.

Bedroom options: Alarm on bedroom door. Voice-activated computer. Blacklights. Kitchen with milkshake machine and rubber toasters. Bathroom with whirlpool bathtub and hairstyling machine. Furniture stored in ceilings or walls when not in use. Swimming-pool bedroom with floating furniture.

10

Special Interests A to Z—And Even More Great On-line Places

"I get to talk to people who are 17, 18, 19, all the way up to 45, without having to worry about what I look like, and all that stuff. The people that I talk to, especially guys, probably wouldn't take much more notice of me than a fly if I met them in person. But since we are on-line, they respect me as a person, instead of ignoring me 'cause I'm eight years younger than them."
—Charlotte, thirteen, Middle Haddam, Connecticut

ASTRONOMY

On CompuServe, GO ASTROFORUM for the Astronomy Forum. Amateur and professional stargazers gather here to talk about astronomy news, events, and equipment and techniques for watching the heavens. This forum also contains public domain software, articles and reference materials, and a treasure trove of GIF images for downloading. This is an extended service, costing $4.80 an hour above the basic CompuServe rate.

You can also find out what is worth viewing in the skies and what equipment you'll need to enjoy the sights in the Astronomy Club on AOL (KEYWORD: ASTRONOMY); it's hosted by the associate editor of *Sky and Telescope Magazine*. GEnie's Space & Science RoundTable (KEYWORD: SPACERT) is an area where kids can talk with professionals in the scientific world.

BROTHERS AND SISTERS

Talk about your sibling problems on-line. Give advice, get advice (or just revenge!) on-line. "I can't stand my brother," says RyGibs. "If I said what I thought of him, I'd get arrested. He gets so annoying sometimes I want to hit him!" WTKS complains: "It crawls through day. It's scared of a bug. It's my sister!!!!" Sound familiar? They're annoying, they embarrass you, they get you in trouble for no good reason. Don't get mad, get even. The message boards in the Kids Only OnLine area of AOL (KEYWORD: KOOL) are full of kids dissing their siblings. "My sister plays with baseball cards half the day and spends the other half saying moo," writes BearShark. "On a good day however she won't moo, and returns the favors. Good days don't come very often." Prodigy's Kids' Club Bulletin Board is another good place to dish on your sibs.

Really good sibling advice is only an e-mail message away when you're on-line. So is really bad advice!

• "Do your siblings annoy you every minute of your life? I've found a quick and easy solution to this problem. After every word they say just simply repeat 'what's that mean?' If that doesn't work after about five minutes walk away and if that doesn't work write me and I promise I'll find you a solution."
—Annoy your siblings, by Viking7000

150

• "There's an easy way to get your brother to stop bugging you. Sell him to the zoo! First you need to get some bait. Then put it in a cage or a big box. Then that will make him go into the box. Then tie, tape, and chain the box shut. Then call the zoo and tell them that you caught a wild animal. Then the zoo will take it. Then you will never be troubled by your brother again."

—Re: Older Siblings, by Sillybark

• "I have an eight-year-old brother and I've learned that all I have to do to control him is to threaten to tickle him to death. Anybody else do this?"

—Tiny terrorist control, by Plenasia

CLOTHES

Take your cues from the 'Net. Before you let your mom drag you off to Target or the Gap or some department store at the mall, log on and check out what's what. Here's what people were telling one another this time last year (fall 1994) about hot rags and way queer outfits:

• "Here in Broken Arrow, OK (Tulsa), if you are a Raver (pretty much a skater) you wear baggy jeans long and Pumas, Airwalks, Adidas, Vans. If you can't skate (skateboard) then you are known as a poseur or a wannabe. And Proges dress with tight hippie clothes. Preps wear jeans that fit and name brands like Vans, Cole-Haans, Dexters."

—Re: Two-color socks, by Melisa3491

• "Waz' I wear: baggy jeans, City Jammers by Reebok, tee shirt, bander, and well it's hard to explain it's like a patch with waz' gang I am in, my beeper, hoop earrings. Very compy!"

—Re:Waz's in and waz' I like, by Suave187

151

- "The cool things to wear are band tees like Metallica and Pearl Jam, or Stussy, No Fear, Quicksilver."

—What's cool, by Stimpy59245

- "COOL: Chucks (All Star), Champion clothes, GAP clothes, flannel and plaid shirts, Life Forum shirts, body suits, '60's style hair, crocheted vests. OUT: bell bottoms, clogs, dresses, New Kids, Marky Mark, stiff bangs."

—Lookin' cool in PA, by DWEEB

- "For guys: frayed baggy jeans, colored jeans, Vans or Air-walks, Rusty, Quicksilver, Stussy, No Fear, long (past your knees) denim or plaid shorts. For girls: body suits, bell bottoms, '60's-'70's look, Birkenstocks, Puma."

—Brian's style, by Kathi652

- "THINK ABOUT IT! What would our world be if we had never invented 'name brands.' Why do people spend $150 on a dang pair of shoes (or any other article of clothing for that matter) when you can get a look-alike for $100 or less. I think it's downright stupid!!!"

—WHAT'S THE POINT!!!, by Sean8963

DOGS AND CATS

No matter what information you need about your pet, you can get it on-line. You can visit rec.pets.dogs and rec.pets.cats—two of the many Usenet newsgroups about pets. The FAQ (Frequently Asked Questions) in rec.pets.cats contains resources for getting advice on choosing a cat, health care, cat behavior, and lots more. Rec.pets.dogs has information on dozens of e-mail lists you can join on many popular breeds of dogs. It even tells you how to set up your own mailing list if there's not one on your favorite breed. And, do you want info on pet care? To get advice written by a veterinarian, try Prodigy: JUMP: PETLINE QUESTIONS. And, since EVERYBODY loves Goldens—except maybe Marian, who is ready to kill hers for jumping into bed this morning at five o'clock and licking her awake—join up in golden retriever chat by sending an e-mail to LISTSERV-@HOBBES.UCSD.EDU. Type in message: Subscribe Golden, and your full name.

ENVIRONMENT

If you're looking for ways to save the planet, or just be more environmentally smart around the house, cyberspace is the place to be. "Now information is power. You don't need money," Don Rittner, the host of the Environmental Forum on AOL (KEYWORD: EFORUM) said recently. "If you can make your case to the public, you can do anything. You can stop anything. You can move mountains. It used to be 'Think globally, act locally.' Now, it's 'Think globally, act globally.' " It's true, cyberspace has become the most important meeting place for environmental activists. The computer has become the tool to save the planet.

• CompuServe's "Earth Forum" (GO EARTH) offers discussions on scores of environmental issues. You can also download files from Greenpeace and EcoNet.

• On Prodigy, the "Green Connection" (JUMP: GREEN CONNECTION) is the place to go. Chosen "Best Environmental Online Service" by *Computer Currents Magazine* in its "Green PC All-Star Award" (January 1995), it features terrific message boards and a well-stocked library with environmental resource guides and a "green product guide."

• The Environmental Forum (KEYWORD: EFORUM) is the place to go on American Online to talk about the environment. Want to know where to buy recycled paper? How about all-cotton clothes? Organic foods? You can find them and hundreds more with the electronic edition of *PJ Grimes' EcoDirectory* online, as well as info about companies and products that are environmentally responsible.

• There are dozens of places on the Internet to discuss the environment. Start with the Usenet newsgroup alt.save.the.earth. There are also a number of good Gopher sites that are easy to reach, including the EnviroLink Network (envirolink.org), Greenpeace (greenpeace.org), and the Environmental Protection Agency (gopher.epa.gov).

FOREIGN LANGUAGES

Escribimos en Español! Join *le cercle français! Parliamo Italiano!* Going on-line is a great way to practice a foreign language with other students or native speakers from other countries.

America Online offers foreign language classes for a fee—usually about $25—as part of Interactive Education Services (KEYWORD: IES). They also have something called International House (KEYWORD: INTERNATIONAL), featuring a large "dining hall," in which a different language is spoken every night. There are shops and libraries, too, filled with cultural information from around the world, and a message board on which you can carry on conversations in over a dozen languages. It's a great place to meet a foreign language keypal.

CompuServe's Foreign Language Forum (GO FLEFO) is for teachers and students of all ages. On Prodigy JUMP: LANGUAGE to visit the Foreign Languages Bulletin Board, where members "speak" to each other in languages other than English.

GEOGRAPHY='NET GEOGRAPHY

Geography and the 'Net go hand in hand since logging on is like getting an open ticket to travel anywhere, any time of day

and night. Why, the other day I (Marian) was looking for libraries. I could have left my apartment and walked over to a branch
of the New York Public Library and been there; rather, I logged
on to the Web, using Netscape, and visited libraries in Helsinki,
at Harvard University, and tried mighty hard—to no avail—to
navigate my way into the Hanoi Public Library. You can find
maps everywhere: try ABC on America Online; try LIBRARY
on AOL, also to find the maps that the Library of Congress has
posted; and *National Geographic* on both AOL and Prodigy is
a good bet. Better still, you need to do the virtual geography
thing by just logging on, heading to Yahoo—the Stanford University search mechanism which makes 'Net navigating way
simple—and taking off from there! (And if you want to do as
I didn't do, you can search the catalogs of the New York Public
Library by using telenet NYPLGATE.NYPL.ORG, then
NYPL/<none>).

HITCHHIKING ON THE 'NET

Hitchhiking the 'Net is a fave pastime of many kids. There's a
great "how-to" source on line, not surprisingly known as the
Hitchhikers Guide. Internet access is by ftp (FTP.EFF.ORG.,
then ANONYMOUS/<your e-mail address>, then pub/internet-
info). And suppose you want to hitchhike to college and get
the scoop on the "ugly roommate" scene—kind of like 'netting
into another episode of "Real World" but set on campus; try
Usenet: alt.flame.roommate. You are bound to hear roommate
from hell stories, but funny ones!

IN-LINE SKATING

How can I learn to skate backward? How do I stop? Log on
and get the answers to all these questions and many more.

Rec.skate is the place to hang out to learn about equipment, maintenance, technique, competitions, and places to skate.

Q: What is the difference between in-line skating and "rollerblading"?

A: In-line skating is the official term for the sport commonly called "rollerblading" or simply "blading." The commonly misused term of "rollerblading" is due to the company called Rollerblade, which wasn't the first to produce in-lines, but managed to popularize in-lines faster and farther than anyone previously (in the States anyway.) Rollerblade was the only company in the in-line market for a while, which has led to the term of "rollerblade" to stand for all in-lines, even if made by different companies. This is similar to the use of "Kleenex," "Coke," "Q-tip," "Xerox," and other products.

Source: Usenet=FAQ for rec.skate

JOKES

Amateur comedians try out their best lines on Prodigy's Punchline (JUMP: PUNCHLINE). Every Tuesday, they pick the best joke of the week and post it at 6:00 P.M. Thursday. Your reward is to see your entry in the Punchline!

They've got a million of 'em. . . .

Police computers take a byte out of crime.

What happens when you lift up all the smog from California?
UCLA.

The limerick packs laughs anatomical,
Into space that is most economical,
But the good ones I've seen so seldom are clean,
And the clean ones so seldom are comical.

A policeman pulls a man over for speeding. The man insisted he was not speeding. "Just ask my wife," he said. The policeman looks at his wife and asked, "Was he speeding?" The wife replied, "No, but I never argue with him when he's been drinking."

If they ship Styrofoam, what do they store it in?

Keep the day job, gang. . . .

KIDS HELPING KIDS

"My parents are getting a divorce," says Dana362, "and I am used as a stepping stone for them to fight." SteveP posts: "I have been to over 10 different schools in a 5 year period! And it was HORRIBLE." "My uncle Billy had HIV. He found out about 5 months ago," writes Rose. "It's even worse since there is no cure. Sooner or later he will develop AIDS."

If you think nobody else in the world understands what you're going through, a visit to message boards in Kids Only OnLine on AOL (KEYWORD: KOOL) will surprise you. Kids talk about their problems and get advice from other kids who have been through the same thing.

On Prodigy, the Just Kids area (JUMP: KIDS) features a Teens BB and The Big Help BB for kids to talk about serious issues. Teens meet nightly in GEnie's Teen Chat Club to discuss whatever's on their minds. The kids are in charge and they keep adults out. KEYWORD: CHAT

LONDON, ENGLAND

There's no place like home—except, of course, a great foreign capital. How about 'netting off to Merry Old England for an afternoon? Try the British Travel Agency by logging onto Prodigy. JUMP:BTA for the British Tourist Authority. And there are often English people to talk with on CompuServe and eWorld. You just need to be a-lookin'. And, another way to find English keypals is to post on one of the zillions of newsgroups that cater to English culture. Foreign keypals from the 'Net can be found on Usenet—soc.penpals. Kids and others often post information about themselves and their interests. (Parents may want to supervise 'Net usage since postings ARE NOT reviewed for the appropriateness of their content for younger people.)

MUSEUMS

You can visit the Smithsonian without going to Washington, D.C., and the Louvre without traveling to Paris. How cool is that? Stroll through art galleries, get information on art and artists—even upload your own artwork for evaluation by a museum curator! Check out the Miró exhibit!

NICKELODEON

Need to know the words to Ren & Stimpy's "Happy Happy Joy Joy" song? Will new episodes of "Rugrats" come out soon? Which is the best show, "The Adventures of Pete and Pete"? "Roundhouse"? "Clarissa Explains It All"? The answers to these questions—or debate about the answers—can be found on the Internet in alt.tv.nickelodeon.

From daytime soaps to late-night talk shows, there are dozens of TV discussion groups on-line. Use the Internet access of your on-line service to take part in newsgroup discussions about "Mystery Science Theatre 3000" (alt.fan.mst3k/alt.tv.mst3k/rec.arts.tv.3k), "The Simpsons" (alt.tv.simpsons), "Roseanne" (alt.tv.roseanne), "Melrose Place" (alt.tv.melrose-place), "X-Files" (alt.tv.x-files), MTV's "Real World" (alt.tv.real-world), "Beavis & Butt-Head" (alt.tv.beavis-n-butthead), and far too many others to list here.

Commercial on-line services have lots of places for TV talk. ABC, NBC, MTV, The Ricki Lake Show, and Extra all have areas on America Online. Television Viewers Online on AOL has discussion threads on over two hundred shows and The Remote Control room, where you can watch your favorite shows with your friends on-line. CompuServe's Entertainment Drive (GO: EDRIVE) is home to over fifty entertainment companies. On Prodigy, JUMP: TVBB for discussions on all kinds of shows.

PERSONALITIES

Everyone's going on-line . . . How about linking up, virtually, with one of the hipper on-line heroes, former MTV veejay Adam Curry? Adam makes it his business to get companies, including Reebok, on-line. His address is adam@metaverse.com.

Have a newsy opinion? Write to Tom Brokaw at nightly@nbc.com.

Aerosmith, which has been raising funds for the Electronic Frontier Foundation, can be reached by writing to Sweetemail@aol.com.

Want to chat up *People* magazine's editors, or pass along a celeb's e-mail address for potential inclusion in its new "Cyberchat" column? Write to them at 74774.1513@compuserve.com.

159

Besides the possibility of e-mailing a celeb, you can join an on-line fan club. Most major on-line services now offer access to Usenet newsgroups. And that's where you'll find fan clubs for a bewildering number of celebrities and others. A quick search of the subject ''fan'' among newsgroups on AOL (KEYWORD: INTERNET) turns up over 230 fan clubs. These range from the basic (alt.madonna, rec.arts.startrek.fandom) to the weird (alt.itchy-n-scratchy), to the surprising (alt.fan.amy-fisher, alt.fan.dan-quayle) to the totally off-the-wall (alt.fan.lemurs. cooked).

STAR TREK

The Starship *Enterprise* may have been boldly going where no one has gone before, but it ended up in cyberspace. ''Star Trek'' is one of the most popular subjects on-line. There are several Usenet newsgroups devoted to Trek Talk, and it's a big topic in CompuServe's Science Fiction and Fantasy Forum (GO SCI-FI).

Whether you're a fan of the original ''Star Trek'' series, ''The Next Generation,'' ''Deep Space Nine,'' or ''Voyager,'' the Star Trek Club on America Online (KEYWORD: STAR TREK) has something for you. The club has meetings several times a week; Trekkers gather there to meet one another, chat about ''Star Trek,'' or play some trivia. You can also read the latest issue of the club newsletter, ''Dateline: Starfleet,'' download original stories written by club members, and download pictures and graphics in the Star Trek Record Banks. The bulletin boards are filled with Trek debates from Kirk vs. Picard to which was the best Trek movie.

JUMP: STAR TREK BB on Prodigy, to get in on the action. There are over two dozen discussions going on—about characters and aliens, clubs, conventions, memorabilia, and lots more.

TALK SHOWS

"Get Real! He's no good for you!" "Guys are easy—I can get any man I want!" "I like making out in public and you can't stop me!" You can talk about those topics and dozens more on The Ricki Lake Show Online on AOL (KEYWORD: RICKI LAKE). Or you can send in your suggestions for topics to the show's producers.

TV and radio talk shows are going on-line to make it easier for you to have your say. Real-time forums for shows like CNN's "TalkBack LIVE" on CompuServe (GO CNN) and National Public Radio's "Talk of the Nation" on AOL (KEYWORD: NPR) ask viewers to send in questions and comments on-line while they're watching or listening at home.

It's easier to participate on-line than to call in. It's nearly impossible to get your question on the air by calling a TV talk show, because thousands of people are watching and calling in. But on-line viewer forums usually have only a handful of participants.

Most talk show forums let you post messages for the show on the message board or chat with other viewers while the show is on the air. Talk shows on the "America Talking" network take viewer questions on Prodigy (JUMP:CNBC). And scores of local radio and TV talk shows give out their e-mail addresses for on-air Q&A.

UFOS

Want to meet someone who claims to have been abducted by aliens? There are more than a few such people in cyberspace. UFO true believers gather in alt.alien.visitors to discuss everything from crop circles to their favorite conspiracy theories. You can also check out alt.paranet.ufo. This is a UFO forum from the ParaNet BBS gated onto the Internet, which prides itself on being a forum for serious discourse, and not too much nonsense.

There are no areas specifically dedicated to UFOs on America Online, but it's a hot discussion topic in The National Space Society (KEYWORD: SPACE) and the Astronomy Club (KEY-WORD: ASTRONOMY). UFOs and extraterrestrials are also discussed in the Space Forum (GO SPACEFORUM) on CompuServe.

VIDEOS

There are downloadable video clips on all the commercial services, movie trailers, great promo spots, and even an occasional celebrity interview or two. A great place to start is America Online where downloading instructions are about as clear as they come. But, beware of the minute eater when you're downloading video. It sucks up the time—and quickly. At a baud rate of 9600, expect that a VERY short clip might take fifteen minutes to download.

X-MEN

The X-Men are in cyberspace. Don't believe us? Go XMEN on CompuServe. And that's just one of the many comics forums on-line.

DC Comics, home of Superman, Batman, and Wonder Woman, has an area on America Online (KEYWORD: DC) with chat rooms and message boards for readers, writers, artists, editors and anyone else who's into comics. There are previews of upcoming issues in the What's Hot section (a sneak preview of Superman #100 was downloaded 1,000 times in just six days earlier this year), and a Who's Who picture gallery of characters from the DC universe.

The Comics RoundTable on GEnie (KEYWORD: COMICS)

has fan clubs for comics collectors and help for aspiring comics writers and artists. It provides kids an opportunity to meet comics writers and artists and get advice. If you want to try your hand at comics, check out Cartooning Classes in GEnie's Visual Arts RoundTable (KEYWORD: ARTS), where kids can discuss techniques in cartooning with experts. There are lots of graphic files to download, too.

11

Freebies—
Downloading Cool Things

As you have probably figured out already, the on-line world is jam-packed with all kinds of fun stuff to download. You can get cool games, photos of your favorite celebs, maps, articles, software programs, transcripts, fonts, recipes, multimedia clips, TV listings, sports stats—you name it, it's there.

Cyberspace is like a gigantic mall where you and your friends can hang out and find cool things you want to own. A big difference, though, is that in the cybermall, just about everything is FREE! (That is, it's free UNLESS you're specifically there to shop at one of the on-line stores.) To find all kinds of cool stuff to download, you just need to know where to look—and that's where we come in:-) There's no way we could tell you how to find everything that's out there—if we did, you'd probably be old and gray before you finished reading the book!—but this chapter will give you a basic rundown on what's available on the major services and on the 'Net. Get those downloading fingers ready!!

SOFTWARE

We hope you have a whole lot of RAM on your computer, because lots of newbies in cyberspace go CRAZY downloading

Free for the Taking

Free Stuff from the Internet, by Patrick Vincent, provides tons of info on all kinds of stuff you can get for free on the 'Net. The book is priced at $19.99.

Here are just five places Patrick Vincent recommends heading:

1. For those who crave way cool fonts, head, via FTP, to garbo.uwasa.fi. From there go to windows/fonts/*, windows/fonts-atm/*, and windows/fonts-tt/*. Definitely download at least one of the weird fronts that are yours for the taking.

2. Free articles galore from magazines that include *Discover, Internet World,* and *Outside.* Use Gopher to go to internet.com, and then go to Introduction to the Electronic Newsstand.

3. Interested in Bart Simpson trivia? If so, use Gopher to head to quartz.rutgers.edu. Once you're into that computer server, go to pub/tv+movies/simpsons.

4. To download neat geography stuff, use FTP to oak.oakland.edu, and from there go to SimTel/msdos/geogrphy/usgeo11-0.zip. The book claims that this piece of software actually makes geography just like video games!

5. Get free stickers by e-mailing NASA! You can receive stickers that commemorate the Apollo and space shuttle missions, as well as other memorabilia. Send e-mail to kdurham@smtpgate.osu.hq.nasa.gov. Ask for the stickers and for information on other free stuff they may have for kids. Be sure that you include your name and full snail mail address since they can't exactly zap you the stickers through your modem!

software. It's so tempting to just grab everything in sight. In fact the only thing that will probably stop you from doing that—in addition to a lack of RAM—is the time it takes to transfer files to your computer. Some programs can take hours to download, especially if you're not connected at a high modem speed.

SHAREWARE VS. FREEWARE

"I would be a total download junkie if my parents weren't so uptight about having to send a fee for the shareware I decide to keep . . . Shareware is usually pretty inexpensive, around $10 or $20, depending on what you want. When I feel broke, I go for freeware since my parents pay my on-line bill."

—RonXV28, a ninth grader from Canton, Massachusetts

As Ron (not his real name) has learned the hard way, there is a big difference between freeware and shareware. **Shareware** is software you can download and *try out* for free. If you decide you like it and want to keep it, you have to send in a small fee to the creator. No, the cyberpolice aren't going to show up at your house and lead you away in handcuffs if you don't pay for your shareware. Shareware works on the honor system: The creator makes the software available free of charge on the understanding that people who try it and decide to keep it will pay the specified fee.

Why would anyone distribute their software free of charge? There are lots of reasons. First of all, no software store has enough shelf space to stock all the computer programs that are available. Only the best-selling titles are worth the money it takes to distribute and display them. As a result, some software developers take their product directly to the consumer: you! They let you try it out for a while to see whether you like it. If you do like it and decide you want to keep using it, you fork over the cash. It's really a great deal.

Why should you pay for shareware when you can get it for free? For one thing, the people who created the shareware worked very hard on the program, and they should be reimbursed for their time and effort. For another thing, if a lot of people use shareware but don't pay for it, the whole system will collapse. Software developers will stop providing shareware, and none of us will be able to download these programs anymore.

Freeware is an entirely different story. You can download freeware and use it to your heart's content without ever owing anyone a cent. You can even copy it as many times as you want and give it to all your friends. The only thing you're not allowed to do to freeware is modify it in any way. That's because it may be copyrighted. The one exception is if the freeware is in the **public domain.** That means that no one owns the rights to it, so you can do anything you want with it.

Developers very often put freeware on-line either to test it or as a demonstration (''demo'') version. If they're testing their freeware, they want people to use it so they can detect any problems with the software and make suggestions for improvements. If they're making a demo version available, they usually want people to try it and like it, and then pay for a more complete or advanced version that's for sale. Either way, you can end up downloading a lot of fun and useful programs for free.

Software Sources

Where do you find the best shareware? On CompuServe, Delphi, and GEnie, the best shareware treasures are typically in SIG libraries. So, if you're in the market for something in particular, search the service's index for whatever it calls SIGs or special-interest groups. AOL and CompuServe are the easiest services to search for shareware. On AOL, everything is in the Software Center. So you don't even need to consider which SIG or Club library is most likely to have the file you're dying to download. CompuServe has a ''FileFinder'' feature which makes it easy to search all SIG libraries at one time—and fast.

No matter which major commercial service you join, you're

bound to find lots of software to download. And, needless to say, there's also tons of software available on the 'Net. Here are a few of the major sites:

AMERICA ONLINE

AOL is a downloader's paradise. All of the shareware and freeware are stored in one place: a systemwide library called the Software Center. Click on the types of files you're interested in, such as games, graphics & animation, or Windows, and a word that describes the type of program you're looking for. Click and *voilà*—you'll be shown a list of what's available.

Here's an example of how it works: When you log on to AOL, you type in KEYWORD: SOFTWARE, which brings you directly to the Software Center. Once there, you can run a search through the database or click on one of the icons. For example, one icon is titled "Macintosh Top 20"; it lists the most popular software that was downloaded in the previous month. Here's what you would have seen if you had clicked on the icon in February 1995:

MACINTOSH TOP 20
Top Files January 1995

1995 Postal Rates—Business

Highway Navigator 2.0—Business

Asphodel Font (TT)—Desktop

epsConverter 1.2.2—Desktop

C string <-> number—Developer

Cool MacsBug Tricks—Developer

Lighthearted Clipart—Education

Vocab. Puzzle Creator—Education

Doom: Hell on Macs—Games

Tank Splatter—Games

ImageBrowser—Graphics

Thumbnailer—Graphics

DeskTape 2.0 Demo—Hardware

Calendar '95 Pro—Hypercard

Mortal Kombat Stack—Hypercard

MacAnim View 1.0.5—Multimedia

Sparkle 2.3.1—Multimedia

Dave's Online Sounds 2.1—Music

WaveWindow v2.5—Music

As you can see, you can download everything from hardware to graphics to multimedia software and games.

COMPUSERVE

As you might expect, CompuServe also has masses of shareware and free files, and finding them is almost as easy as on AOL. CompuServe keeps shareware and downloadable files in its hundreds of forum libraries, but it is possible to search most of the libraries at the same time.

If you have only a general idea of what you're looking for, start with the FIND command and locate whatever subject you're in the market for locating "stuff" on. That will give you a list of services that have something to do with your area of interest, and the GO command you need to get there. Use the GO command to reach the forum, and once you're there, you can ransack the forum's library for the files you want. Say you're into studying foreign language. You'll find the Foreign Language Forum (GO FLEFLO) and there you can download software programs to help you learn everything from German to Portuguese, from French to Italian.

And, in terms of the most general shareware areas, try these to get started. But, remember that downloading can become an addiction and very few kids need 247 fonts.

GO IBMAPP—DOS and Windows shareware
GO MACAP—Macintosh shareware
GO WINSHARE—Windows shareware
GO WINSOURCES—Windows shareware
GO PBSAPPS—DOS and Windows shareware
GO ZIFFNET*—DOS, Windows, and Macintosh shareware

---

*Surcharge of $2.50/month to add Ziffnet to your CompuServe subscription

THE INTERNET

The best place for shareware on the 'Net seems to be FTP sites. For Macs, try the Info-Mac archive at sumexaim.stanford.edu/info.mac. For DOS and Windows shareware, try ftp.cica.indiana.edu.

PHOTOS, GRAPHICS, AND MULTIMEDIA FILES

In addition to software, the on-line services have all kinds of photos, graphics, and other files to download for free. If you have a favorite actor, musician, or athlete, the odds are good that you'll be able to find a photo of him or her, which you can download and then print out. Some of the services even let you download multimedia clips of movies and news events, and music recordings.

The following are samples of some of the downloadable files that are available on-line. We happened to find all of these on AOL, but you can find similar files on most of the major services and on the 'Net. [For example, on CompuServe you'll find free fonts, utilities, software, templates, and art in the Desktop Publishing Forum (GO DTPFORUM).]

T-REX TO BARNEY (KEYWORD: SOFTWARE)

Leaping Ceratosaurus (picture)	Dinosaur Primordial (picture)
Jurassic Park vs Barney (text)	DinoDesktop (picture)
Jurassic (picture)	Dinosaurs
Vicious Utahraptor (picture)	Dinosaur Skeleton (picture)
Leaping Antrodemus (picture)	Dinosaur Morphing
Electric Dinosaur (picture)	Barney Dies Giggling (sound clip)

EXTRA GUEST ALBUM
(all photos black and white)
(KEYWORD: EXTRA)

Jim Carrey

Teri Hatcher!

Untamed Brad Pitt!

Kevin Costner

Gillian Anderson

David Duchovny

Patrick Stewart

Keanu Reeves

Steven Seagal

Wesley Snipes

Arnold Schwarzenegger

Jane Seymour

Denzel Washington

Mel Gibson

BABYLON 5

Tim Allen

Jean Claude Van Damme

Drew Barrymore

LOLLAPALOOZA IMAGES (all photos)
(KEYWORD: MTV)

Beasties Stage with crowd

Chalk Girls

Flava Flav singing

George Clinton

NYC Mosh Pit

Perry Farrell dancing

P-Funk All Stars dancing
L7 Hairdo

Bad Seeds' Stage

Beastie Boys Freak Out

A Tribe Called Quest

Rollerskate Skinny

Smashing Pumpkins

The Breeders

The Verve

YO! MTV RAPS IMAGE BANK (KEYWORD: MTV)

Fab5Freddy's Top 5 Picks (sound clip)

Ed Lover's Top 5 Picks (sound clip)

Dr. Dre's Top 5 Picks (sound clip)

Mic Geronimo (photo)

Lil' Vicious on YO! (photo)

Ice Cube, Tyra Banks & Omar E . . .
(photo)

Heavy D (photo)

Notorious B.I.G. (photo)

Digable Planets (photo)

Black Sheep (photo)

Ed Lover, Dr. Dre, T Money (photo)

BEAVIS & BUTT-HEAD (KEYWORD: MTV)

B&B Home Vid "Neighborhood"

B&B Home Vid "Work Sucks!"

Beavis & Butt-Head Screensaver

Poster

Cow Tipping

Young, Gifted, and Crude

Washin' the Dog

Trailer Ladies

This Rocks!

Snot Bad

No Laughing Please, Part 1

Have a Nice Day (tattoo)

Life Sucks (tattoo)

Good Credit

French Flies

Drive-In/Beware of the Butt

Chicks in Glasses are Cool

Sometimes Art Doesn't Suck

Beavis's Butt

ABC SPORTS SUPERBOWL VIDEO CLIPS (KEYWORD: ABC)
HOW TO PLAY SUPER VIDEO CLIPS!!

R U Ready?—Tim Allen, Tom Landry

R U Ready?—Andre Agassi

R U READY?—Space Shuttle

Raiders/Chargers CRUNCH!!!!

R U READY? Little Richard!

ABC Sports Super Bowl Animation

Steelers BIG HIT!!

Scott Norwood Missed Field Goal

Crashing Helmets 49ers/Vikings

Crashing Helmets Cowboys/Saints

Crashing Helmets Chiefs/Dolphins

Crashing Helmets Raiders/Chargers

Crashing Helmets 49ers/Saints

Crashing Helmets Giants/Oilers

Crashing Helmets Bills/Steelers

Crashing Helmets Giants/Cowboys

GAMES

Do you like to play computer games? Then, boy, are you going to LOVE cyberspace! The on-line world is jam-packed with all kinds of games you can download, including flight simulators, role-playing and adventure games, strategy games, puzzles, word games, and video games. (See Chapter 8 for information on games you can play on-line.)

■ ■ ■ ■ ■
■ ■ ■ ■ ■   •
■ ■ ■ ■ ■
■ ■ ■ ■   # Map News
■ ■
■

Are you nuts about geography or topography? If so, have we got the place for you! CompuServe offers Magellan Geographix maps on-line. Basic Maps offers maps of the seven continents and a frequently updated Hot Spots topical map. Maps of the World contains more than six hundred maps of places and regions worldwide. And MGDigitalAtlas offers vector maps of cities, countries, regions, states, and other areas of the world. You can also discuss maps in the Maps Forum. GO MGMAPS.

• •

Here's a list, for example, of some of the more popular games that you can download from AOL:

GAMES (KEYWORD: SOFTWARE)

Maelstrom 1.4.1	Arashi v.1.1
Tetris Max 2.4	Risk III
Jewelbox v.1.0	Glider v.3.14
Seahaven Towers	3Tris v.2.1.1 Color
Quagmire! Color Action Game	Gunshy v.2.0
Galactic Empire v.2.0	Movod Color
Solarian II v.1.04	MacBzone v.1.3.1
Medieval Trader v.1.0	MacAir Hockey
Klondike 5.1 Solitaire	Roboids II v.1.1
GNU Chess v.3.02	Canfield 5.1 Solitaire

Fun Product: Vivid 3D, a quirky electronic device by NuReality, unleashes the hidden sounds in games—and their music.

For $80, you can hear it all! Say, when is your birthday, anyway?

DOWNLOADERS BEWARE!

As we mentioned at the beginning of this chapter, downloading can be downright addictive—particularly when you first join a service. To keep things under control, bear in mind the following cautions:

* *Time is money.* Even though you don't have to pay a special fee to download software and other files, you do have to pay the regular connect charges. If you're logged on at 14,400 baud, this may not seem so bad, but if you're at 2400, you could end up paying through the nose. Ouch! Before deciding whether to download a particular file, take a look at its description. This will tell you a) approximately how much time it will take to download, and b) what equipment (hardware and software) you need to use the file. Don't waste your money downloading huge files that you'll never use. And, remember, if you decide to keep any of the shareware, you're honor bound to pay for it!

* *Don't space out.* Don't forget that when you download a file, you need somewhere to keep it. If your hard drive is stuffed to the max and your room is littered with dozens of computer disks that you rarely use, you may want to rethink a particular download. Ask yourself these questions: Do you really need the file? Will it be something that you use a lot? Do you have room for it on your computer? Do you have the equipment you need to support it? If you answer no to any of these questions, you may want to rethink the download.

* *Play it safe.* If there's one thing that strikes fear in the heart of even the bravest cybertraveler, it's the word *virus.* EEEEEEKKKKKKKKKKK!!!!!! Though not all computer viruses are destructive, those that are can really wreak havoc on your system. They can delete your files, mess up your hard

drive, and make your life miserable. Don't let this happen to you!

What exactly is a virus? It's a program that invades your computer without your consent. Some people create viruses just to stir up harmless trouble or amuse themselves, but other people create viruses that are purposely destructive. How do you catch a virus? Viruses are spread when people share infected programs or disks. If you have an infected disk, for example, and you make a copy for your friend, your friend's computer will be infected too. Imagine how quickly a virus can spread from a single downloading site on the Internet!

The good news is that there's lots of effective antiviral software available. Antiviral software will let you know when a file is infected, screen inserted disks for viruses, and get rid of the viruses. Depending on what service you join, you can probably download Disinfectant, which is distributed free of charge. You'll also be happy to hear that all of the major on-line services let you know whether each particular file you can download has been screened. That way you'll know what's safe and what's not. Take particular caution should you decide to download software from an unknown source, especially some anonymous 'Net site.

12

A Touch of Class

"The reality of doing school in cyberspace is that learning is much more fun when you can log on and actually discuss an idea with someone with an interesting point of view. I have a friend from Houston with whom I swap brain teaser math problems in pre-calc class. That's really cool."
—KevinD6417, a ninth grader from Southborough, Massachussetts

The elementary school students in Patricia Weeg's computer lab meet in a glass-enclosed corner of the media center in Delmar Elementary School in Delmar, Maryland. There's barely enough room for the eight computers in the lab, let alone the students who crowd around them. But the tiny lab is the school's gateway to the world. Mrs. Weeg's kids meet in the lab, but by using a modem as a group passport, they also meet in Egypt, Russia, Japan, the U.K., Iceland, the Netherlands, Germany, Guam, South Africa, Malaysia, Brazil, and dozens of other countries.

They're not the only ones. Schools are leading the way into cyberspace. Kids from Omaha to Oshkosh, from Toronto to Tulsa are learning on-line. From classrooms and computer labs in small towns and bigger cities, from private schools and parochial schools, they're heading into cyberspace to do research, interview experts, learn about history and geography, study foreign languages, and talk to people all over the world. What are they learning? Just about everything—including about the daily life, customs, and traditions of kids in lots of other places. The most interesting part of this learning—besides the real-life experience of its *really* being a small world after all—is that the computer and modem have more in common with an aircraft and a spaceship than they do with a calculator or a VCR. "Like who would believe that we went to the Arctic today?" says ten-year-old Amy, a fifth grader from a quiet suburb of Nashville, Tennessee. "But we did. And it was awesome. I wish I could see a real penguin!"

"Are we linked to a larger teaching and learning community? You bet we are!" says Mrs. Weeg enthusiastically. "The world is our classroom! All are welcomed in. Our subjects aren't divided into neat pockets of match, science, social studies, and language arts. In the global classroom the curriculum is a 'living' curriculum with real people—not textbooks—feeding our desire to learn and explore. Once you are part of the global community you can't settle for less." But, back to school. Why should you use the Internet and on-line services when you're in the classroom? And what arguments can you make to your teachers and parents to help you win the battle for more technology?

WHY IN-SCHOOL TECHNOLOGY IS SO IMPORTANT

If your school isn't hooked up to cyberspace yet, you shouldn't feel like an outcast. The sad truth is that relatively few schools are on-line today. Vice President Gore and other politicians are working toward a goal of someday hooking *every* school to a huge on-line system, but that's probably years and years away.

What can you do to speed up the process? For one thing,

177

you can write your political representative and school district, and tell them how important it is for your school—and all schools—to have access to the incredible resources in cyberspace. Here are a couple of points to get you started:

• Cyberspace puts an incredible amount of information at your fingertips. Once you're wired in, you instantly have the biggest personal library in history. Why you could never, ever read all the stuff that's available on even one commercial service, especially since it's always changing, let alone the trillions of books in all the libraries that are connected to the 'Net.

• The Internet isn't going away. It's becoming a part of life in education, in business, and in people's personal lives. You'll need to learn how to use it sooner or later. And, just as parents always tell you when they want you to do something, there's no time like the present to get up and go, even if where you're heading is on-line.

This chapter will discuss some of the interesting and innovative things teachers and students are doing on-line, and show you how to get your school involved. Even if your school isn't as technically up-to-date as Mrs. Weeg's, there are many ways to get your class involved from your home PC.

WAYS TO GET YOUR CLASSROOM/SCHOOL INVOLVED

KidLink

KidLink is a grassroots, global project based in Norway aimed at getting kids from ten to fifteen involved in a worldwide dialog. Since it started in 1990, KidLink has involved over thirty thousand children from sixty-five countries on all continents in all kinds of activities, including a keypal exchange, educational projects, live chat, and a gallery of computer art. The coolest thing about KidLink is you can join via e-mail.

How to: All you have to do is send an e-mail message! Send your request for KidLink to LISTSERV@VM1.NODAK.EDU. In the message body, type: subscribe KidLink (your name). It's a great way to use the Internet to connect with other kids all over the world!

KIDSPHERE NETWORK

The Kidsphere Network is a growing international network of students and teachers. The main "Kidsphere" list is mainly for teachers. It links classrooms looking to cooperate on projects. St. Robert's school, London, Ontario, for example, asked other classes on the Kidsphere list to e-mail them descriptions of outdoor games they play in other parts of the world. Another list, called simply "Kids," is for kid-to-kid communications.

How to: To subscribe to Kidsphere send e-mail to: kidsphere-request@vms.cis.pitt.edu. In the body of your message write: subscribe kidsphere (your name). Subscribe to Kids by sending e-mail to: kids@vms.cis.pitt.edu. In the body of your message write: subscribe kids (your name).

ACADEMY ONE

Academy One is part of the National Public Telecomputing Network (NPTN), which is to the on-line world what public TV and National Public Radio are to broadcasting. Academy One is an on-line resource for teachers, students, parents, and administrators from kindergarten through high school. Academy One organizes on-line projects that let students share their creative writing, artwork, science experiments, or research with other students via computer. They can also exchange messages with schools in foreign countries or in foreign languages, and share their involvement in projects that help their community or address social issues.

How to: To register in the Academy One program and receive project updates, or to receive additional information send e-mail to: a-1@nptn.org or contact Linda Delzeit at 714-527-5651, or write, by snail mail, to: Academy One, 7151 Lincoln Avenue #G, Buena Park, CA 90620.

Electronic Schoolhouse

The Electronic Schoolhouse on America Online (KEY-WORD: ESH) is a meeting place for teachers who want to join or create on-line class-link projects. Over the past few years the Schoolhouse has grown to the point where there is now a continuous selection of interesting projects that cover a wide variety of topics. There is a "SCHOOL TO SCHOOL: PROJECTS" board where teachers gather participants for structured class-link projects and adventures. Click on "STUDENT TO STUDENT," and find students hard at work and play. The oldest ESH project is the "ScrapBook Writing Project." The ScrapBook Library contains ScrapBook chapters of student essays from more than 250 schools in thirty-five states.

How to: Contact Emery "Ted" Roth (ESH Tooter@aol.com) or Leni Donlan (ESH Leni@aol.com).

Global Schoolhouse Project

The Global Schoolhouse is a project of the Global SchoolNet Foundation, funded in part by the National Science Foundation and supported by many local and national businesses. They connect schools and students nationally and internationally over the Internet. Kids do collaborative research and use videoconferencing to communicate with each other and national and international leaders, including U.S. senators, Dr. C. Everett Koop, and anthropologist Dr. Jane Goodall. If your school is not up to speed on computers and the Internet, tell your teacher about the Global SchoolNet Foundation's teacher workshops, including "Hello Internet," which introduces teachers to Internet resources useful to the classroom.

How to: To be placed on the Global Schoolhouse listserv, send an e-mail message to fred@acme.fred.org with the body of the message containing "SUB HILITES." Or you can write to Yvonne Marie Andres, Global Schoolhouse Director of Curriculum at: andresyv@CERF.NET.

I*EARN

I*EARN (the International Education and Resource Network) helps teachers and students (K–12) to work together in a thousand elementary and secondary school sites in twenty-five countries, including the United States, Russia, China, Israel, Australia, Japan, and Kenya. Students and teachers gain experience with the Internet, cross-cultural communication skills, and global awareness, as well as an enhanced motivation for learning about their world. On-line I*EARN student projects, designed by the teachers and students themselves, facilitate the learning about other cultures and encourage active group participation in improving the social and environmental conditions of the planet.

How to: Send e-mail to: iearn@copenfund.igc.apc.org.

REAL SCHOOLS, REAL PROJECTS

Each and every school day, kids go on-line to do research, to visit distant cities and other countries, and to work on projects which often bring them into collaboration with other classrooms the world over. Here are just some 'Netter classrooms and projects:

• A second grade class at Indian Creek Elementary School in Indianapolis, Indiana, learns about Chinese New Year from on-line kids who celebrate it.

• Fifth graders in Holden, Massachusetts, keep in touch with a sister class in Melbourne, Australia.

• Fourth graders at L'Ouverture Computer Magnet School in Wichita, Kansas, studied different tribes by contacting Native Americans on-line to discuss their heritage with the class.

It's easy to get in touch with other kids and schools on the Internet. In fact, we learned about every school project in this chapter by using KidLink, Kidsphere and the other resources we told you about. Here are some real stories of adventures in cyberspace we collected from teachers and students we met on-line:

"We are a very small village school in the interior of Alaska. We have been doing Internet projects for about two years now. One of my favorite projects is the Journey North Project out of Minnesota. We get a class map showing which animals to watch for as they migrate from South America. These include swallows, song birds, tundra swans, and whales! The kids read the messages and stick little flags in the map following the sightings as they are posted. Then when our kids spotted the migratory birds, it was our turn to share the findings. It was great fun! The Internet is a priceless tool for me in my classroom!"
—Joy Hamilton, Innoko River School, Shageluk, Alaska

"Seventh grade students are currently in the middle of a collaborative project on wetlands ecosystems. We are gathering data from about twenty partners around the U.S. Eighth grade students are

using the World Wide Web to find information about pollution to create their term research reports."
—Terrie Gray, Chico Jr. High School, Chico, California

"We have in our school participated in many projects and the kids love to have friends all around the world. They have been 'Santa Clauses' and organized psychology research, have pen pals and so on."
—Kaisa Vahahyyppa, Puolalanmaki Secondary School, Turku, Finland

"My students have used AOL and the Internet to research water and air pollution, to find students in other parts of the country eager to participate in studies such as measuring ozone levels, to do research for science fair projects, to get answers from 'Ask the Scientist,' to get ideas on how to approach a problem, to use on-line encyclopedias, to search back issues of newspapers on specific topics, to download weather data used in projects, to download programs that can be used in classwork such as graphic converters, to see what NASA is doing, and just to become awed at what is out there and how much fun it can be. We do not have enough modems to go around!"
—Doris Ranke, West Bloomfield High School, West Bloomfield, Michigan

"I teach third grade at a magnet school for math, science, foreign language, and technology. My students have been learning how to use the Internet and all have keypals in different places around the world. My students have been 'On-line' with Mark Szorady, a cartoonist from Ohio. I found him through Cleveland Freenet, where he had offered his services to surrounding schools as a guest speaker. My students read and studied his cartoons (called 'George') and then interviewed him via e-mail. It was a wonderful experience for us!"

—Margaret "Kip" Mitchell, Bay Point School,
St. Petersburg, Florida

"As a class we wrote to a classroom of German students. Our students who were taking German language classes wrote in German. We also told the German students what the eighth grade American history class was learning about the American system of government and we asked questions about the German system of government ... We have convinced seventeen teachers to get Internet accounts and we've been teaching them how to use the Internet during computer classes, consultations, and after school. The geography teacher is in the process of having his students join KidLink."

—Donna Graves, English and journalism teacher,
Olympus Junior High, Salt Lake City, Utah

"A group of our students took a three-day field trip to the Okefenokee through AOL and CNN. They spent about an hour each day on-line talking to the experts about swamps in general and the Okefenokee in particular. They chatted with experts and other schools while simultaneously viewing a live video of the swamp and experts and students trudging around in it. Some of our hearing impaired students (we are the county middle school for all hearing impaired) correspond with other hearing impaired students in Washington, Iowa, and Texas. Last year we also participated in a project aimed at building the self-esteem of less successful students. The kids exchanged 'artifacts boxes' containing items indigenous to our area. We sent, among other things, a Coca-Cola bottle—full, of course—and a rock, leaf and some good ole Georgia red clay."

—Sandy Ewanowski, Sweetwater Middle School,
Lilburn, Georgia

"We have a large project beginning in February which will involve the study of five companies globally located. The project is multifaceted, but one of the goals is for students to locate as many people as possible in countries their companies are located in, thereby gaining information about doing business in that country, cultural considerations to be made, etc., and basically to find as much information about that country as they can through their e-mail pals."

—Patti Tuma, teacher, Midland High School,
Midland, Michigan

"Here in Texas we are fortunate to have a statewide communications network—the Texas Education Network (TENET). The network has been up and running for four years now and has over twenty-five thousand educators with accounts. I am so thrilled about more folks using telecommunications in schools—I find that students enjoy the interactivity and the ability to 'expand' the walls of our classroom!"

—Hollye Knox-Green, Bryson Independent School District,
Bryson, Texas

"I am media coordinator and technology facilitator at Pine Valley Elementary School. We have approximately six hundred students. I have been working with fifth graders this year on Internet projects—we participated in 'Day in the Life,' in October and November. Our fifth graders as well as several first and second grades will also take part in projects through Scholastic Network—Magic School Bus, live chats with the president, etc."

—Paula G. Futrell, Pine Valley Elementary School, Wilmington, North Carolina

"In 1994 my class were communicating with Davis Station in the Antarctic. In 1992 my class also communicated with yachts in the Steel Boat Challenge, a yacht race from Britain travelling around the world in reverse. We are also trying to organise an exchange of photos between classes around the world."

—Peter Lelong, Fahan School, Hobart, Tasmania, Australia

ON-LINE PROJECTS FOR SCHOOL

Study geography by plotting the locations of your school's on-line keypals on a map. And, to learn social studies, how about e-mailing kids in other countries to learn more about the holidays they celebrate? What do they eat for dinner? What do they do on Sundays? How do they celebrate their twelfth birthdays? There's no end to what you can learn on-line! Here are just a few of the hundreds of examples of cool school projects we collected:

A DAY IN THE LIFE OF A STUDENT

Tell other kids all around the world about a day in your life. The project involves keeping a chronological account of a single prearranged day from wake-up to bedtime. Student entries can be compiled into a class file and shared with other participants. Classes compare student responses, attitudes, and schedules to learn about other types of schools and other cultures. "We read daily logs of students in Argentina, Alaska, Japan, England, Raleigh, North Carolina, and from all over the USA and Canada," says Paula G. Futrell of Pine Valley Elementary School, in Wilmington, North Carolina. "Our students compared language (cookies in America and biscuits in England), sports, what students did after school, what kind of classes they took, music they listened to, etc." Contact: Sheldon Smith (shsmith@ctp.org).

Project Outdoors

Les Williams's tenth grade biology students at Hot Springs High School (President Clinton's alma mater) in Hot Springs, Arkansas, run an annual project called Project OUTDOORS! Teachers and their classes from all over the country and as far away as South Africa and Estonia take part, studying their local school grounds as an ecosystem. The kids in each school exchange information and compare notes with all the other schools around the world, and learn how scientists work and gather information. Contact: Les Williams, Hot Springs High School, 701 Emory, Hot Springs, AR 71913. By e-mail to williamsl@hshs2.dsc.K12.ar.us.

Teleolympics: A "Virtual" Olympics

Students compete every year in a series of track events in their own schoolyards, posting the winning scores in each category to the computer network. Results are compared, and international winners receive recognition. "Chesapeake has had world winners for the past three years," says Mrs. Linda Scott, the principal of Chesapeake Center for Science & Technology. "Our first was a student in a wheelchair." It's a great way to integrate geography, writing, math, computer science, and physical education! Contact Shelly Benner (sdb@nptn.org).

Peace Project

Cynthia "Sam" Foley, a librarian at the R. C. Buckley Elementary School in Lansing, New York, came across a message on the Internet from a high school class in Israel, describing what peace meant to them. Inspired by the spirit of a group of kids in the violence-plagued Middle East, Ms. Foley sent a message out over the 'Net asking elementary school students all over the world to write to her third grade students and tell what peace meant to them. All the responses were posted on a map of the world and used for a discussion about peace and conflict resolution in class. In a separate project, kids at Eastern Avenue School in Davenport, Iowa, developed a Declaration of Peace to share with other students around the world via the Internet. Contact: Cynthia Foley, library media specialist, R. C. Buckley Elementary School, Ridge Road, Lansing, NY 14882; send e-mai to sfoley2@onondaga.bitnet.

Bug Survey

Kids at the Rose City Park School in Portland, Oregon, studied insects in science class by conducting an on-line "bug survey." They heard from kids all over the country about the kinds of bugs most common to their areas, and bugs unique to their states. After getting results from classes in more than half the states in the U.S., the kids posted the results on the Internet to everyone who took part. Contact: David Berkham, Rose City Park School. By e-mail: dberkham@teleport.com.

Inter-generational Exchange

This Academy One project brings different generations together on-line to compare how traditions, sports, music, and family roles have changed over the years. There is value in the memories of each generation and opportunities to learn through the sharing process. Contact: Lou Schwartz (xx141@nptn.org).

The Landmark Game

Mount St. Joseph Academy in Flourtown, Pennsylvania, devised this geography game for classrooms on KidLink. Each class chooses a landmark anywhere in the world. Students research facts concerning their landmark and come up with nine interesting clues. They post three clues per week to the Kidproject board over a three-week period. All of the other schools get to ask one question per week of each clue-posting school. Questions require a yes or no answer. At the end of the three weeks the school which guessed the most landmarks is declared the winner! Contact: Carol Siwinski, Computer Teacher and coordinator, Mount St. Joseph Academy. By e-mail: mountsj@rbs.org.

International Holiday Exchange

Students around the world compare their holiday customs. This is a real eye-opener and learning experience as students not only share their favorite customs, but recipes, and reasons behind what makes the holiday season such a special time of year. Contact: Shelly Benner by e-mail at sdb@nptn.org.

Egg-a-Thon

This egg-citing event is organized by the Electronic Schoolhouse. Last year's event involved thirty-six classrooms in three countries. Classes compete in different events, with students working in teams. Drop containers designed to let eggs inside survive the fall; drop ''naked eggs'' onto a specially constructed landing platform; and send eggs through the mail to other schools for the ''International Egg Toss'' (just hope the school front of you has really smart kids!). Egg survival is the mission of the teams in all events. Event results and outcome stories are shared in the America Online Egg-a-Thon folder. Teams will discuss their design success, experimentation, and modifications with other teams around the world. Contact: Stewart Clements by e-mail at stewclem@aol.com.

SIMULATED SPACE SHUTTLE PROGRAM

Schools around the world assume various roles in a simulated space shuttle mission. These could include being another shuttle (doing a docking maneuver), a secondary mission control, and alternate landing site (weather station), a solar disturbance observatory, and so forth. Electronic mail is exchanged, hourly reports are posted, and even real-time electronic "chats" can occur between mission control, astronauts, and supporting units. Contact: Bob Morgan by e-mail at xx118@nptn.org.

IDITAROD ON-LINE

This project revolves around the annual Iditarod Sled Dog Race, an eleven-hundred-mile trek from Anchorage to Nome, Alaska. The University of Alaska each year sets up IDITANET. For two to three weeks in March, students from the the villages of Anvik, Grayling, Shageluk, Takotna, Nikolai, and other places along the Iditarod trail send, via University of Alaska Computer Network, Iditarod Race data, weather information, geographical information, and local cultural information to students in McGrath. These students then send the information to participating schools around the world. The participating schools are asked to send similar information to the students in McGrath, who forward it to the other schools along the Iditarod Trail, as well as all the other schools participating in the project. Contact: Bob Kuhn, Technology Coordinator, Iditarod Area School District, McGrath, AK 99627. By e-mail: rsrck@aurora.alaska.edu.

Titanic Search

A fifth grade student in Selah, Washington, went on-line to add color to a report about the *Titanic* and its disastrous voyage in 1912. She read lots of books and encyclopedia entries, but wanted something more human and "real." So she posted a message on the Kidsphere e-mail list searching for a person who survived the sinking of the *Titanic*; a historian with specialized information on the event or era; or anyone who is employed as an ocean navigator with iceberg experience. It's a good example of how, with a little imagination, any school project can go beyond the books and come to life. Contact: Ken Newkirk, Selah School District, Selah, WA 98942, or by e-mail: knewkirk@destiny.esd105.wednet.edu.

Virtual Field Trips

Fourth graders in Nadine Hinton's class at Emerson Elementary Magnet School in Westerville, Ohio, became keypals with a class in New York City. After writing back and forth, the kids from Ohio went on a "virtual field trip" to visit their e-mail friends in the Big Apple. The kids "traveled" by Amtrak, departing from Cleveland, changed trains at Albany, then rode along the Hudson River before going sight-seeing in New York City. They learned all about the areas they passed through from people they met on-line who lived in those cities, whom Ms. Hinton had contacted in advance over the Internet. Contact: Nadine Hinton by e-mail at hinton@cedar.cic.net.

Surveys

On-line services and the Internet give you a great opportunity to get opinions on important (and not-so-important) issues from other kids all over the world. Fifth and sixth graders in Springfield, Illinois, sent a questionnaire on school prayer over the Internet. Kids from Mandeville Middle School's National Student Research Center in Mandeville, Louisiana, posted questions about gun control on the Internet. Mr. Carbone's fourth grade math class at the North Stratfield School in Fairfield, Connecticut, did a nationwide survey of gasoline prices. (Guess which state had the lowest prices? Georgia was the cheapest for "regular" gas.) And, hundreds of kids write to Channel One each week—Chanone@aol.com—to talk about their favorite news segment and to even ask the on-air anchors for homecoming dates. (For more ways to get involved with Channel One Online, see pages 139-140.)

VIRTUAL CARNIVAL!

Every other year, Osprey Central School, in Maxwell, Ontario, Canada, holds a Winter Carnival on the second week during February. It's modeled after the famous winter "Carnaval de Québec." The entire school, kindergarten through eighth grade, gets into it, beginning with history of "Carnaval," art activities, and other projects. The school has now taken its Winter Carnival into cyberspace, searching the Internet for kids around the world who will share information about their local celebrations—New Orleans' Mardi Gras, the festival in Rio de Janeiro, and dozens of other cities. Contact: Tim Noxe by e-mail at timnoxe@village.ca.

GLOBAL GROCERY LIST

Imagine a "global grocery shopping spree" where you could buy food from anyplace in the world. Where would you get oranges, or hamburger? What do they call hamburger in other countries? What type of money would you spend? To take part in the Global Grocery List project you simply collect your local grocery prices for a group of selected items, post them on the Global Grocery List Project newsgroup, and keep checking the newsgroup (or your mailbox) for the price lists of other participants. Contact: David F. Warlick, Instructional Computing Consultant, North Carolina Department of Public Instruction. By e-mail: dwarlick@dpi.state.nc.us.

CYBERSTARS SINGING CONTEST

The University of Song, Global SchoolNet Foundation and On Ramp/Media America, in cooperation with the United Nations' "Children's Summit," launched the first-ever talent contest to be held over the Internet! The program earlier this year allowed children around the world to share their singing talents with up to thirty million people, in more than forty countries via the Internet. The six winners were flown to New York to perform live at the United Nations' "Children's Universal Summit" from June 23–29, 1995.

BIRD MIGRATION WATCH

Bird migration makes for an interesting and educational experience. Students record their observations about the birds in their area and post the results for other students to compare and read. Two special weeks are set aside as concentrated bird-watching sessions in October and in March. During the remainder of the year postings can be made on observations from home or school. Special files on birds, bird migration, and the hobby of bird watching are available for on-line research. Contact: Judson Elliot or Nick Barber (xx132@nptn.org).

TIP: If your school is considering going on-line, check into the possibility of joining a freenet. It'll probably be a lot easier to talk your school board into the purchase of a modem if they know they won't also have to cough up big bucks for on-line usage! For a list of freenets, see Chapter 3.

Fun Stuff for Families

13

Just a few decades ago, computers were MASSIVE machines in office buildings and government headquarters. And very, very few people knew how to work them. There's *no way* anyone would have had a computer at home! Just twenty years ago, the idea of computers in schools was amazing!

Times sure have changed, haven't they? Today, just about four out of every ten households has a computer. And that number is expected to jump to six out of ten by the year 2000. Families use computers to write reports, play games, keep track of money, and explore the world. Since you're reading this book, the odds are pretty good that you already have a computer at home. Some kids actually have their own computers, which they keep in their bedrooms. Other kids share a computer with their parents and brothers and sisters.

How is your home computer used? Does everyone use it, or just you? Did your parents teach you how to use a computer—or are you teaching *them?* That's one of the funny things about computers. In many families, the kids know a lot more about them than their parents do. That's because many kids learned how to use computers in school.

Another funny thing about computers is that some families never, ever think of doing things *together* on a computer. Mom uses it to keep track of bills. Dad uses it to write a monthly newsletter. And the kids use it to play games and do assignments for school. Sheesh, what a waste!

There are so many fun and interesting things for families to do on a computer—especially on-line. It's so easy to spend time with our families without actually *doing* anything. Oh, sure, we eat dinner and watch TV. Sometimes we go out to the video store together or go to the mall, but that's just not the same thing as really participating in an activity together.

Another great thing about being a "family in cyberspace" is that you can reach out and connect with long-lost relatives near and far. Remember Aunt Ethel from Wichita? The one with the toy poodles? Oh, wait, maybe that's Aunt Eunice ... It's all too easy to lose track of our relatives when we don't get to see them very often. That's why lots of people are hooking up with long-lost relatives in cyberspace. And you can, too.

In this chapter you'll learn about all sorts of things you can do on-line with and for your family. There are so many activities out there that we couldn't possibly list them all, but these examples should give you a good starting point. Have fun!

Play Games on the ImagiNation Network.

Jocelyn, a fourteen-year-old from western Massachusetts, enjoys playing computer games with her twin brother, Jason. It's also one of the few activities that both of them enjoy sharing with their dad. "Dad wigs out when Jas and I try to get into the 'sexy' rooms on-line," says Joci, "but he's kind of cool about how much time we spend playing OK stuff, like the board games and the card games on ImagiNation Network." One of the fun things to do on ImagiNation is a math race for kids that launches a rocket: It's called Rocketquiz (found in Sierraland, select ROCKETQUIZ). ImagiNation's Clubhouse is a great gaming area that features everything from checkers and chess to backgammon.

For more information about ImagiNation! call 1-800-IMA-GIN-1 (1-800-462-4461) from 8:00 A.M to 10:00 P.M., seven days a week. (**NOTE:** ImagiNation! has no Mac platform at this time—your computer must be IBM compatible.)

Turn a Family Member on to Cyberspace.

John, a twelve-year-old from Malibu, California, takes friends and family members on tours of America Online. He shows them his favorite places and answers all their newbie questions. John's cousin, a year older, reports that John even showed her how to download photographs from the on-line gallery.

If someone in your extended family has a computer and modem, why not surprise them by asking your parents to order free on-line software for them? America Online and Prodigy give away their software and offer free trial periods, so it won't cost your relative anything to try the service out. Some on-line services have limited-time offers of free software; check computer and other magazines for these. For example, ads in *NetGuide* and *U.S. News and World Report* have offered free CompuServe memberships, and rumor has it that *Sports Illustrated* will be running a promotion with Prodigy in *SI For Kids*.

Keep in Touch Via E-mail.

Brian V., a fifteen-year-old from Houston, Texas, told us that his aunt turned him on to America Online. He sends her occasional e-mails to keep her up-to-date on all the stuff he's doing.

A mom in northern Virginia told us that she had a modem line installed in her mother's nursing home just so her kids could stay in touch with their grandmother. This mom explained, "Nannie was hardly about to give up daily contact with Jack, Eric, and Lexie." And, "the kids felt much better about the fact that their communication with their Nan wasn't in any way affected just because her arthritis had become so bad that she could no longer live completely independently."

Join the America Online Family Album.

If you're a member of AOL, you can upload a family picture to be included in the AOL family album! You can find out how by entering the Family Room within the Family Computing Forum (KEYWORD: FC).

Post Your Artwork for the World to See.

Do you have a drawing that you're particularly proud of? Then why not post it on the cyberrefrigerator? Refrigerator Door, an interactive program on AOL, lets kids upload and post their artwork on-line. So the next time your grandma asks you how you're doing in school, you can tell her, "Didn't you hear? They're showing an exhibition of my art in cyberspace!"

If you haven't created your art on a computer, you'll need to scan it in. If your family doesn't have access to a scanner, don't fret; you can get things scanned in cheaply at Kinko's and other copy shops. Go to the Refrigerator Door area on AOL for complete details (KEYWORD: FAMILY COMPUTING).

But what about the rest of your family? Don't Mom and Dad get to post their artwork, too? Sure they do! Adults of all ages can upload their artwork to be posted on the Freezer Door. You can even have a competition to see whose artwork is best!

Adopt a Virtual Grandparent.

If you don't have a grandparent or other older relative who wants to communicate on-line, why not adopt one? There are lots and lots of older people who would love to hear from a kid your age. Many of the services have special bulletin boards for older members. See if you can strike up a friendship by letting people there know you're looking for a keypal. When you find someone who shares your interest, start typing away! (Remember: Be sure to check with your parents before establishing an on-line relationship.)

Organize an On-line Scavenger Hunt.

This is a really cool thing to do with your entire family. First, you need to have someone create a list of thirty items that can be found on-line. Then, each of you takes a turn going on-line for half an hour and finding and downloading as many of those items as you can. The person who downloads the most wins!

What kind of items can you include in your scavenger hunt? The sky's the limit. They could run the gamut from David

Letterman's top 10 list to a soccer player's photograph, to an instant message from someone from North or South Dakota. It all depends which service you belong to and whether or not you have Internet access.

Get Advice. No matter how much you love your brothers and sisters, we'll bet they can drive you absolutely, positively, no doubt about it, one hundred percent CRAZY at times. [At least ours could:-)] When you're fed up with a brother or sister—or even one of your parents—don't get into big fights about it, go on-line and vent. You can tell other kids your age what you're going through, and they can give you comfort and advice. Here are some postings taken off the message boards in the KOOL area on AOL. We've changed the screennames to protect the post-ers' privacy:

"My little sister is annoying. If I let her alone in my room she would tear all my stuff if she could. She can be good sometimes. If she does anything just tell your mom or dad but don't tattle."
—My little sister, by Robbyl

"Hi I am Robbyl's sister. Robbyl is annoying but sometimes he can be a little obnoxious and he can be nice but sometimes he takes my stuff and bothers me when my friends are over and I just want to throw him in the garbage can. He helps me sometimes when he can; he crosses the street for me when we walk home from school especially when we are alone. I love him."
—My big brother, by Sis333

"My brother and sister are always hitting me (hard) & bugging me. I would do something but I'm the baby of the family. So I'm too small to do anything about it. If any of you feel the same way please e-mail me."

—My annoying brother & sister, by Lily85

"My sister is really annoying. She's younger than me, so she gets what she wants."

—My sister's annoying!, by Annie1863

"I have 2 annoying sisters who always bug me. I don't like them. They don't like me. Uh-oh, gotta go! My sister's coming! (If she sees this she'll give me a . . . you don't want to know.)"

—Two annoying sisters, by JakeC

"I'd like to get a club for sisters who have annoying little brothers. We could give each other advice on how to ignore them. If interested please post a note to me."

—Bratty brothers, by COOL123

"I have an older sister and a younger brother. My brother's OK, but he's spoiled. My sister is the worst though!!! Sometimes I can't stand her!! She became friends with all my friends (she only has 2 good friends) and now she comes with me everywhere my friends and I go, but she won't let me go anywhere with her friends!!!!"

—All siblings are terrible, by Sarah1

"My sister would always follow me around when I was with friends, too . . . but I didn't mind. When we were younger, the only time we would get along was when friends were around. Now we've gotten older, and we get along very well . . . even when we don't have to. My parents are both very busy, so it's also nice to have someone older around to talk to."

—Re: All siblings are terrible, by Scott1

"Scott1: My sister is also 14, we still can't get along. How old are you??? I'm 12. Maybe it's just because we're so close in age? Please answer."

—Re: All siblings are terrible, by Sarah1

"We are about two years apart. We are both homeschooled, so we are around each other a lot. I guess we've just gotten used to each other. We spend a lot of time telling each other about all the things my mom does that gets on our nerves . . . and it's even better when my dad is home. I guess it's one of the only things the three of us have in common."

—(Not) all siblings are terrible, by Scott1

"I bet that whoever wrote what I just read about was very annoyed with their brother. And I also bet sometimes she/he loves him sometimes. I know either she did something wrong she is not aware of or her brother did something wrong. I say she should just relax and do something fun with her brother. My little brother is really annoying sometimes and sometimes he's an angel. He's usually annoying. I'm probably actually annoying to him too though. Whatever I like he doesn't and my mom usually says he can do what he wants and it's usually the opposite of what I want. The disgusting thing is he knows that."

—Little brother, by JaneyS

200

Give Your Parents a Clue.

Do you and your parents ever seem to be speaking two entirely different languages? If you use a lot of slang, you probably are! Why not give them a break and tell them where to look for the latest slang—*and* definitions?

On AOL, they can head to *Disney Adventures* Online (KEY-WORD: DISNEY). Each issue includes a list of some of the latest slang used by a particular group. Here are a few examples of current volleyball slang:

> Facial (n)—when the hitter slams the defender in the face with a spike
>
> Lollipop (n)—soft serve; a team will get licked if it serves too many of these
>
> Roofed (adj)—blocked—also known as "clamped" and "serious Jed" (as in Jed Clampett of "The Beverly Hillbillies")
>
> Spader (n)—an ace serve (as in ace of spades, the best card in the deck)

Send a Personalized Greeting Card.

Families are so busy these days, that it's easy to let a friend's or relative's birthday or another big occasion slip by without sending a card. One way to avoid this is by shopping in the Electronic Mall's Hallmark Connections store on CompuServe. Using GIF images of card selections, you can choose your cards, fill in the blanks with your own personalized greeting, and tell Hallmark when to mail it. Hallmark will print out the card with a simulated signature and mail it to the designated addressee to arrive by the date indicated. The cards cost $2.95 plus postage. To order them, GO HALLMARK.

Be a Spy for the Net Nomad.

Family PC is one of many magazines on-line; it's on AOL. To help families find their way on-line, *Family PC* has dispatched the Network

Nomad to wander the commercial on-line networks. She searches for fun family treasures and cool destinations and then sends back missives from around the on-line world. If your family comes across any cool destinations in its own on-line travels, drop into *Family PC* Online and let them know ... Or e-mail the Net Nomad at screenname FPCNomad@aol.com.

Travel the World in a Weekend.

Sometimes traveling with your family can be a major hassle. There's fighting over who gets to sit next to the window or whining over where to go for lunch. But not in cyberspace! When you're cybertraveling, your whole family can go mile after mile without so much as a complaint! But how do you travel the world in a weekend? It's easy! The first thing you should do is download the article "Travel the World in a Weekend" by Seth Godin in *NetGuide* (February 1995). The author will show you how you and your family can visit thirteen different places, from Scotland to Vietnam and Laos, over the course of a relaxing, hassle-free weekend. The only bad news is you don't earn frequent flier miles. . . .

To download Seth Godin's article off the Web, visit the *NetGuide* home page at http://techweb.cmp.com/net. Or, if you don't have access to a Web browser, send an e-mail to netmail-@netguide.cmp.com and request a copy of the article. Be sure to reference its title and the author's name if you order it by e-mail.

Hunt for Relatives.

You may have relatives around the world that you've never even heard of. One easy thing you and your family can do on-line is conduct membership searches for people with the same last name as yours. You can then e-mail them and try to figure out if you're related. Be sure to give them a few details about where your family is from, names of grandparents, etc. Who knows, you could end up locating a great-aunt in Hawaii who would love to have your family visit over winter vacation!

Your Family Tree

Some people search out long-lost relatives just for fun because it's interesting to learn about relatives they've never met. But some people search for relatives for more serious reasons. For example, a recent issue of *People* magazine told the story of a young woman who had a seriously ill baby. This woman needed to find out about her family's medical history, but was unable to do so because her own mother had been adopted and didn't know who her birth parents were. The young woman went on-line and was able to track down her mother's brothers and sisters. The amazing part of this story is that it turned out that this woman's mother had been working in the same store as her own sister and didn't even know it!

Become a Genealogist. If your family really wants to get into researching your family tree, you can become genealogists. Genealogy is the study of ancestors. You can try to find out neat stuff about your great-grandparents, great-great-grandparents, and beyond. Find out if your ancestors were Pilgrims or explorers or farmers or nobles. Some families will be easier to research than others, but being on-line will give you a real head start.

There are several places on-line in which you'll find great information to get you started. If you have access to the 'Net, a good place to start is the Gopher at the University of Toledo: GOPHER alpa.cc.utoledo.edu. At this location, you'll find how-to information, including how to interview family members, access the University of Michigan databases of locations, and even tips to avoid being disappointed as you start to search out long-long relatives and family histories. On the Web, there's a home page devoted to researching family roots [http://www.ftp.cac.psu.edu/~saw/genealogy.html].

The commercial on-line services all offer lots of ways to get you started. Here are a few of the basics:

CompuServe has a Genealogy Forum (GO ROOTS), which features bulletin boards with last names, places of origin, and general strategies for playing gene sleuth.

Prodigy's genealogy bulletin board is chaotic (JUMP:GENEALOGY BB), since some post-ers post whatever they want, wherever they want. However, the basic layout is sensible (surnames A–H, surnames I–Z, and state resources).

Delphi and AOL both have a roots venue (on Delphi, GO CUST 68; on AOL, KEYWORD: ROOTS), but they're fairly weak. Maybe by the time this book is published these areas will be better organized; for now, though, it's not very easy to find what you're looking for.

Plan Your Next Family Vacation.

If you subscribe to AOL, check out a series of guidebooks that are available in the on-line bookstore. Published by John Muir Publications in Santa Fe, New Mexico, *Kidding Around* is a wonderful series of books written specifically for the young traveler. You and your family can read through the guides to select major attractions and points of interest you want to visit before you even leave home. And because the guides are written with kids in mind, you can be sure that you won't end up in some stuffy place where kids are only barely tolerated.

To order any of the titles in the series, go to KEYWORD:

TRAVEL FORUM and then click on Travel Books. You can order the guides through Read USA Mail Order, Inc., and because you're an AOL member, you'll receive a ten percent discount!

If you don't belong to AOL, don't worry—you can get plenty of travel info on all of the major commercial services. In addition to bulletin boards for travelers and would-be travelers, many of the services offer local newspapers from travel hot spots, as well as on-line travel agencies.

Show Off Your Geography Skills.
One fun game to play on-line with the entire family is Where in the World Is Carmen Sandiego? You'll find it on Prodigy (JUMP: CARMEN). If you watch the show on TV or if you've taken geography classes in school, you might even beat your parents. Place your bets now!

Get Organized.
With all the stuff there is to do on-line, it's easy to lose track of fun activities to do with your family. One way you can solve this problem is by creating your very own "family on-line" reference shelf. You can keep the shelf stocked with on-line–related magazines and books (you can start with this one!) and articles that you've clipped or downloaded.

To build your reference area, ask your parents if you can subscribe to one or two computer magazines—even if it's only on a trial basis. If you subscribe to CompuServe, you'll receive their magazine automatically every month. Check out reviews of books and magazines on-line to see which are must-haves.

Expert Advice

"The best thing about AOL is that it's easy to use. When we got AOL, a friend of ours installed it in my sister's PowerBook, and we were totally psyched because we could figure it out. Then my father ordered a guidebook from America Online. Once we read it, getting around was even easier. Always get a book when you are learning something new on the computer. Otherwise, you might be ready to tear out your hair."

—Jeremy, eleven, North Miami Beach, Florida

ALMOST THE LAST WORD!

There are tons of tricks of the trade that will make your computing, your 'Netting, your cyberchatting, and your cyber-researching a lot easier—and a lot more fun. Lots of this info was included in earlier chapters of this book, but we wanted to give you a few of the most important tips all in one place, so you can refer to them as you get going in cyberspace. Once you master these things, your on-line experience will be that much more exciting.

Be an expert. Get to know your on-line service, and start

with one service at a time. We recommend America Online and Prodigy as the first places to consider, since they both have user-friendly interfaces, and enough newbies that you won't stand out.

There are plenty of books about the major on-line services, and enough Internet books to fill a small library. (You can even order books on-line and have them delivered to your home.) Pick one up and see what experienced cybernauts say about your on-line service. Another way to get help is to ask for it. In the "new members" area on AOL, for example, newbie questions prevail. Also, if your service has a free "members helping members" area, hang out there, read the postings, and get all the free advice you want. This is one time when the adage "You get what you pay for" doesn't apply.

Beware of the time vampire. Time flies, especially on-line. And, as the hours fly by, so does your money—or your parents' money, as the case may be. Since your on-line service is keeping a very careful eye on the clock—and billing you accordingly—it makes sense that you keep track of your on-line time, too. Learn how to check the on-line meter on your service—and check it often. That way, your parents won't freak when the bill arrives.

E-mail Usually Is Cheaper Than Chat.

Have a friend you like to spend time with on-line? It's usually much cheaper to keep in touch via e-mail, even if you log on several times a day. An hour of chat costs an hour of on-line time. But you can send and receive mail in just seconds. One fun activity that lots of kids do is send one another questions, almost like interview scripts, and then exchange lots and lots of info, mostly written off-line to keep costs down.

Get an Off-line Reader.

If you receive a lot of mail and read a lot of bulletin board messages, you'll save a significant amount of money by using a front-end program that grabs material of interest off the network as quickly as possible. You read

Five Questions Sure to Give You a Good Sense of a 'Netting Friend

1. What's the funniest experience you've ever had?

2. If you were a breakfast cereal, what kind would you be? What brand? How sweet? And how wet would you choose to be?

3. Pretend you're stranded on a deserted island. Who would you want to be with you? (You can name up to seven others.) What items would you most like to have with you? (You can name up to twenty items; be sure to tell why you picked each one.)

4. Take your keypad on a tour of your bedroom. What's on the walls, in the closet, under the bed? Do you have any very cool collections? How about hidden stuff that is just for your eyes only?

5. The year is 2020. Write a letter that describes exactly what your life is like then. What city or state or country or planet will you live in? What will you eat? What will you do for fun? Use your imagination!

and respond to it off-line, at your leisure. The program then posts your responses in another single, lightning-fast session.

Slow Down and Save. Some on-line services charge you higher hourly rates to connect at 14,400 and 9600 baud rather than 2400 and 1200 baud. So it might be cheaper to surf at the slower speed and go into high gear only when you need it (such as when you're downloading large files and software). Experiment, and see which speed works best for you.

Don't Be a Jerk. As you will soon find out, cyberspace is full of nice, funny, helpful people of all ages. But it also has its fair share of opinionated jerks. Don't become one. Flame only when ABSOLUTELY necessary, and pick your battles wisely. Cyberspace is a big place, but not so big that you can't get a bad reputation fast, especially if you hang out in the same places all the time. A little 'Netiquette (see Chapter 4) will go a long way. And once you've learned the rules, have patience with those who haven't. We were all newbies once.

Take Advantage of Free Services and Trial Memberships. Almost every on-line service will give you anywhere from a few free hours to a free month to try it out. Take advantage of these offers. It's the best way to find out which service is best for you. You may like AOL, but how do you know CompuServe or Prodigy doesn't offer things you like even more? The best way to learn your way around is hands-on!

Get Out of Your Neighborhood. Once you're an experienced cybernaut, you'll probably find a few fave on-line hangouts. That's fine. But every now and then, take a trip to another part of the service ... to someplace you've never been. And check your service's list of new features on a regular basis to see what's new on-line. Keep exploring—cyberspace should NEVER get boring ... how could it?

Don't Hog the Phone. Don't forget that when you're on-line, it's the same as making a phone call and keeping the line occupied. You may be the most popular kid in cyberspace, but if your family has only one phone line and you're constantly on-line, you're going to be the least popular kid in your house. Be considerate. Or sell your parents on getting you a second line. Establishing household rules is a good idea. If everyone knows that your regular pattern is to log on to the computer from 7:00 P.M. to 8:00 P.M., it's less likely that someone will pick up an extension and inadvertently knock you off-line.

Read a Book/Have a Life. Books are highly interactive, fully browsable, and totally portable. Don't become so caught up with cyberliving that you use it as a substitute for the real thing. Read a book, call a friend, and yack it up by telephone, or just take a walk with your favorite hound every now and then.

Expert Checklist

• Use your on-line network for technical support. Hundreds of software and hardware vendors run forums on all the major services. Post your questions and problems on-line, and you'll get help from both the manufacturers and from other users who've already beaten your problem.

• If you have an area of special know-how, help others out by jumping in with solutions.

• Step back and reevaluate things periodically. Can you really afford the time and money you're spending on-line?

• Disable call waiting. The breaking noise used to indicate an incoming call will throw your modem off-line every time. Your phone company has a way to disable call waiting temporarily (usually by dialing *70). Use it every time you go on-line; otherwise, you may find yourself disconnected mid-sentence or even as you are locating the final source you need for that assignment due tomorrow morning.

15

Kidspeak On-line

When you go on-line for the very first time, you'll be entering a world full of adventures and discoveries. You'll meet new people and be introduced to new ideas and points of view. Cyberspace is an exciting place to be—no matter what age you are.

As you explore this new world, you'll find that the content and people—and maybe even the rules—are changing rapidly. And you'll be one of the people who are influencing these changes. As a pioneer in cyberspace, you're on the cutting edge of new technologies. Buckle your seat belt, adjust your controls, and hang on for the ride of your life!

Here's what some of your fellow pioneers have to say about the adventure:

"I am relatively new on America Online, but I feel like an expert. It is so easy to use. Even a total computer illiterate can use it! When I first logged on to AOL, they took me on a 'tour' of all the areas. It was very easy."

—Joellen, fifteen, Chicago, Illinois

"Being on-line is a whole lot of fun! Before, I never used computers. Now I love using them, and they're a whole lot of fun—especially on-line."

—Krista, eleven, Willow Grove, Pennsylvania

"One thing I like about being on-line is that I can 'talk' to people all over the world. I have many friends that I talk to through e-mail. It's a lot of fun!"

—Michelle, thirteen, Cleveland, Ohio

"I like making new friends. I have had America Online for a year! It's fast and easy and has many fun clubs. When I get on, I check for new mail then go to a chat room. I usually go to the teen rooms. I like the fairy-tale section in KidsOnly!"

—Abby, fourteen, (hometown unknown)

"I would describe being on-line as a great way to get information and a new experience that everyone should try at least once to see if they like it. Also don't think that it is for techno-nerds or whatever they are called. It is for everyone."

—Kevin, sixteen, Cupertino, California

MEET AN OFFICIAL CYBERNAUT KID

Kara Kaleen Mead is an eleven-year-old girl from a remote part of West Virginia. She uses on-line services for everything from studying Gaelic to swapping corny jokes with keypals across the country. We asked Kara to tell us a bit about her on-line experiences. Here's what she had to say:

• **On the Role the On-line World Plays in Her Life:** "I live on a mountain in West Virginia, but I am everywhere because I have a computer and a modem (and AOL). I am never out-of-date because I can go to the reference section of AOL and look up the latest stuff on whatever I am studying. I can't check out reference books from the library in town but I can read,

212

copy, and keep lots more information from the on-line libraries than from our library (which Daddy calls the 'dead tree version')."

• **On the Best Way to "Dive into" the On-line World:**
"I am eleven, and I have always had a computer. I expect my daddy will have to try real hard to keep up with me!

"Daddy says that, before on-line services such as Prodigy and Delphi and AOL, getting a computer to do anything was tough. There were all kinds of secret strings of letters and numbers. He says there was probably a secret handshake somewhere, too. I like AOL because it is colorful, it is big enough that I will never get to all of its rooms, and because it has special sections for kids, study, and chat rooms. Daddy likes AOL for me because it has monitors on the kid sections. I sent a person my address once to be a pen pal and the monitor caught it, sent it back to me undelivered, and told me it wasn't a good idea to do that. If I had been out on-line on my own without a service, I wouldn't have known that."

• **On Her Favorite Place On-line:** "I sign on to AOL and click on Kids Only on the main menu. I go to Hobbies and Clubs and read the latest for American Girls (I love 'em), dogs (I have a big one!), stamp collecting, ghost writers' corner, ice skating, and gymnastics. Then I click to Funtime for jokes and funny stuff. I like going through the Compton's Encyclopedia and finding the pictures, articles, and stuff I haven't seen before. For example, since Daddy is Scottish, I told the computer to search for mentions of Scotland, Scot, Scottish in the Compton's and came up with 256 references!

"I love shopping, so I try, if Daddy is brave enough to let me, to look around Marketplace. They have an Online Bookstore, which is good because our local bookstores are tiny and slow in ordering stuff. Then I go to Internet connection. I have Daddy with me to make sure everything is OK and I don't go to bad places. In newsgroups I searched for my hobbies and

213

interests and found groups for skiing, French, Spanish, and Scotland.

"Back at the main menu I go to its reference section and search the BBSes for anything interesting. Then I can also use Barron's Book Notes (this family is into reading in a BIG way), CNN Newsroom guides, a great computer terms dictionary, take a tour of the National Academy of Sciences and the Microsoft Knowledge Forum.

"There are also times when my favorite authors are in the large room for an open question-and-answer time. I got to talk with the author of the Magic Schoolbus series and really enjoyed it."

• **On the Most Unusual Thing She's Done On-line:** "While waiting for the author to show up for an on-line conference, a few of us talked to each other. I found out that one lady was a teacher of fourth grade in North Carolina and the whole class was watching our conversation! She asked me about home-schooling and my studies. That was cool. Then the author showed and I got to visit some more with her and other people. All for a local phone call in north central WV!"

• **On How She Expects Computers to Change the World:** "Jobs will change because people can sit at computers and tell them what to do. There won't be as many people going to work in cars, and that's good. Libraries will be on-line or out of business, I think . . . especially if they don't like kids checking out reference books!!! I wish that there could be some way to protect people from the idiots and flamers but I don't see how that could happen. Best advice? Daddy—don't enter cyberspace without him!"

16

The LAteST Word on 'Netting

THE WORD FROM AUTHORS OF RECOMMENDED BOOKS

• **On 'Netters Making History—BIG HISTORY:** ''You may not realize it, but by the simple act of reading this book you're making history. You're becoming an accomplice to the greatest revolution mankind has ever realized. Bigger than the French Revolution. Bigger than the Russian, American, and Chinese revolutions combined. Times 10. Times 100. And not a shot has been fired. A revolution in communications is raging around the world, and it's called the Internet. And whether you realize it or not, you are now on your way to being the latest foot soldier in this latter-day Information Crusade. Welcome to the Internet.''

—Patrick Vincent, *Free Stuff from the Internet,*
Coriolis Group Books, 1994

• **On 'Net Clutter:** ''You can't walk into a bookstore these days without stumbling over a pile of books about the Internet. I'm not criticizing. Certainly I have done my best to raise high the roofbeams of bookstores across the land with every Internet book I could nail down and then nail together. I hope, however, that my carpentry is better than most."

—Alfred Glossbrenner, *The Little Online Book*, Peachpit Press, 1995

• **On Being Street Smart:** "If we can think of the telephone lines that carry our data as an electronic highway, we can certainly think of our destination as a huge city. In fact, the online community has a population larger than any city in the world. It's smart to treat it just that way—the largest city in the world—with the associated perils. It's easy to compare ourselves, as individual users in our comfortable homes and offices, with the apple-cheeked Iowa farm girl who goes to the Big City for the first time. We know who we are and expect the same attitude and value systems from everyone else. It's a big mistake. We all need street smarts."

—Pamela Kane, *The Hitchhiker's Guide to the Electronic Highway,* MIS Press, 1994

• **On Log On—and Travel:** "What can I do on the 'Net? You can start relationships, fire off insults, publish your own writings. You can get help on your screenplay. You can get updates on the TV soaps you've missed. You can play games. You can send and receive electronic mail. You can search through libraries around the world. You can trade advice, ask and answer questions, and exchange opinions . . . You can lose yourself in a new medium and a new world."

—A Michael Wolff Book, *Net Guide,* Random House, 1994

BIG THREE CONSUMER SERVICES POST DOUBLE-DIGIT GAINS

"Despite intense competition, the big three consumer services—America Online, CompuServe and Prodigy—posted double-digit or better sales and subscriber gains in 1994, according to Electronic Information Report. Subscribers to the three services reached 5.36 million at the end of 1994, up 71.2% from

3.13 million in 1993, according to Electronic Information Report estimates.''

—Cowles/SIMBA Media Daily, January 18, 1995

• **Overheard on the 'Net:** ''Those without modems (in the year 2000, say) will be like those without telephones today. It will be the preferred method of conducting business, being entertained, and gathering info.''

Glossary:
Cyberspeak

ALADDIN: Communications software that makes it easier to use the GEnie on-line service.

AOL: America Online, the fastest-growing commercial on-line service in the U.S. (See Chapter 2.)

AUDITORIUM: The area in which moderated conferences are held on some of the on-line services. On eWorld, the auditorium can hold up to two hundred members and one or more hosts on a stage. AOL's four auditoriums are called the Odeon, Coliseum, Globe, and Rotunda, and hold up to two thousand people each. Attendees "sit" in rows of up to eight people who can talk among themselves, send questions and comments to the stage, vote, and bid.

BAUD RATE: The speed at which a modem sends and receives data. The higher the baud rate, the faster the speed. Baud rates keep getting faster and faster, but at the moment, a 1200-baud modem is an antique; a 2400-baud modem is slow but will get you around; a 9600-baud modem is pretty much standard; and the 14.4 (14,400-baud) modem is quickly gaining ground.

BBS: Bulletin Board System—a central system that posts data that can be accessed via modem. Most BBSes include databases, message boards, and libraries. AOL, Prodigy, and CompuServe are each huge BBSes; most BBSes are much smaller than that.

BITNET: A large-scale computer network that primarily connects colleges and universities.

CHAT: When you're connected to a service, you can chat with people who are also on-line at that time. You "chat" by typing in words that the other person or people can see on their screens.

CIM: CompuServe Information Manager; software that makes CompuServe easier to navigate for Mac and Windows users.

CIS: CompuServe Information System

COMMUNICATIONS SOFTWARE: Software that connects computers to one another (via modem). CompuServe, GEnie, and Delphi can be reached with any communications software. AOL and Prodigy provide their own software.

CONFERENCE: A live, scheduled discussion on-line, often involving a celebrity guest.

CONNECT TIME: The amount of time you are connected to an on-line service. Since most services charge by the minute (after your "free" hours run out each month), the price you have to pay for connect time can really add up.

CONTENT: All the stuff that's available on the on-line services, including publications, databases, forums, etc. Every time you post something on-line, you're adding to the content.

CYBERSPACE: The world you are in when you are on-line. Sometimes called the INFORMATION SUPERHIGHWAY, IN-

FOBAHN, ELECTRONIC HIGHWAY, etc. The term *cyberspace* was coined by William Gibson in his novel *Neuromancer*.

DATABASE: A collection of information. There are thousands of databases on-line, drawn from magazines and newspapers, encyclopedias, phone books, etc. The most useful databases allow you to search for information by name, title, or keywords.

DELPHI: One of the commercial on-line services (See Chapter 2.)

DEMO: Demonstration software, usually lacking some of the features and functions of the real thing. Publishers often make "demo" versions of software available on-line as shareware or freeware to get people interested in buying the finished version.

DISCUSSION BOARD: eWorld's name for Message Boards (See Message Boards).

D-LITE: Communications software that makes it easier to use the Delphi on-line service.

DOWNLOADING: To retrieve a file from another computer. You can download software, for example, from all of the major on-line services.

E-MAIL: Short for "electronic mail"—a private message you send or receive via modem.

EMOTICONS: See **SMILEYS.**

eWORLD: The on-line service launched by Apple Computer in 1994 (See Chapter 2.)

FAQ: Frequently Asked Question. Many newsgroups/forums post a list of answers to FAQs; be sure to check this first if you have a question.

FLAME: Sometimes funny but often nasty insults sent via e-mail or posted on-line. When two or more people start bombarding each other with flames, it's called a FLAME WAR.

FORUM: CompuServe's name for Message Boards (See Message Boards.)

FREENET: An organization that provides free Internet access in specific parts of the country.

FREEWARE: Software that you can download and copy free of charge. This software may be copyrighted, though, so you cannot modify it in any way.

FTP: File Transfer Protocol. One of the main ways you can retrieve information from the Internet.

GATEWAY: A gateway allows you to send e-mail and information between different on-line services—sending e-mail to Prodigy from CompuServe, for example. The Internet is the gateway for e-mail on commercial on-line services.

GENIE: A commercial on-line service owned by General Electric (See Chapter 2.)

GOPHER: A huge menu system for the Internet. It was developed at the University of Minnesota, whose mascot is the Golden Gopher. It will "go-fer" information from the Internet. Get it?

GUI: Graphical User Interface; a GUI (pronounced "gooey") interface is easier to use than a text-based interface.

HACKER: Someone who knows a lot about computers and spends a lot of time on programming and other computer-related activities. Some hackers are PIRATES, meaning that they (often illegally) break into computer systems, usually to extract information or simply to cause trouble.

ICON: A picture on a computer screen that you click on with your mouse. For example, on AOL you would click on the icon of the hand holding mail in order to read your e-mail.

INSTANT MESSAGE (IM): On some of the on-line services, you can send a message instantaneously to anyone else who is on-line at that time.

INTERNET: A massive network that links computer networks all over the world. It is maintained by the National Science Foundation and is said to connect as many as thirty million people worldwide. (See Chapter 3.)

LIBRARY: This is where files are stored on-line.

LURKERS: People who read message boards or discussions on-line but don't post any messages of their own.

MAILING LIST: A list of people who receive postings on a particular subject. For example, if you're really into the game Dungeons & Dragons, you could subscribe to a mailing list that will send you regular e-mail on this topic. Almost all mailing lists are free.

MEMBER: Person who belongs to a particular on-line service. Some services call their users *subscribers,* but most prefer to call them *members* to promote a feeling of community.

MESSAGE BOARDS: A place where you can read and reply to public messages, or create your own topics. In addition to the actual message boards, many of these areas also contain downloadable software, archives, and a chat room. There are message boards (called Bulletin Boards on Prodigy, Forums on CompuServe, Discussion Boards on eWorld, Newsgroups on the Internet) on thousands of topics and every imaginable subject on commercial on-line services and the Internet. Sometimes, these are the best places to find up-to-the-minute information about a subject.

MODEM: A device that lets your computer send and receive data over telephone lines. Modem stands for **mo**dulate and **de**modulate. You can't connect to any of the on-line services without a modem.

MODERATOR: A person (almost always a volunteer) who reads submissions to a newsgroup/forum before posting them to make sure they're appropriate.

MOSAIC: Probably the best-known Internet navigator program (called BROWSERS); it was invented by a twenty-three-year-old named Marc Andreessen, and it makes it easier to access graphics and photos, sounds, and text on the 'Net.

'NETIQUETTE: On-line manners (short for " 'Net etiquette").

'NETTING: The act of logging on(line) and chatting it up.

NEWBIE: The new kids on the virtual block. People who are new to cyberspace, or a particular area on-line are sometimes teased for being "newbies."

NEWSGROUP: The Internet's name for Message Boards (See Message Boards.)

ON-LINE: When your computer is connected to another machine via modem, you are on-line. When you are not connected, you are OFF-LINE.

PASSWORD: The secret code that lets you log on to an on-line service—and prevents others from using your account.

PRODIGY: One of the major commercial on-line services (See Chapter 2.)

PUBLIC DOMAIN SOFTWARE: This is like freeware, but it's not copyrighted, so you can modify it in any way you want (and can also copy and distribute it for free).

SCREENNAME: Names used by AOL members to identify themselves on-line.

SCROLLING: Programming in sounds and repeating them again, and again, and again. It's kind of like repeating the word "cat" (or any other word) again and again, until anyone listening wants to shoot you or at least shut you up. A definite cyberspace no-no!

SHAREWARE: Software that you can download on-line and try out free of charge. Many games, utilities, and applications are published as shareware. If you find a shareware program useful and decide you want to keep using it, you are obligated to send a small fee to the creator. Shareware is distributed on the honor system, so no one's going to *make* you send in the fee. Remember, though, if no one pays for shareware, the people who produce it will stop making it available on-line.

SHORTHAND: Speedy abbreviations for common phrases. Shorthand helps make conversation in live chats and forums quick, easy, and colorful. Common examples include G (grin),

VBG (very big grin), and LOL (laughing out loud). (See Chapter 6.)

SMILEYS: A combination of punctuation and characters used to mimic facial expressions during on-line conversations. There are hundreds of known smileys, and people make up new and more elaborate ones all the time. The most common and useful ones are :-) to indicate a smile, ;-) to show that you are winking, and :-(to show you are sad. If smileys don't make sense to you, try tilting your head all the way to the left. (See Chapter 6.)

SNAIL MAIL: Mail sent the old-fashioned way: through the U.S. Postal Service. It's called snail mail, because—compared with e-mail—it's SOOOOOOOO slow!

SUBSCRIBER: See **MEMBER.**

USENET: A network made up of thousands of discussion groups on all kinds of topics.

USER ID: Your identification number on CompuServe, Prodigy, or another service (also called USERID).

USERNAME: If you belong to one of the three major on-line services, your ''username'' is either your screenname (AOL) or your user ID (CompuServe and Prodigy).

VIRTUAL COMMUNITY: Groups of people who hang out together on-line. These communities can be made up of thousands of people who hang out in a particular area on-line or of a handful of people who meet in a chat room every week.

VIRUS: A program that travels from computer to computer via floppy disks, networks, or telecommunications systems. Some viruses are benign, meaning that they don't cause any trouble. Other viruses can be very destructive and can even erase your entire hard drive. It's a good idea to use anti-viral software programs to keep your computer virus-free.

WORLD WIDE WEB (WWW): Also known as "the Web," this service makes it easier to surf the 'Net and find text and pictures.

Address Book

Celebrity E-Mail Addresses

Government
President Clinton: president@whitehouse.gov
First Lady Hillary Clinton: root@whitehouse.gov
Speaker of the House of Representatives Newt Gingrich:
   georgia6@hr.house.gov

Entertainment/News
Aerosmith: Sweete-mail@aol.com
Tom Brokaw: nightly@nbc.com
Former MTV veejay Adam Curry: adam@metaverse.com
The editors of *People* magazine: 74774.1513@compuserve.com

The Authors
Robert Pondiscio: RPondiscio@aol.com
Marian Salzman: Marian Salzman@chiat.com

Popular Newsgroups/Sites

Animals
Horses: rec.equestrian
Pets and pet care: rec.pets

227

Kid Chat

Discussion group for kids: alt.kids-talk

Discussions for students in grades K-5: k12.chat.elementary

Discussions for students in grades 6-8: k12.chat.junior

Discussions for high school students: k12.chat.senior

Kid Company: KidCompany@aol.com (radio show)

Entertainment (TV, Movies and Music)

"Beavis and Butt-Head": alt.tv.beavis-n-butthead

'Beverly Hills, 90210'': alt.tv.bh90210

CBS (web site): http://www.cbs.com/

"The Late Show with David Letterman": alt.fan.letterman

"Melrose Place": alt.tv.melrose-place

MTV's "Real World": alt.tv.real-world

"Mystery Science Theatre 3000": alt.fan.mst3K/alt.tv.mst3k/
  rec.arts.tv.3k

"Roseanne": alt.tv.roseanne

"The Simpsons": alt.tv.simpsons

"Star Trek": rec.arts.startrek.info

Star Trek Fan Club: rec.arts.startrek.fandom

"Tiny Toon Adventures": alt.tv.tiny-toon

"Tonight Show with Jay Leno": http://www.nbctonightshow
  .com

"X-Files": alt.tv.x-files

Disney: rec.arts.disney

Madonna fan club: alt.madonna.fandom

Music videos: rec.music.video

The Rolling Stones: http://www.stones.com

Hobbies

Celebrity autographs: alt.collecting.autographs

Comic book exchange: rec.arts.comics.marketplace

Family roots research on the Web: http://wwwftp.cac.psu.edu/
  ~saw/geneaology.html

Sports and other collectible cards: rec.collecting.cards

UFO forum: alt.paranet.ufo

Games
Nonvideo:
Board games: rec.games.board
Chess: rec.games.chess
Miscellaneous games: rec.games.misc
PC Gamers: 74431.3433@compuserve.com
Pinball: rec.games.pinball
Tiddlywinks: alt.games.tiddlywinks

Video:
Arcade video games: rec.games.video.arcade
Games and computer games: rec.games.misc
Home video games: rec.games.video
Nintendo game systems and software: rec.games.video.nintendo
Sega game systems and software: rec.games.video.sega
Street Fighter 2: alt.games.sf2

Miscellaneous Clubs
Amy Fisher Fan Club: alt.fan.amy-fisher
Dan Quayle Fan Club: alt.fan.dan-quayle
Off the Wall Fan Club: alt.fan.lemurs.cooked
Silly Fan Club: alt.itchy-n-scratchy
Weirdnetters: alt.usenet.kooks

Sports
Basketball: rec.sport.basketball.misc
Ice skating and roller-skating: rec.skate
skydiving: rec.skydiving

SHOPPING

Free stuff on the Internet: garbo.uwasa.fi (FTP)
Godiva Chocolates: http://www.godiva.com
Good deals on clothing, sporting goods, gifts, books etc.: http://
www.onramp.net/shopping_in/

229

Nordstrom: Nordstrom_PT_America@MCI-MAIL.COM
Pennywise shopping: http://www.onramp.net/goodstuf/
Pizza Hut: http://www.pizzahut.com
Shopping 2000: http://shopping2000.com/shopping2000/

PERIODICALS AND RESEARCH SITES

Campus newspapers online: http://ednews2.asa.utk.edu/papers
.html
Family PC Magazine: FamilyPC@aol.com
Library of Congress, library stack: http://lcweb.loc.gov/
Library of Congress Archives: ftpSEQ1.LOC.GOV,ANONY-
MOUS/<your e-mail address>
People Magazine "Cyberchat" column: 74774.1513@compuser
ve.com
The 'Net (free issue): 800-706-9500 (voice)

THE ENVIRONMENT

EnviroLink Network: envirolink.org
Environmental Protection Agency: gopher.epa.gov
Greenpeace: greenpeace.org

HOMEWORK HELP

AAC's Homework Help: Homework24@aol.com
Electronic Schoolhouse on AOL: ESHTooter@aol.com (E-
mail), ESHLeni@aol.com (E-mail)
Global Schoolhouse Listserv: fred@acme.fred.org (E-mail), and
resyv@CERF.NET (E-mail)

PLACES TO EXPLORE

Outerspace
NASA visuals: http://stardust.jpl.nasa.gov/planets/:

NASA stickers commemorating the Apollo and Space Shuttle Missions: kdurham@smtpgate.osu.hq.nasa.gov (E-mail)
"Welcome to the Planets" visual images for NASA: kgreenb@-panix.com (E-mail)

Paris
A Tour of Paris: http://mistral.enst.fr/~pioch/louvre/

Miscellaneous
Disneyland Fun Fact: ftprtfm.mit.edu from there you go to pub/usenet/new.answers/disney-faq/disneyland
Geography stuff: SimTel/msdos/geography/usgeoll0).zip (FTP)
MGDigitalAtlas: Magellan Geographix maps on-line (compuserve)
Ozark Regional Information On-Line Network, Annie Linnemeyer: annie@ozarks.sgcl.lib.mo.us (E-mail), 217-2244-3299 (voice), ozarks.sgcl.lib.mo.us (Internet), 417-869-6100 (modem)

CLASSROOM PROJECTS

Big Sky Telegraph, Frank Odasz: franko@bigsky.dillon.mt.us (E-mail), 406-683-7338 (voice), 192.231.192.1 Frank (Internet), 406-683-7680 (modem 1200 baud)
Bird Migration Watch, Judson Elliot or Nick Barber: xx132@nptn.org
Bug Survey, David Berkham: dberkham@teleport.com (E-mail)
Channel One, Surveys: Chanone@aol.com
A Day in the Life of a Student, Sheldon Smith: shsmith@ctp.org:
Egg-a-thon, Stewart Clements: stewclem@aol.com (E-mail)
Global Grocery List, David F. Warlick: dwarlick@dpi.state.no.us (E-mail)
Iditarod Online, Bob Kuhn: rsrck@aurora.alaska.edu (E-mail)
I*EARN (the International Education and Resource Network): iearn@copenfund.igc.apc.org

231

Inter-Generational Exchange, Lou Schwartz: xx141@nptn.org
International Holiday Exchange, Shelley Brenner: sdb@nptn.org
The Landmark Game, Carol Siwinski: Mountsj@rbs.org (E-mail)
Project Outdoors, Lee Williams: williams1@hshs2.dsc.k12 (E-mail)
Peace Project, Cynthia Foley: sffoley2@onondaga.bitnet
Simulated Space Shuttle Program, Bob Morgan: xx118@nptn.org
Titantic Search, Ken Newkirk: knewkirk@destiny.esd105.wednet.edu (E-mail)
Virtual Carnival, Tim Noxel: timnoxe@village.ca
Virtual Field Trips, Nadine Hinton: hinton@cedar.cic.net

COMMERCIAL ONLINE SERVICES

America Online: 800-827-6364 (voice)
CompuServe: 800-848-8990 (voice)
Delphi: 800-695-4005 (voice)
eWORLD: 800-775-4556 (voice)
GEnie: 800-638-9636 (voice)
ImagiNation!: 800-462-4461 (voice)
Prodigy: 800-Prodigy (voice)

FREENETS

Buffalo Freenet, James Finamore: finamore@ubvms.cc.buffalo.edu (E-mail), 716-877-8800 ext. 451 (voice), freenet.buffalo.edu (Internet), 716-645-3085 (modem)
Ciao! Freenet, Ken McClean: kmcclean@ciao.trail.bc.ca (E-mail), 604-368-2233 (voice), 142.231.5.1 (Internet), 604-368-5764 (modem)
The Cleveland Freenet, Jeff Gumpf: jag@po.cwru.edu (E-mail), 314-882-2000 (voice), freenet-in-a.cwru.edu (Internet), 216-368-3888 (modem)
Columbia Online Information Network, Bill Mitchell: bill@

232

more.net (E-mail), 314-882-2000 (voice), bigcat.missouri.edu (Internet), 314-884-7000 (modem)

Dayton Freenet, Patricia Vendt: pvendt@desire.wright.edu (E-mail), 513-873-4035 (voice), 130.108.128.174 (Internet), 513-229-4373 (modem)

Denver Freenet, Drew Mirque: drew@freenet.hsc.colorado.edu (E-mail), 303-270-4300 (voice), freenet.hsc.colorado.edu (Internet), 303-270-4865 (modem)

Freenet Erlangen-Nuernberg, Dr. Walter F. Kugemann: Walter-Kugemann@fim.uni-erlangen.de (E-mail), +49-9131-85-4735 (voice), 131.188.192.11 (Internet), +49-9131-85-8111 (modem)

Great Lakes Freenet, Merritt W. Tumanis: merritt_tumanisa@ fc1.glfn.org (E-mail), 616-961-4166 (voice), not available (Int ernet), 616-969-4536 (modem)

Lorain County Freenet, Thom Gould: aa003@freenet.lorain.oberlin.edu (E-mail), 800-227-7113 ext. 2451 or 216-277-2451 (voice), freenet.lorain.oberlin.edu or 132.162.32.99 (Internet), 216-366-9721 (modem)

Medina County Freenet, Gary Linden: aa001@medina.-freenet.edu (E-mail), 216-725-1000 ext. 2550 (voice), not available (Internet), 216-723-6732 (modem)

National Capital Freenet, David Sutherland: aa001@freenet. carleton.ca (E-mail), 613-788-2600 ext. 3701 (voice), freenet. carleton.ca or 134.117.1.25 (Internet), 613-564-3600 (modem)

Ocean State Freenet, Howard Boksenbaum: howardbm@dsl.rhil inet.gov (E-mail), 401-277-2726 (voice), 192.207.24.10 (Internet), 401-831-4640 (modem)

Prairienet, Ann P. Bishop: abishop@alexia.lis.uiuc.edu (E-mail), 217-244-3299 (voice), prairienet.org or 192.17.3.3 (Internet) 217-255-9000 (modem)

Rio Grande Freenet, Don Furth: donf@laguna.epcc.edu (E-mail), 915-775-6077 (voice), rgfn.epcc.edu (Internet), 915-775-5600 (modem)

Seattle Community Network, Randy Groves: randy@cpsr.org

(E-mail), 206-865-3424 (voice), not available (Internet), not available (modem)

South Eastern Ohio Regional Freenet, Damien O. Bawn: bawn @oucsace.cs.ohiou.edu (E-mail), 614-662-3211 (voice)

Tallahassee Freenet, Hilbert Levitz: levitz@cs.fsu.edu (E-mail), 904-644-1796 (voice), freenet.fsu.edu or 144.174.128.43 (Internet), 904-576-6330 or 904-488-5056 (modem)

Tri-cities On-Line, Bruce McComb: nelva@delphi.com (E-mail), 509-586-6481 (voice), not available (Internet), 509-375-3548 (modem)

Tri-State Online, Michael King: sysadmin@cbos.uc.edu (E-mail), 513-397-1396 (voice), tso.uc.edu (Internet), 513-579-1990 (modem)

Victoria Freenet, Gareth Shearman: shearman@cue.bc.ca (E-mail), 604-385-4302 (voice), freenet.victoria.bc.ca or 134.87.16.100 (Internet), 604-595-2300 (modem)

Wellington Citynet, Richard Naylor: rich@tosh.wcc.govt.nz (E-mail), +64-4-801-3303 (voice), kosmos.wcc.govt.nz or 192.54.130.34 (Internet), +64-4-801-3060 (modem)

The Youngstown Freenet, Lou Anschuetz: lou@yfn.ysu.edu (E-mail), 216-742-3075 (voice), yfn2.ysu.edu or 192.55.234.27 (Internet), 216-742-3072 (modem)

Index

America Online (*cont.*)
parental controls, 62
rating of, 30
resource information,
130–31
software, 167, 168–69,
173
special interest forums,
103
Star Trek Club, 160
statistics concerning,
216–17
talk shows, 161
television, 158–59
travel, 204–5
trial memberships, 196
UFOs, 161–2
videos, 162
Web and, 37
American Dialogue, 85
Archie program, Internet, 35
Artwork, posting, 197
Astronomy, 149–50

B

BBSes. *See* Bulletin Board
Services
Bulletin Board Services
(BBSes), 38–39
freenets, 43–48
SFNet, 39–40
The Well, 39

C

Careers, 141–42
Channel One, 139–40
Chat rooms, 78–79
conference, 81–84
vs. e-mail, 207
guidelines for, 89–90
private, 80–81
public, 79–80
"Child Safety on the Information Highway,"
60, 61–62
on-line pledge, 61
Clothes, 151–52
College prep tests, 142
Comics, 162–63
Communication:
historic revolutions in, 4
shorthand, 88–89
symbols, 56, 84–88
CompuServe, 12, 16–18, 20
astronomy, 149
charges, checking, 26
chat rooms, 79, 84
e-mail, 73–74, 76
environmental issues, 153
features (table), 72
foreign languages, 154
forums, 98–99
games, 105, 106, 107,
109–10
genealogy, 204
homework assistance, 136
Internet e-mail and, 65–67

N

O

P

MARIAN SALZMAN and ROBERT PONDISCIO are the ultimate information superhighway pioneers, although each has staked out a different virtual turf. Marian is fascinated by on-line chat and by the popularization of the commercial on-line services; Robert is a big Internet fan and a subscriber to literally hundreds of newsgroups, including ones on global affairs, education, religion, and culture.

In 1990, Marian Salzman was virtually computer illiterate. She considered her computer a word processor—nothing more. Now, five years later, she is director of emerging media (and resident futurist) at Chiat/Day, one of the twenty-five largest advertising agencies in the world and the first to go "virtual." Marian is now responsible for introducing all new technologies and related marketing approaches to Chiat/Day and its clients.

Marian, 35, graduated from Brown University with honors and attended the Harvard University Graduate School of Arts and Sciences. She is the creator of American Dialogue™, the first on-line market research facility and is coauthor of several books for kids and teens.

Marian's first on-line experience took place in January 1993. Since that time, she has logged an average of forty or more hours per week on America Online, eWorld, CompuServe, Prodigy, and, lately, the 'Net. She commutes between New York City, her hometown, and San Francisco, her second home, every couple of weeks. Her dogs, Sam and Tyler, live in New York City full-time. They're not 'Netters at all. In fact, they occasionally bark at the computer while Marian 'Nets: "Sam especially hates the sound, which I happen to adore, [ping] You have mail.''

Robert Pondiscio is *Time*'s public affairs director. He is the magazine's principal spokesperson on trade and consumer issues. Robert is actively involved in *Time* Online, the magazine's computer on-line service, and is the host of the magazine's weekly "on-line news conferences" with *Time* journalists, authors, and newsmakers. Widely quoted as an expert in on-line publishing, Robert frequently speaks on the subject at conferences and seminars for publishers, editors, and advertising executives.

Among the most critically praised interactive publications, *Time* Online logged over three million visits in its first year. It features the full text of each issue of *Time* the day before it is available on newsstands, and allows readers and journalists to interact with each other via message boards on current events and issues raised in the magazine. The service also includes a daily news summary, fully searchable back issues, and other interactive services.

Robert, 32, spent several years as a radio reporter and anchor at the NBC Radio Network and several local stations in New York prior to joining Time Inc. in 1989. A native of Long Island, he currently lives in New York City. On an avocational basis, Robert is working with a nonprofit organization to create a freenet and easy access for less-privileged kids in the greater New York area.